MW01114697

# ONE MORE DANCE

## Kay Francis

WITHDRAWN

For my friends and family without whose encouragement this book would never have been written.

And to my new husband who allowed me to spend so much time in this world.

Copyright © 2011 by Kay Francis.

| Library of Congress Control Number: | | 2011910999 |
|---|---|---|
| ISBN: | Softcover | 978-1-4628-9757-5 |
| | Hardcover | 978-1-4628-9758-2 |
| | Ebook | 978-1-4628-9759-9 |

All rights reserved. No part of this book may be reproduced or transmitted
in any form or by any means, electronic or mechanical, including photocopying,
recording, or by any information storage and retrieval system,
without permission in writing from the copyright owner.

This is a work of fiction. Names, characters, places and incidents either are the
product of the author's imagination or are used fictitiously, and any resemblance
to any actual persons, living or dead, events, or locales is entirely coincidental.

This book was printed in the United States of America.

**To order additional copies of this book, contact:**
Xlibris Corporation
1-888-795-4274
www.Xlibris.com
Orders@Xlibris.com
100451

# PROLOGUE

*It wasn't fair*, was Rob Waterford's first thought. He was an excellent pilot, never drank twenty-four hours before a flight, always filed a flight plan, and always checked the weather. He flew enough hours that his skills stayed sharp. He was in good health. This shouldn't be happening to him.

Flying was his passion. Since retirement, he had entered a lot of hours into his logbook. There was the fishing trip to Canada, a flight to Texas that Beth and he thought would never end, a wedding in Wisconsin. It was a wonderful way to keep in touch with their widely scattered friends—just climb in the plane and go. The sense of freedom was the kicker. He was up above all the traffic, able to rest his mind in the quiet drone of the plane's engine.

He was a good pilot, except for one weakness. He liked to play pranks. Like a naughty boy daring to risk a spanking, he would buzz a friend's ranch house almost low enough to dislodge a brick from the chimney or scatter the rancher's cows, ignoring the raised fists of the riders.

His wife's voice pulsed in his head. "You're an excellent pilot. I'm not afraid to fly with you, but you pull one more stunt like that and I will never fly with you again. You're too low." His wife always meant exactly what she said, so he didn't pull any more stunts . . . when she was with him.

His friends knew Beth was riding copilot when he flew over at the prescribed altitude. "There are no old bold pilots. If you don't allow for the unexpected, you'll kill yourself." His wife repeated the old saying to him often. A "pinch hitters" flying course had given her the skills to land and fly the plane. She knew the safety rules, and she was going to be seriously pissed at him because there was a good chance he wasn't going to survive this little prank. He was grateful she wasn't with him. If he died here, much better he do it alone.

Beth had gone to Canada on a horse trip with her gal pals. He found himself wandering around the house, missing her, restless. She would be home two days from now, but he needed something to fill today.

The cherries in the orchard were ripe. He had picked what the birds missed, phoned his ranching friends. Did they want pie cherries? Could they meet for lunch?

It had been a perfect day to fly, sunny and warm with smooth air at his cruising altitude. Wyoming was lush from above-average rainfall, and the August sun had cured the prairie grasses to the color of honey. The surface wind rippled through the tall growth, giving the effect of wave action on an inland sea.

His landing at Lusk, Wyoming's small airport had been perfect in spite of the usual brisk breeze. Friends waiting for him helped him tie down the plane. As they drove to town, they had talked about old times, Beth's trip to Canada, and the couples' hay and calf crop.

The café was full of Harley riders heading to Sturgis, South Dakota, for the annual huge motorcycle rally. He knew several of them, which led to slapped backs and traded insults.

"How about flying with me on a short leg over to the tower before you go home? It's a perfect day for it." He had pushed his plate back and looked hopefully at his friends.

"Can't. We have to pick up a load of hay this afternoon. We better get you back to the plane so we can hitch up the trailer. We'll have to do it some other time."

There had been hugs all around before he climbed into his plane. He had flown north and east to the spectacular volcanic plug called Devils' Tower, made a big loop around it, and headed back to Highway 85. Would any of his friends be on the highway so he could send them off to Sturgis with a flyby?

Now here he was, too damn low. The cream and navy Beach Bonanza was only a hundred feet above the highway. *Not fair*, he thought again as he stared in disbelief at the power line straddling the highway where it went through the cut at the top of the hill. The power line that had been invisible until now, when he was almost on it—the power line that might possibly kill him.

What idiot took that line across the road when it had been on the right side of Highway 85 all the way from Lusk, Wyoming? Then again, what idiot was this low when planes are supposed to be at least five hundred feet above the deck, except for landing and takeoff?

*Think or there won't be time for blame. Too close, too close. Not enough space to try to turn east for open country.* There were more hills to the west. No time to gain enough altitude to go over the power line that crossed the highway. The only option was to try to go under. *Keep the wheels up, hold your breath, and pray, dummy,* he thought. *You finally got yourself in a life-or-death situation. It's only going to be a few seconds before you deal with the consequences.*

Dare he lose altitude? Too low, he would hit the ground. Not low enough, the tail would hit the power line. He dropped the nose of the plane slightly, nudged the left rudder to line up with the highway. He hoped to God there wasn't a car coming up the road on the other side. The Harley riders he was pursuing had just gone out of sight. He wished he had time to bleed off more air speed, but if he was going too slowly, he wouldn't make the hill.

He fought the urge to go lower. His altimeter said he was on the ground, so it didn't look like an option. Hold steady, just a few more feet. He realized he was hunched down in his seat. As if making himself shorter would give the plane more clearance.

The plane slid under the power line.

"I made it," the pilot shouted. His relief lasted only a second. The plane's tail hit the wire. It shuddered liked a dying animal as the tail tore off. The impact forced the pilot's body against his seat belt so hard it dislocated his hips. He screamed.

He felt the right wing tip of his crippled plane hit the ground. The force of the second blow flipped the aircraft. The pilot saw blue sky for an instant. Then the top of the hill rotated into view.

"I'm sorry, love," he whispered.

The plane hit the side of the cut at an air speed of 175 miles an hour.

# CHAPTER 1

The dream started as it always did. She was in the rubber raft, her head resting on her dead husband's shoulder. She knew he was dead, that she was dreaming but . . . Rob tilted her chin upward, kissed the tip of her nose. With trembling fingers, she gently skimmed the deep smile lines time had engraved on his face and sighed, "Oh, how I've missed you since you died." She snuggled against his body, feeling safe and content.

Her gaze traveled over the other occupants of the raft: her husband's brother killed in Vietnam; her father, victim of a car crash; her ninety-year-old grandmother. Tom had been her favorite of Rob's three brothers. Divorce had separated her from her father until she had a chance to know him just five years before his car accident. Grandma Steffy had been her only grandparent, the one source of uncritical love when she was growing up. She taught Beth to spin daydreams when troubled, a skill Beth had always treasured. Too much death, but the faces of her loved ones were peaceful, and that gave her comfort. They didn't seem to be aware she was in the boat, hadn't reacted when she tried to speak to them. Sighing, she turned back to her husband and kissed his neck, inhaling the scent of his Old Spice cologne.

Her voice husky with emotion, she tucked her head under Rob's chin and talked of past times. "Oh love, do you remember how much you enjoyed our float trip in this canyon? You said you would go back again the following week. It was almost a religious experience, wasn't it? Remember how astounded we were about the numerous waterfalls that flow into the canyon? How we hiked up to several of them for some exercise and to wash off the grit of the river? The marks of water wear on the canyon walls . . . remember the pool of tiny frogs? And how relaxing it was? The water was so low. It was so peaceful."

Her husband nodded.

Beth sighed with pleasure and looked down river, watching the walls of the Grand Canyon slide past. Their rubber raft rode the surface of the Colorado River as it ground deeper, hour by hour, heading toward layers of fossilized mud laid down at the beginning of time.

A Sandhill Crane lifted off the river in front of them and winged silently down the canyon ahead of the raft, seeking the solitude they had intruded upon—a dusky blue-gray wraith. Beth could smell the dankness of the river, feel the heat of the sun, and she felt like she had when they ran the river that September, enthralled with the beauty of the experience.

The canyon of the Colorado is a cathedral of nature—timeless, brutal to those who misjudge its dangers. The guides had told them that their group was, in many ways, as helpless as the early explorers who came down the river in awkward wooden boats. They were totally ignorant of the lack of game and the fact that the canyon was over a hundred miles in length with only two exit points.

Trapped between the sheer walls of stone, the explorers found themselves totally committed to the river. They were ants floating through the huge environment, at the mercy of the careless placement of a giant's foot. Many of them died.

Even today, once the Little Colorado and the Colorado River converge, rafts are the only possible way of travel through the canyon until the takeout point ninety miles downriver. The modern-day trips end north of Lake Mead, where the rafters can go back to the rim by mule or helicopter.

Beth smiled and closed her eyes as she remembered the enervating heat, the sudden storms of wind and rain that battered their camp without warning during the darkest part of the night. The sand got into everything. The mice and bats caused shrieks from the women. It was one of those gems you relive in old age, proud that you survived the experience intact.

A soft mutter intruded on her memories. She raised her head from her husband's shoulder as the raft began to slide into a lazy turn to the right. The river picked up its pace, waves replacing ripples, causing the pontoons to bob as the water slapped their sides like ghostly hands urging more speed.

The mutter increased to a roar as the raft came through the turn. She could see rapids now, and the river was definitely going downhill. She frowned up at her husband, but he seemed unconcerned.

Their speed increased as the raft entered the section of the canyon that was almost a mile deep. Here the river was in a savage mood. It thrashed and threw itself into standing waves as high as a house. Not tame like the last trip, not tame at all.

The raft fell forward toward the first wave. She screamed and shifted away from her husband to grab the straps that secured the pontoons to the body of the raft. The raft hit the water wall with a blow that lifted her bottom off the container she was sitting on. The roar of the river hurt her ears. She held on with all her strength as the raft slid toward the next wave. She closed her eyes and tucked her chin hard against her chest.

Shock rattled her shoulder sockets as the raft twisted its way through the barrier. She fought to keep her balance, to stay in the raft, but was ejected into the icy water.

The shock was mind-numbing. She surfaced, gasping. A wave crashed over her, driving her back under, rolling her beneath the surface until her lungs were burning. A pulse of the current brought her head above water. She drew in great gasps of air as she paddled in a clumsy circle, wiping her eyes as she treaded water.

Where was the raft? She looked around frantically. There. It was traveling too fast for her to catch up. The indifferent river moved it rapidly downstream, taking her loved ones, leaving her behind. Alone. Again.

"Noooo!" she screamed.

\*     \*     \*

Beth Waterford's body convulsed as she tore free from the dream. The loss of her husband hammered at her heart, and she cried in the cold darkness of her bedroom until she felt like an old wrung-out dishrag. *Please don't let me dream of him anymore*, she prayed. Her breathing gradually slowed, tears ceased, and the dream began to fade. She drifted away from her grief as sleep carried her back under to forgetfulness.

Hours later, the early morning light gently woke Beth. Slowly she came to full consciousness, blinking sleepily. She realized she had been dreaming about Rob again, but most of the details mercifully stayed with the night. *It was probably just as well*, she thought. The dreams were so real. Although being with her husband was wonderful, she could hardly bear the sense of loss when she woke to the reality of her widowhood.

*Another morning*, she thought, *get on with it.* Beth stretched, her joints cracking, hamstrings tightening, and sat up in bed. She pushed pillows behind her back to cushion the headboard. "Good morning, Lord. Thank you for this day and the strength to get through it. Please take this sadness from me and let me be a blessing for someone," she prayed. She gazed out her picture window as she tried to ignore the lingering sadness of the dream.

Twenty miles away to the west, the front range of the Colorado Rocky Mountains swept abruptly upward from the drylands in various shades of blue toward the awakening sky. Hay fields still lay dormant, and the plowed fields added texture and pattern as they waited for the spring seed. She watched the light grow stronger, turning the clouds to hot-pink streams edged with gold. Each morning, this view was a gift, even when the weather was bad.

Beth threw back the covers and wiggled to the side of the king-sized bed. Yawning, she stepped into a pair of gray felt slippers as she ran her fingers through her short reddish hair. It was trying to stand straight up, visible proof of her uneasy night. The house was cool, she decided, and bumped the thermostat up a notch. She shrugged into her worn red robe, grateful for its warmth, pulled the bedspread into temporary order, and left the bedroom.

A growl from her stomach as she wandered down the hall to the kitchen surprised her until she remembered she hadn't eaten anything but popcorn the night before. What was needed was a big breakfast before chores. She put the kettle on for tea and opened the refrigerator. The offerings were meager. All she could find was a couple of English muffins. What had happened to the bread? Beth sighed. The muffins would have to do.

A long-haired cat stalked into the room and twinned around Beth's bare ankles. It looked up with eyes that appeared to be made of blue crystal. Its face was marked with strips of brown and black that gave the cat a knowing expression. The rest of its coat was a combination of brown, cream, and white.

"Morning, Taz. Thank you for keeping me safe from harm last night." Beth bent down and stroked her hand along the cat's body.

With a plaintive meow, the cat moved out of the kitchen, heading for the back door. It looked over its shoulder at Beth in a demanding way, meowed again.

"All right, all right, go kill something." Beth opened the door. The cat streaked outside, intent on prey.

Half an hour later, Beth pulled a blue down vest over her faded denim shirt, zipped it up, opened her front door, and stepped out into the crisp spring morning. The melodious sound of a meadowlark caught her attention. She listened with delight, for they were Beth's favorite birds. They raised their young in the high grass of the waste area to the north of her pasture. This lark seemed especially thrilled with the new spring day.

Beth's ten acres boasted a grove of ponderosa pines to the north of the house and an orchard with peach, apple, cherry, and apricot trees to the east. When they bloomed, the fruit trees looked like full-skirted ballerinas dancing flirtatiously with the spring winds.

North of the orchard sat a large metal storage building. It had a three-sided matching lean-to attached to its east side. A small corral made of panels made it possible for Beth to shut her horse out of the pasture. She was careful to keep him slim. The old-timers used to say you should just see a rib when a horse took a deep breath, and Beth abided by that saying.

A pass-through gate let her into the loafing area. Making a face at the numerous manure piles, she decided they would be the first chore. How could one animal produce so much waste?

Minutes later, she attacked the mess, forking the manure into a large wooden wagon. The pungent smell of horse droppings tickled her nose as the exertion warmed her quickly in the cool morning air. She hung her vest on the fence and continued scooping, her thoughts drifting back to a spring day a year ago.

"You know you'll marry again," May McIntosh said that day as she placed another card on the table. A small dark bird of a woman, May wore her long hair piled carelessly on top of her head. Her yellow blouse and blue jeans were bright accents of color. Her feet were bare, toes painted a clear, bright red.

Beth stared thoughtfully at May, shook her head, and sighed. "I can't imagine getting involved again. After spending forty years with one man? How do you get past that?"

The two friends sat across from each other at a table in May's cheerful kitchen. The walls were painted an off-white, which the sun warmed to butter yellow. Playing cards were spread in a pattern on the table. A blue vase filled with daffodils sat on the window sill, and the smell of cookies baking perfumed the air, promising culinary delight.

"I only know what the cards tell me. I see a man. He's tall, nice looking, with sandy hair. I see marriage there. It is up to you to make the decision of course." May gestured at the cards with brightly polished nails. "The cards are very clear about this marriage."

"You know, I believe you. But it doesn't seem possible," Beth said. Her green eyes were sad. "It's still hard, at times, to believe it isn't a dream. All that first year, I would be in the middle of doing something when the fact that he was dead would come out of nowhere. It would just lay me out. Rob's dead. I'll never see him again. Maybe if I could have seen him after he died. Maybe if I could have looked at his face, told him good-bye, it would have been easier. After three years it still hits me unexpectedly. How long does it last? We were supposed to grow old together." A single tear rolled slowly down her cheek.

"You didn't get to say good-bye? I didn't realize that." May's voice was warm with sympathy. "That's hard."

"Rob was badly burned. They didn't say I couldn't look, but they strongly suggested it wouldn't be a good thing to do." Beth bit her lip, turning her wedding ring back and forth. The diamond sparked fire from the sun that filled the room. "I was afraid to look. I would never have been able to think of Rob as he was before he died if I had. But I needed that closure." She concentrated on her ring. "I had a dream about him the night he died. It was brief, and he didn't speak, just smiled at me. I woke knowing he was telling me he was all right. It comforted me." She looked at her friend, her lips quivering.

May reached across the table, gently squeezed Beth's hand. "I know you've had a bad time, but you've really been strong. You dealt with everything as soon as you could. I don't know that I could have done as well."

"I didn't feel strong. I was a quivering mess. And I was so mad. After the funeral, when everyone left, I remember sitting in the swing on the patio in the middle of the night screaming, furious at him for dying. For leaving me alone when we had barely begun his retirement.

When I tried to look down the road into the future, being alone for twenty more years just overwhelmed me. If he hadn't been dead, I'd have killed him." Beth gave a weak laugh, took a sip of tea. "I've forgiven him finally. I think." She sighed. "What else do you see?"

"This man comes to you unexpected." Beth made a dismissive gesture. May smiled, turned another card.

"You are concerned about your son, but he will be all right. He will find work."

"I worry about him so," Beth said. "He has too much to deal with. His wife's family has had one crisis after another since they were married. Steve is the one everyone turns to for help. And he's been out of work for almost a year. He sure didn't need me giving him more problems. I think that helped me try to stand on my own two feet." Beth sighed and then laughed softly. "My mother said I was just like her mother, sighing all the time. I never noticed it until she mentioned it."

"Losing your mother just a year before you lost your husband, then having that hip replacement the fall after Rob died was way too much to handle. At least in my opinion," May said. She picked up the dark-blue teapot, poured fresh tea into both cups.

"Thanks, May." Beth stirred a teaspoon of sugar into her tea. Her hands were strong with long fingers, the nails clipped short. "The orthopedic doctor was a little hesitant to do the surgery because he thought it might put me into a depression because of Rob's death and all. I told him I was already depressed, so to heck with it. I might as well get it all over at once. In a way, having the surgery to deal with helped me start to put the pieces of my life back together again." She said slowly, "I had to focus on something besides my loss."

They both sat quietly, lost in their thoughts, letting the peace of the bright room settle on them. "Let's talk about something else." Beth turned and looked out the window. "Your daffodils are just glorious."

\*　　\*　　\*

*I wish I could get that conversation out of my head,* Beth thought, picking up another pitchfork of manure. *But it wanders into my mind whenever it pleases. Where would I meet a man? I go to the grocery store, ride with my woman friends, get gas, and go to church. The men at church are all married or a hundred and five. Didn't I always say I would never get remarried if something happened to Rob?*

*But in spite of that, I find myself looking at men from time to time, wondering. Are you the one May said will come along? It does give me something to hope for, helps me get through the bad times when I look forward at twenty or however more years I have left. Living in my big house alone except for a cat seems really dismal.*

A hoof clicking on a stone distracted Beth from her thoughts. She looked up and smiled as she watched a gray Arabian gelding come toward her, his dark eyes intent. He stopped two feet away and stretched his neck out until his nose was almost touching her chest.

"Looking for a handout, are you, Far Horizon? I don't think so. You look like you could foal any minute," Beth added with a laugh as the gelding bumped his nose against her pocket. She waved him away so she could finish cleaning the loafing area. Far followed her around like a dog, asking for attention. Beth gave him a good-bye scratch. He hung his head over the corral panel, watching her with reproachful eyes as she walked to the house.

After a quick shower, Beth made herself a peanut butter sandwich, carrying it into her office to eat as she answered her e-mail. She needed to deal with the piles of paperwork on her large rolltop desk. She sighed, resigned to being inside all afternoon on this beautiful day. Sorting would be the first step. She really needed to keep up with her desk work every day.

A picture of her husband taken on their last trip to Europe sat on the bookcase as though he was watching her work. Right after Rob's death, Beth had put all the family pictures away because the sight of his face made her loss unbearable. But in time she was able to look at them again. This picture was taken just after his retirement. Bearded, smiling joyfully into the camera, it showed his zest for life. Looking at his face still occasionally caused Beth pain, but she felt he was watching over her, so the picture stayed on the bookcase. The meadowlark was still singing outside her open window hours later as Beth finished her paperwork.

\*   \*   \*

That evening, Beth sat in a big leather chair in her living room, watching TV. Her cat was sprawled across her lap on its back, so fast asleep it looked dead. It was a pleasant room, an Indian-patterned couch and matching chair with a footstool faced the fireplace, where a gas insert waited for winter. Paintings that depicted Western themes were prominent, and the west wall had a huge window to take advantage of the spectacular view.

An old black-and-white movie starring Fred Astaire and Ginger Rogers was playing on the Turner Movie Channel. "This is the story of Vern and Irene Castle, dancers in the year before the Great Depression, if you want to know, my sweet girl," she said to the unconscious cat. In the scene, pilots were being trained to fly. Astaire, wearing his new uniform, got into a plane, took off, and Beth tensed. *Oh, I think I remember how this goes,* she thought. *I shouldn't watch it.* But her eyes were frozen to the screen.

The plane flew a pattern around the air field while officers below went through their dialogue. Beth started wriggling in her chair. Another plane was in position for takeoff as Astaire was on his final approach. He didn't notice it start to taxi because the second plane was slightly behind him and underneath his airplane's wings. The two planes traveled almost in unison—one descending, the other ascending. The pilots were obvious to each other. Almost to the point of collision, Astaire looked down and saw the other plane. He made an attempt to avoid a crash by pulling his plane off to the side and up. Beth watched as the plane stalled out, nosed over, and crashed. It burst into flames.

"Oh God," Beth cried, tears streaming down her face. She broke into crashing sobs, rocking herself in the chair. The cat hung on for a few minutes, jumped to the floor. It watched as Beth moved back and forth, holding herself, moaning as though she had been hit hard in the stomach. Sobbing, she turned the TV off, stumbled down the hall into her bedroom, and threw herself on the bed. She cried, wailing at times. She was hiccupping as she finally fell into an exhausted sleep. After she quieted, the cat carefully crept onto the bed and snuggled into the curve of Beth's hip.

As she poured cat food into a bowl the next morning, Beth said, "That was quite a show last night, wasn't it, Tazmeralda?" She looked out the window as the cat started eating. "I thought I was doing better, but I started off the morning in tears and finished the day the same way." She put her hand on the cat's head and ran her hand gently along its body. Taz continued eating, but her back rose in response to the caress. "Let's hope it's the last time. I'm getting tired of crying and kicking pillows. It helps, I guess, but I'm just flat sick of it." Beth stared at the cat another few seconds, blew out a huge breath, and walked away, saying, "Are you going to come help me feed or what?"

# CHAPTER 2

"Damn, damn, damn!" Beth kicked the side of the four-wheeler as hard as she could and then yelped. "Arrrgh, that was smart. Break a couple of toes, why don't you?" She limped over to the workbench, wiped her hands off on a rag, turned, and glared at the offending machine. *Some days, it just doesn't pay to get out of bed*, she thought. *Can't get the wheeler started, the lawn mower battery is dead because I didn't turn the switch off yesterday. I hate trying to deal with all this stuff.*

Taz came into the shed, walked over to Beth, and looked up at her with a mouse firmly clenched between her jaws. She dropped it at Beth's feet. "Oh, my mighty huntress," Beth enthused. She stroked the cat with loving hands and told it what a great mouser it was. Tired of the praise, Taz picked the mouse up, went under the saddle racks, and started to feed. "Ugh, glad that isn't my special treat," Beth said as she listened to the cat crunch the mouse's bones.

She stood for a few minutes, her hands on her hips, eyes flicking irritably around the interior of the shed until she glanced at the sliding door that opened into the lean-to. Far Horizon stood there, his chest pushed against the metal gate that kept the horse out of the storage shed but let a breeze through. He nickered.

Beth laughed. "Let's go do something I know how to do." She crossed to the gate, waved the gelding backward, and walked out of the lean-to. "How do you manage to produce so much manure?" Beth gave Far Horizon an accusing stare as she surveyed the loafing area. "To heck with it, I can scoop later. Since I got you all cleaned up, I think you need some exercise. In fact, we both do."

In fifteen minutes, she had her gelding saddled. She slapped a large straw hat on her head, pulled on a pair of riding gloves. "Come on, you sluggard," she coaxed as Far Horizon planted his feet in protest when she tried to lead him away from the shed. She tugged gently on the reins. The gelding heaved a huge sigh as she led him out of the loafing area.

Beth led Far Horizon to the gate on her south fence line and passed through into her neighbor's corrals. There were several pens of different sizes to the north of a large barn with a round pen to the west and a roping arena to the east. Her neighbors, Len and Nancy Delagon, allowed Beth to use their arena anytime they weren't. It was the only reason Beth had been able to retrain Far Horizon when she bought him shortly after Rob died. They had needed that confinement.

She used the mounting block in the middle of the arena and was walking Far to warm him up, when the door to the barn opened. A small blonde woman came out, carrying several feed buckets.

"Hey, Nancy," Beth yelled. She watched, amused as Nancy's five horses milled around her, ears back, biting at each other like starving sharks as they eyed the buckets their owner was carrying. "Are you going to have time to ride on the canal?"

Nancy shook her head. "We've got to do some work in the yard, maybe tomorrow." She dumped the buckets in the feeder, spread out hay in separate piles, and vanished into the barn.

Beth decided to stay in the arena rather than ride on the irrigation canal like she preferred. She walked and trotted Far to warm his muscles and then focused on being in rhythm with her horse. Far Horizon was responding so well Beth was riding him without using the reins, just her seat and legs, when she realized a man was standing just inside the barn door, watching her. It wasn't Len or anyone she recognized. How long he had been there, she had no idea.

She turned Far Horizon and rode to the fence. "If you're looking for Nancy or Len Delagon, they're in their yard," she called.

He smiled, walked to the arena, put his hand on the top rail of the fence. *What my grandmother would have called a well-made man*, Beth thought as she watched him.

He said, "He's working well. How long have you had him?"

"About two years," Beth replied. "He's been a lot of work because he really didn't know anything. He'd been used for endurance racing. I think all they did was haul him to a race, point his nose up the trail, and let him go as fast as he wanted. But he's been worth it. He's the best horse I've ever had." She laughed. "That's probably more information than you needed or wanted."

He smiled slightly, looking up at her.

There was a silence as they stared at each other.

Beth pulled her hat off, ran her hand through her sweaty hair. "You weren't looking for Len or Nancy?"

"No," he said, "I was looking for you." He peered up at her. His eyes were green like hers, Beth noticed.

She jammed her hat back on her head. "Are you the guy from the solar company?"

"Nope," he said, smiling slightly. "You don't remember me, do you?"

Beth narrowed her eyes, really looked at him. He was a big man, tall and stocky, no extra weight on him. About her age, she guessed, with short sandy hair well on the way to going gray. He was dressed in well-worn jeans and a lightweight short-sleeved shirt. His boots were shined or had been until he stepped out into the dust of the corral. He had strong features, a good face, she thought.

"No." She shook her head. "Your voice rings a bell, although dimly." He had one of those low velvet voices that make movie stars out of some men. "You do seem familiar. Are you someone I met at one of Rob's bank functions?"

"Further back than that. In fact, I knew you before you met your husband," he said. "I was at your place, but your neighbor saw me and said you were over here." He looked at her, still smiling.

Beth glared at him with irritation. "Well, this is what I call a Mexican standoff. I'm blank. If you want to play games . . ." She picked up the reins.

"Remember Dale Runnington?" He was serious now.

Beth's mouth dropped open.

"Guess you do, finally."

Beth gulped, tore her gaze away from his, looked down at her saddle, back at him, and said, "Uhh . . ." Her mind seemed incapable of engaging further.

"Could we go over to your place and talk?" Dale asked.

Dazed, Beth just stared at him, swallowed, and said, "Ah, sure, I guess so. Would you open the gate?" When he did, she walked her horse out of the arena, her mouth dry.

She could feel his eyes on her as she nudged Far against the gate in her pasture fence, leaned down, opened it, and rode through. Beth dismounted, made sure Dale shut the gate, and they walked to her shed, where she started unsaddling. He leaned on the fence, watching her while she watched him out of the corner of her eye. When she put the cinch through the cinch keeper, Dale moved over, easily picked the saddle off the gelding's back, and asked, "Where do you want this?"

"Throw it on the first saddle rack inside the door, please." She watched him put the saddle in place. He turned. They looked at each other. Beth ducked her head, said to her knees, "Why don't you come up to the house? I'm hot and dying for a drink . . . I think I have some iced tea." She waved vaguely toward the house and managed to get her feet in motion.

Unable to come up with small talk, Beth led the way to the deck, motioned to chairs that were drawn up to a green wrought-iron table, and said, "Just sit at the table. I'll go wash up, get us some tea, and be right back."

Beth splashed some water on her face at the kitchen sink, opened the refrigerator, and stood looking inside as though it might give her answers to the questions that whirled through her mind. She shook her head, pulled out a pitcher of tea, and put it and two glasses on a tray. Staring at the tray solved nothing; she took an enormous breath and returned to the deck.

"Do you take sugar?" she asked as she gave Dale a glass of tea. "I don't use it, so I never remember to have it handy."

"No, thanks," he said as he watched Beth plop into a chair across the table. They drank in silence.

Dale said, "I imagine this is something of a surprise."

"A surprise?" Beth licked her lips. "How on earth did you know where I was? I haven't seen you for over forty years, and you show up. A surprise," she said to her glass as she rolled it back and forth between her hands.

"I've always known where you were," Dale said. Beth frowned as he continued. "I knew where you were when you lived here after you married, and when you went up to Wyoming, I kept track of you up there. Your husband had a lot of newspaper articles written about him. I knew people that knew you." He paused. "I was sorry to hear about your husband. Losing him like that must have been hard."

Beth nodded, carefully put her glass on the table.

"What caused the plane crash?"

"He caused it himself. He was following friends that were on motorcycles down the highway, didn't see the power line across the road. It tore the tail off the plane. It was so awful for our friends that saw him die." She bit her lip.

"You didn't like to fly with him?" Dale asked.

"Yes, I did, but I was on a ten-day pack trip in Canada, back in one of the wilderness areas. He was killed the day I returned to Banff. Getting home was a nightmare." Beth looked down at her hands. Her right hand started twisting at her wedding ring.

"I'm sorry. I didn't mean to upset you," Dale said. He turned in his chair, looked at the yard. "You really have a beautiful place."

Beth showed him around, talking about the frustrations of trying to learn to do all the outside work her husband had always taken care of while her mind ran in circles. How could she not have recognized him? He really hadn't changed that much—filled out, aged, but as they talked, he became the young man she had known, had been crazy about.

"How's your family?" Beth asked when they were again sitting at the porch table. "Did you go on to get a teaching degree like you said you were going to?"

"I did. I taught math and coached in Sterling until I retired. I decided to move to Fort Collins a year ago. There isn't much in Sterling for a single."

Beth frowned. "A single?"

"Marian and I got a divorce. We didn't survive the empty nest syndrome."

"Oh, I'm sorry. That must have been rough." After a brief silence, Beth asked, "How many kids do you have?"

"We have a girl who's a nurse. She's never married. She has a condo next to mine." Dale shifted on his chair. "How about you?"

"I have a son that's given me two beautiful granddaughters who are just starting school. They keep Grandma hopping when they come."

They were exploring mutual friends when Dale looked at his watch and whistled. "Whoa, where did the time go? I better get home. My daughter is coming over for dinner tonight. If I don't hurry I won't get it made in time." He stood up.

Beth got out of her chair. "Well, this was a surprise, you showing up out of the blue, very unexpected." She suddenly looked at Dale's hair, thought about May's prediction, and turned bright red. Flustered, she stuck out her hand. Bad mistake, she thought as a shock ran up her arm as he engulfed her hand in his. She pulled away, turned toward the door. "Nice to see you again. Good-bye." She opened the screen door, tripped on the sill, and almost fell into the house.

*Well that was sure smooth,* Beth thought as she watched his blue SUV going down her lane. What on earth was he doing showing up here? She dropped into a chair, fanned herself, got up, and hurried to the bathroom. The image in the mirror made her cringe with dismay. *God, I look like I'm at least ninety. I'm sure he was impressed.*

She fiddled around the kitchen, took a shower, put on clean clothes. Muttering to herself, she called May.

"Well, I think he showed up," she said as she looked distractedly out the bay window in the dining room at the mountains. The sun was almost down, the sky every shade of red and yellow possible.

"Who?" May asked.

"I thought you were a psychic. You know who, the guy that was going to come unexpected with sandy hair. What do you mean who?"

"Ah, and who is he?"

"I dated him before I met my husband."

"So how did it go?" Beth could tell May was smiling on the other end of the phone line.

"Oh, just peachy. I looked like the Wicked Witch of the West, no makeup on, ratty clothes, probably smelled. I was riding, and he just showed up over at my neighbor's arena." Beth hesitated. "We went back to my place. I showed him around. We sat on the porch, drank iced tea, and talked about old times.

"And?" May prompted.

"He's divorced, recently moved to Fort Collins." Beth sucked in a breath and plunged on. "These out-of-the-blue situations are really quite unfair. They always catch you looking your absolute worse, and you end up acting like your brains have leaked out your ears."

"Did his visit upset you?"

"I was all right, well kind of, until he shook hands and I really looked at him, and I finally realized he might be the guy you were telling me about, and I bolted into the house and left him standing there. He must think I'm an idiot," Beth groaned.

"Well, you don't want to get involved with anyone anyway, right?"

Beth could hear the amusement in May's voice. "Absolutely right, I just got my life put back together again. I have enough money, have my riding friends, travel when I want, have my family . . . he sure looked good."

"Did he ask you out?"

"No."

"Well then, you don't have to worry about it, do you?" After a brief silence, May added, "Look, I'm going into Fort Collins tomorrow. Join me, and you can tell me all about this guy." She was chuckling when she hung up.

Beth didn't sleep much that night.

\*　　\*　　\*

Beth yawned as she pawed through a rack of slacks in Sears the next morning. Losing interest, she looked for May. Spotting her friend, who was looking at purses, Beth wandered over, glancing at the merchandise displays on the way. "Oh God, enough shopping, I'm exhausted. Let's get a drink or something so I can sit down."

May looked at Beth, shook her head. "We have only been shopping for an hour. As Nancy would say, get a grip."

"Yeah, but that's more shopping than I do in a month . . . except for groceries," Beth clarified. She grabbed May's sleeve. "Let's go to the food court."

"If the U.S. economy depended on you, we would all starve," May grumbled.

Settled at a table in the food court, Beth took a long drink of her Coke. She sighed. "That's better. I was really parched."

"Good excuse anyway." May took a sip of her bottled tea. "All right, tell me more about Dale. You dated him before you met your husband?"

Nodding, Beth looked away.

"Do I have to pry it out of you? I deserve the whole story. After all, I predicted he would show up."

"Usually your predictions take years before they come about. I guess that's why I didn't tumble to it right away." Beth leaned forward in her chair. "All right, you asked for it."

Eyes unfocused, Beth went back to her past. "When I was in college, I went on a double date without knowing the guy. I guess you could say I was flying blind." She snickered. "It's the only time I ever did, and I wouldn't have, except my girlfriend vouched for him. It was like a collision between two stars." Beth made an explosive motion with both hands. "We started going out, spent most of our time together. I've never had that sort of total attraction before or after Dale. I felt like I couldn't breathe if he wasn't supplying the air."

"I have to meet this man."

"I never really figured out the attraction. I had dated guys that were a lot better looking and . . . nothing."

"Maybe you knew him from a previous life."

"Could be, it was instant."

"So go on. How long did you date him?"

"It's hard to remember that far back, but I know we went together all one summer into early winter because I remember snow at the end of things. It was on again, off again. No explanation, he would just vanish. It almost killed me that summer. I couldn't eat, I couldn't sleep. It got so bad I even thought about suicide." She rushed on to quell May's horrified look. "You know, like young people do occasionally because they get so miserable, nothing serious."

"Didn't you ever call him?"

"No, I didn't want him to feel like I was chasing him." Beth drained her Coke, rattling the ice at the bottom of the glass. She stared into the glass as though she could see herself there all those years ago. "The last time I saw him, he came to see me in the hospital. I was having some tests done, nothing serious. He found out about it through a friend of his, who worked there as an orderly. Don't they call them male nurses now?"

May nodded.

"Anyway, Dale popped in, handed me some roses, told me he hoped I was better soon, and left. They were lovely yellow roses . . ."

The friends were silent for a moment, their eyes tracking the people passing through the food court.

"And then I met Rob. He wanted me, was determined to convince me of the fact. Dale called when he heard about Rob, said he was going to get a teaching degree. Would I wait? By then I had already committed to Rob. I never saw Dale again until yesterday."

"Well, good thing you don't want to get involved. Do you think history might repeat itself?"

"I'm not going to worry about it. He probably was just curious to see what I looked like after all these years."

"Mmmm. I'm not so sure of that, my friend."

On her way home, Beth's mind was filled with memories stirred up by her visit with May. If she was honest, she had gone over Dale's visit constantly, making it through one whole day without thinking about her husband. She didn't know how she felt about that. She even had a dream about Dale but couldn't remember the details. She hadn't felt the sadness her dreams about Rob always left with her. Somehow she felt almost unfaithful. Wasn't that silly? Her husband died almost four years ago; she had hardly run after the first man she saw. Dale was the only man that had approached her since she became a widow, and he had her all fuzzed up. What had he wanted anyway?

*　　*　　*

Slow moving and sleepy eyed, Beth nursed a cup of coffee on the east deck the next morning. Far Horizon was in the corral, staring back at her with his "Are we riding?" look. She sighed. She should ride; they both needed to stay in condition. She just didn't have the energy; it had been a long night. The unexpected appearance of her old flame had unsettled her more than if she found herself riding Far Horizon down a street, clad only in long hair. She hadn't thought about Dale more than a dozen times in forty years. Now she couldn't get him out of her head. How could he still have the power to turn her inside out? *No more thinking about Dale's visit or her grand exit from the deck,* she told herself firmly. It was embarrassing.

She sipped her lukewarm coffee, frowned. *Wasn't there something this morning . . . her farrier was coming.* She gulped the rest of the brew and headed to the shed. She needed to get her morning chores done.

"You get your tippy toes done today, old man." Beth said as she put on Far's halter. She sprayed him so he wouldn't be kicking at bugs while Chad was trying to work. *Better clean out his hooves.* She grunted as she picked up each of Far Horizon's feet, scraped the debris out of the frog, and sniffed. No thrush, it had been too dry this year. That stuff did stink when it got started in the cracks around the frog of the hoof. She stroked the Arabian's neck as she removed his halter. "All done. You're gorgeous. Just hang out until Chad gets here."

Lunch was another peanut butter sandwich for her and wet cat food for Taz. She was just about out of both items. *I'd better put them on the list,* she thought as she put her plate in the dishwasher. She surveyed her kitchen, hands on hips, shook her head. *Better plan on some serious cleaning in here soon.*

Why had Dale come? Had his reaction been anything similar to hers? Beth felt like she wanted to scream. Her fists were clenched. She was in such a state her stomach hurt. She needed an off switch.

She heard someone knock . . . no, she felt it as if someone was knocking on a door inside her head. Her windows were open; maybe one of her neighbors was making a banging noise. She shrugged. Probably just imagining things; it was pretty plain she'd better cut back on the coffee. Grumbling, she headed back outside, nearly tripping over the cat, who tried to beat her out the door.

Chad was supposed to come at twelve-thirty, but Beth knew her farrier would probably run late. There were too many horses without manners. It was closer to one-thirty when Chad's pickup and trailer came down her lane.

"I'm sorry, I'm sorry. Seems like I'm always behind, but I had a real son of a gun to deal with," Chad Sanger puffed as he hauled his anvil into the shed. He was a stocky, good-looking man with a sunny smile.

Beth haltered Far while Chad brought the rest of his tools into the shed and put his leather apron on. As she led her horse into the shed, Chad let out a huge breath. He grinned as he looked at Far Horizon. "They should all have this guy's manners," he said, stroking the gelding's shoulder. "It's a pleasure to work on a real gentleman."

"Sounds like you had a real doozy." Beth got Far set up square on his feet so he would feel balanced while Chad was working on him.

"Oh yeah, and the woman hadn't even caught him before I showed up. She had to run him all over the pasture before she could get a halter on him." Chad snorted. "I sometimes wonder why I'm in this business."

Beth laughed. "You know you love it. You're just too forgiving of people's stupidity."

"I guess I think they will eventually get it, but some of them are really thick between the ears." Chad picked up Far's left front foot, placed it between his knees, and started nipping off the excess hoof.

"Are you getting any roping done this spring?"

Chad shook his head as he placed Far's foot on the cement. "Pretty hard to get much roping in with the boys both in baseball. We have a couple of houses under construction. That's another story. I think my shoeing clients drive me nuts . . ."

Grinning ruefully, Chad launched into a tale about the Texas woman who seemed determined to constantly change the house plans.

It took close to an hour to trim Far's feet and shoe him. The gelding had good feet; Arabs are known for that. Beth and Chad believed in letting him go barefoot most of the year, but it was time for shoes to protect him from the rocky areas Beth would be riding in through the summer.

Chad finished rasping the last hoof, gently set it down on the cement floor. He looked critically at the gelding's feet and nodded, satisfied. He leaned on Far's rump, wiping sweat off his forehead.

"Do you have lots of riding planned for the summer?"

Beth shrugged. "Only the week at Chugwater with my trainer. The rest will just be day trips with my friends. It's kind of hard to get away this time of year, too much work."

"You need a man around here, woman." Chad started gathering his tools.

"Yeah, that's what everybody tells me," Beth said dryly. She was tempted to tell Chad about Dale showing up but knew he needed to get to his next appointment. Really, what was there to tell?

They had their usual squabble about who would sweep up the hoof parings. Winning as usual, she did while he put his tools back in his trailer.

"You be sure and tell Peaches I said hello, and hug those twin boys of yours," Beth said as Chad shut the trailer door after checking that Taz hadn't decided to slip in undetected.

She turned her head as a huge black pickup rolled slowly past her hedge. It came to a stop in the parking area. The truck had enough chrome on it to dazzle a blind man.

"Now who . . . ah, heck . . ." She sniffed in disgust as she watched a big dark-haired man slide out of the pickup and stride toward them.

"Problem?" Chad moved away from his trailer to stand shoulder to shoulder with Beth.

"Just an irritation." Beth put her hands on her hips. "That's far enough." *Mr. Chrome*, she thought, even to the fancy sunglasses. The black-clad man stopped a few feet away.

"No, don't say anything. You come here every year. I tell you no every year. My husband did the same." Beth gritted through tight lips.

"Your asphalt needs redoing," Chrome said.

"Yeah, I know. If I was going to keep it up, you sure wouldn't get the job. Which is what I tell you every year. What part of no don't you understand?" Beth walked a couple of steps toward the man. "If you come back here one more time, I'll call the police on you since you don't seem to be able to remember you're not welcome at this place. Now get out." She turned her back on him, walked back to Chad. "Now where were we?"

As he watched the man in black stomp back to his pickup, Chad reached over and patted Beth on the arm. "I guess I can quit worrying about you being able to take care of yourself."

"I can't stand that guy." Beth watched the pickup go out of sight. "Who knows? He might be the best asphalt guy in the business. He showed up the first year we were here. He insisted we needed his services, informed us the driveway job hadn't been done right to start with. For all I know, he could have done the job originally. And I don't deal with someone that hides his eyes behind dark glasses."

Chad rubbed his chin thoughtfully. "If I was him, I don't think I'd come back again. I think he got it this time." He opened his pickup door, sat under the wheel, scrabbled around in the cab, and brought out his appointment book. "We'd better reset those shoes in six weeks."

Beth watched as Chad drove slowly out of her yard. She was grateful for his caring. They had become close over the last decade as he shod her horses. *I've watched him grow up*, she thought as she let Far Horizon out to graze. *We went to his wedding, listened to his struggles with his changed life, worried about his baby boys when they were born too soon.* It did startle Beth that he had worried about her.

\* \* \*

The following morning, Beth drank coffee in Nancy's kitchen. Nancy's dog was shoving her nose against Beth's knee while her cat lay on Beth's lap, doing a good job of shedding hair.

"Oh, just swat them away. You know my animals have no manners." Nancy poured cream into her second cup of coffee. "So who was the guy that was wandering around your place?"

"When?"

"Last Wednesday. We were slaving away in the yard when we saw him. I knew you were in the arena. So I went through the fence to see what he wanted. When I found he was looking for you, I sent him to the barn. I spotted you together later when I was putting stuff in the dumpster, so I know he found you.

"Mmm." Beth stirred her coffee.

"Oh come on, is it a secret?"

"No, just a surprise. He's an old boyfriend." Beth gave Nancy the story and then shook her head as she watched her friend's eyes brighten. "Now look, I think he was just curious."

"He didn't ask you out?"

"Nope. We caught up on each other's lives and he left."

"Oh." Disappointed, Nancy huffed out a breath. She thought a moment and slowly brightened. "I bet he calls."

"Doubt it."

"Bet you a bar of dark chocolate." Nancy's eyes danced with glee.

Beth sighed. "Okay, but be prepared to buy the most expensive brand. He won't call."

# CHAPTER 3

But he did, two weeks after his sudden appearance. Beth was working a jigsaw puzzle after dinner, determined to avoid watching the brainless TV programs.

The phone rang.

"Hi, how's it going?" It was Dale.

Beth dropped the puzzle piece she was holding. Her hands started sweating. *Oh, grow up*, she snarled to herself. You certainly aren't a teenager anymore. But she felt as awkward as she had at that age.

They did social talking while her mind ran like a hamster in an exercise wheel.

She answered in tiny affirmative or negatives until he finally got to the point. "Would you go out to dinner with me?"

A rather prolonged silence resulted.

"Are you there?" Dale finally asked.

"I'm here. I'm not sure I want to do that."

"Why not?"

"I'm not sure, probably because I haven't been out with a strange man for forty years. Yeah, that might be part of it."

Dale laughed. "I'm really not all that strange, if you remember."

"Oh yeah, I remember. I remember a lot of it," she said uncomfortably.

"I really would like to see you. Why don't we both relax, just go from here. What do you think?"

Beth sighed. "I warn you, I sigh a lot, got that from my grandma."

"I'll try to overlook it or maybe I'll join in," Dale said. "What about Saturday?"

"I'm busy Saturday."

"How about Sunday?"

"Sorry, I'm busy the whole weekend." *Liar, liar, pants on fire*, Beth thought. "You really shouldn't waste your time on me, Dale. I'm not ready for a relationship."

"How about just a friendship?"

"I'm sorry, but thanks for asking." Beth gently hung up the phone and was surprised at the pang of regret she felt. *I wish I had said yes*, she thought with surprise. *I had a chance. I didn't take it. I'm a chicken.*

"Cluck, Cluck."

Beth looked in disbelief at Taz, who was twinning around her ankles, hoping for a treat. "What? Did you say *cluck*?"

Taz gave her a "don't be an idiot" look and sauntered toward the kitchen.

Shaking her head, Beth muttered, "I'm hearing things. I distinctly heard someone cluck."

"I'm hurt. You don't remember me . . . well, it's been a while."

Beth's mind spun. Like a faded echo, an image was trying to form. "The Worry Nag? You're the Worry Nag. I'd forgotten all about you!"

"You didn't need me. You weren't involved with a man."

"I was married to a man for almost forty years."

"Husbands are a different case. I was necessary when you were dating and before you decided to get married. Once you married, my job was done. You've forgotten how you used to worry about the male gender? Oh, the angst!" The Nag looked at the ceiling, brushed back her thin locks.

The image in her mind was clearer now, a sour old spinster who was standing in front of an open closet door. An apron was tied about her waist over a faded housedress.

"Have you been knocking . . . ?"

"Of course, the minute he showed up. You ignored me."

"You look different. You were younger."

"Ha, missy, so were you!"

Beth shook her head. "This is crazy, go away. I don't need you. I'm not going to get involved again."

"So you say. I can feel it starting all over again right now. The fretting and stewing, the clenched hands. I'm getting too old for this, and so are you."

"Fine, go back in your closet."

"Fine. But you'll need me, you'll see." The Worry Nag sniffed, turned her boney body around, and disappeared into the closet. The door slammed shut.

Beth slumped in her chair, staring at the wall. "I'm losing my mind," she muttered to herself. "I can't have just had a conversation with a figment of it."

Taz came back into the room. Beth stood and scooped up the cat. She cradled it in her arms on its back as she walked down the hall to her bedroom. Staring intently into its eyes, she said, "Are you completely sure you didn't say *cluck*?"

*The Worry Nag was right*, Beth thought as she got ready for bed. The episode with Dale when she was a young woman had been rough. Perhaps, in some strange way, the Nag had saved her sanity. Being able to talk to someone, or rather something, might have kept her from going off the deep end all those years ago.

Well, she had turned Dale down. That was the end of it; she didn't need the Nag because there wasn't going to be any this time.

Beth got into bed, opened her latest book. An avid reader since she was a child, she always liked to have a pile of unread books waiting for her on her bedside table. Adjusting her reading glasses, she found her place in Larry McMurtry's *Lonesome Dove*. But the antics of Gus and Call failed to engage her mind. Perhaps the book wasn't that good, although she thought she had been enjoying it.

"Ha."

"You be quiet. I'm not worrying."

"Fretting, stewing."

"Am not."

"Suit yourself. I can hear you. Are too."

In her mind, Beth pointed a finger at the Worry Nag. "I can board up that door if you don't leave me alone or I can imagine any size of lock. I'll throw away the key."

"Have it your way, but you'll worry. I've known you since you were a teenager, although you were a little slow when it came to boys."

"Books were better. Would you like me to pick you up one so you'll have something to do?" Beth's question was asked with exaggerated sweetness. "Oh, sorry. I guess that wouldn't work very well, would it? Your specialty is nagging. Why don't you go practice. In your room."

Looking put out, the Nag stomped back into her room and slammed the door.

*     *     *

The Barnes and Noble bookstore in Fort Collins was on South College Avenue. As always, it was busy. Inside were so many choices, and Beth was interested in so many subjects. She always bought too many books because, she had to admit, she had a book addiction. For that reason, she seldom risked going. Libraries are free, so Beth went often to the ones in the towns of Ault, Eaton, and Greeley.

But it was a real treat for her to go to the huge store in Fort Collins, roam the aisles to her heart's content, purchase a cup of espresso or a latte in the coffee shop, and plunge headfirst into a new story. She believed a treat truly soothed the soul.

Beth took a sip of her latte and sighed with pleasure. Eyes on the page, she carefully put her coffee back on the table without looking up, loath to glance away from the latest Nora Roberts romance.

"That's a handy skill to have," a male voice said from the opposite side of the table.

She heard a chair scrape across the floor and looked up. Dale sat across from her, looking good.

"Uh?"

"Being able to drink and read at the same time. I'd spill the coffee and ruin the book."

He took a sip of his own coffee, leaned forward.

"Years of practice," she said, leaning slightly back in her chair.

"Umm."

They stared at each other.

Beth groped for something to say, but her brain was in freeze mode.

After an eternity, Dale said, "This is my favorite haunt—coffee, a pastry, and the latest crossword puzzle book. Do you do crossword puzzles?" He took another sip. "Supposedly, crossword puzzles are good for the brain."

Beth reached tentatively toward her own coffee. *I'll spill it*, she thought, drew her hand back. "Jigsaw," she managed. "Mostly in the winter."

"Those are good too."

*Maybe I could just faint*, Beth thought frantically. *I don't know what to say. His presence is overwhelming. He isn't doing anything but sitting there, sipping coffee.* She tried on a smile and hoped it wasn't ghastly.

He smiled back, took another sip of his coffee, and got up. "Well, I won't bother you. I've got to run, but it was nice to see you again. Take care." He nodded at her and walked away.

Beth slumped in her chair. How could someone she hadn't seen for over forty years affect her the way he did? Well, that would be the last of it. Between acting like an idiot when he came to the house, turning him down for a date, and staring at him like a deer caught in the headlights of a car during this conversation, he would surely accept the fact she was terminally insane and leave her alone. In fact he was already doing it. If he still wanted a date he would have asked her, wouldn't he? Why didn't he?

She was proud of the fact that she managed to get home safely.

\*    \*    \*

"You sure handled him well. At least you didn't fall out of your chair." The Worry Nag put up her hand to forestall Beth's demand to leave. "Don't tell me to get back in the closet. There's such a stew going on in there from this last encounter I'll die in there."

Beth was cleaning tack in the shed. She dropped a lead line in the bucket of soapy water, sighing. "It wasn't my finest moment."

"You're telling me. I was embarrassed for you. Here this fine man sits down at your table. You sit there with your mouth hanging open."

"Well, he caught me off guard, and for your information, my mouth wasn't hanging open. I just couldn't figure out what to do with it." Beth sloshed the lead line up and down in the bucket. "What difference does it make? There won't be any more to it."

"There are many reasons for me not to believe that. He's already got you hooked."

"It doesn't matter. There are a lot of fish in the sea. He'll go after someone else. I'm certainly not going to contact him."

"Nope, he'll try again and this time . . ."

"I thought you were a worry nag instead of a mind reader. Please go away and let me be. Having you harping at me doesn't help."

The Worry Nag opened her mouth, thought better of it, turned back toward her closet. She disappeared into the darkness, leaving the door open, but returned immediately with a large kettle that smoked profusely.

"I get it—burning stew." Beth shook her head wearily.

The Nag grinned, put the pot down, waved the door back and forth, fanning the air, and then disappeared into the hazy interior. She left the door open.

\* \* \*

When Beth heard Dale's voice on the phone the following day, it was almost a relief. This would end it, one way or another.

"I hope you enjoyed the book," Dale said.

"What?"

"The book you were reading when I ran into you in the coffee shop."

"Oh, yes. Her characters are well done. I still have one chapter to go."

"You certainly were engrossed with it. I stood in front of your table for a couple of minutes."

"Really? Sorry, I can get kind of single-minded at times."

"Look, I still want you to go out to dinner with me. And I'm going to keep asking. You know, water can wear away stone."

Beth smothered a laugh. "True, but it takes eons."

"Right. So take pity on an old guy. My arm will wear out dropping all those drips."

"Dale . . ."

"Let's just try it, maybe for nothing more than old time's sake? What can it hurt?"

*I should say no*, Beth thought. "All right. When?"

"Saturday?"

"Fine."

After she hung up, she sat staring into space long enough for Taz to realize a lap was available. The cat settled itself in happily.

*I wish I hadn't agreed to go out with him*, she thought. *I think I'm starting something I shouldn't.* She didn't want complications. What would it be like to be on a date after all these years? The very thought terrified her.

The Worry Nag popped out of the closet, but she just stood there with her hands on her hips, shaking her head.

*I need to relax.* With that thought, Beth went to the bookcase and dug through her CD collection, looking for her yoga program and spent an hour in various positions.

Even with the exercise, her sleep was fitful.

# CHAPTER 4

"Keep busy" was Beth's mantra Saturday morning. Pansies were planted, and the soil around other plants flew as she dug industriously, loosening the tight soil. She cleaned the loafing area and groomed Far Horizon until he gleamed like a new penny.

About noon, she staggered into the house and made herself a peanut butter and jelly sandwich. As she munched, she watched robins enjoying the birdbath in the aspen grove. She noticed her windows were dirty. Maybe she should tackle that next, but there were too many to do today—she would sweep the west deck, pay some bills, and take a bath.

Dale would be showing up around five.

It was three o'clock by the time she drew her bath. Relaxing in the steaming water, she hoped she hadn't overdone the sweeping. Her shoulders were tight. As her muscles soaked, her thoughts focused on the coming evening. Her mind had been on that subject while she did all her chores.

She wouldn't think about that anymore. It was making her nuts. Instead she wandered back into the past.

*   *   *

When she opened the door to Dale, there had been no immediate reaction. She was so nervous about her first "blind" date she hardly saw him, but when he took her arm as they walked down the steps toward the car, an electric shock had run through her body. *That reaction is still there*, she thought, remembering their handshake on her east deck a few weeks ago.

The foursome had gone to a kegger at the reservoir. The party had not been Beth's type of thing. She didn't like beer and didn't smoke, but she did love to dance. Dale danced well, and they had enjoyed themselves until the cigarette smoke got so thick it started making Beth's eyes water.

The two of them slipped away from the noisy party and climbed a hill in the mild September air, stumbling and laughing under the light of a full moon. At the top they stood without speaking, in awe of the stars that were reflecting their glory in the still lake water.

Beth had been caught off guard by the sensations she experienced. Her body had yearned for his. She knew before he made the first move that he was going to kiss her, and he had taken her breath away with those kisses. Older than her eighteen years he had been a perfect gentleman, not asking for more. They stayed on the hill, talking softly, experiencing the strong attraction that flowed between them until the night chill drove them back to the party.

*If he isn't a gentleman still, I'll probably scream and run all the way home,* she thought as she carefully got out of the deep steeping tub. Glowing from her hot bath, Beth spotted a tube of scented lotion in the basket that held her bath items, a gift that had languished for several years, unnoticed and unused. No time like the present, she supposed, and applied it lavishly.

Smelling like an exotic flower in an Arabian harem garden, she moved across the bathroom until she caught a glimpse of her nude body in the full-length mirror. She stopped reluctantly and slowly turned to look critically at her body. Not too bad from the top of the head to the waist but not so hot the rest of the way down. Weight stuck in places it never had until she was in her late fifties. She sighed and covered up with the thick terry robe.

She spent considerable time putting on makeup and doing her hair, something she had seldom bothered with for the last few years. She was more than satisfied with the result. *I still clean up pretty well,* she thought as she looked at the results in the mirror, switched off the light above her sinks, and walked into the adjoining bedroom.

It was a pleasant room, done in shades of blue with white chests of drawers flanking both sides of the large west window. Lacy white curtains framed her spectacular view and set off the blue and mauve flowered wallpaper. A large wicker chair was draped with a white throw that was beautifully decorated with pansies. Sliding doors opened onto her west deck.

Usually in good order, the room was a wreck with drawers pulled open and most of her wardrobe thrown on the bed. *Man, I don't have anything but grubbies anymore*, she thought. Everything was either too tight, too loose, wrong color, wrong, wrong, wrong.

She finally decided on a pair of jeans and a lime-green knit top. The diamonds her husband had given her sparkled in her ears, on her neck, and on her ring finger. She looked at her wedding ring. It was a quandary; she wasn't married anymore, but the few times she had tried to leave it behind, she had gone back home to get it. Did she need it to protect her? Did she feel disloyal to her husband if she didn't wear it? Beth couldn't find an answer.

She went back to the bathroom to check her hair again and do her lips. She carefully applied lipstick, one eye on the wall clock. Dale would be here in a few minutes. The tube was old and not spreading well. *I guess I need to update my makeup*, she thought in frustration, pressing hard.

The doorbell rang and she jumped. The lipstick broke, smearing a thick layer of Sweet Apricot on her left incisor. She grabbed a Kleenex, wiped off the tooth, picked up the broken piece of lipstick from the counter, and threw it in the wastebasket. Grateful the lipstick hadn't ruined her top, she took another swipe at her hair and hurried down the hall toward the front door.

*I can do this*, she chanted to herself as she hesitated, her hand on the doorknob. The doorbell rang again. She jerked the door open and invited Dale inside.

"You sure look lovely tonight," Dale said as he stood in her foyer.

"Anything would be an improvement over the last time you were here, right?" He sure smelled good.

"You look better than most women without makeup, and the sun made you glow."

Oh boy.

\*     \*     \*

Dale drove them back into Fort Collins, which was twenty miles west of Beth's place. When she had lived in the same area in the sixties, all the towns along Front Range had been small, but they had grown into an almost continuous flow of humanity from Fort Collins through Colorado Springs. Beth was north of the foothill cities of Loveland and Boulder and straight east of Fort Collins, close to Eaton and Ault. At night there was a glowing necklace of lights along the foothills with just a small wave of darkness breaking against the shore of her isolated world. She wasn't looking forward to homes sprouting up in the pastures across the road. It would come, but she was hoping she would be gone by then.

"I really should have just met you somewhere," she said. "It's going to be a forty-mile trip by the time you get back home."

"That's no problem. It gives us lots of time to talk," Dale said.

"That's the only thing I don't like about living where I am," she said. "I love being out in the country, having my horse right out the back door, but I have to drive into town to get everything. But Ault is just three miles away, and by the time I'm too old to drive very far, I hope it has grown out to me."

"You plan on staying on your place then?"

"I didn't at first. It was overwhelming—so much work to do, and I'm not very good with machines. I swear they see me coming and go bad. But I learned to turn on the sprinkler system, who to call to take care of the trees, and found a handyman to do the heavy work."

"I didn't want to give up my horse or stable him somewhere. I had enough of that before we bought this place when Rob retired. This was always my dream." Beth smiled a sad little smile and changed the subject. "Where do you live?"

Dale glanced over at her. "I bought a condo on the west side of Fort Collins when I moved here from Sterling. I just wanted a small place that would be easy to take care of. My daughter has the condo next to mine."

"She never married?"

"No, she's smart and a really good nurse, but she can be difficult to get along with. She and her mother never got along. I manage all right, but I pretty much let her go her own way. Her mother was always trying to change her."

"I don't know why we can't just accept our kids as they are," Beth mused. "It's hard—when you grow up a certain way and raise your kids the way you think is right—to watch them have a completely different way of living. But I've decided they have a right to live life as they choose, not as I think they should. After my son told me to butt out, I should add."

"Sounds familiar." Dale gave a soft snort of laughter. "It doesn't sound like you have a mama's boy."

"Hardly. I taught Steve to be independent and how to work and be responsible for his actions. He's a really good man, and I got lucky with the woman he married too."

"Tell me about your grandchildren. You said you have two granddaughters?"

"Oh, let me tell you. I knew I wanted to be a grandmother, but I had no idea . . ."

The radio played old rock-and-roll tunes Beth recognized from the years she was in college as they drove toward Fort Collins while she told Dale about her beautiful granddaughters in more detail than he probably wanted to know. The soft darkness wrapped around the vehicle, encapsulating them in a warm cocoon.

Dale took her to an Italian restaurant in Old Town, which was perfect. The music was hardly noticeable, and there were no loud large groups. It was a relief not to have to shout to have a conversation. They both chose the fettuccine Alfredo and talked about their likes and dislikes concerning food. The special was very good, and Beth realized she had finally relaxed and was enjoying herself.

She pushed her plate aside and sighed. "I'm going to have to take the rest of that home. I'm stuffed. They always give you way too much food."

She fiddled with her spoon, groping for a subject to fill the silence that was developing. *Just shut up, Beth*, she thought. Her husband always told her she talked too much. She smiled nervously at Dale, and he gave her a slow, easy smile that jumped her nerves up another notch. "Uh, what are you doing with your retirement? Are you finding it hard?"

Dale took a sip of wine and regarded the glass as he frowned. "I didn't realize how much of a change it would be. I guess I really never thought about it. All those busy, hectic years went by and now . . . sometimes I really don't know what to do with myself. I never really had the time or money to develop any hobbies, like golf or hunting, although I did a little fishing." He paused and then grinned at her. "I've learned how to clean house and do laundry, no pink underwear anymore." He put his glass down. "So what besides your grandchildren and your place keeps you busy?"

"I finally decided I wanted to learn to ride, properly instead of just staying on the horse, so I started taking lessons. I wish I had known what I know now all the years I worked cattle when I lived in Wyoming. It's been a long process. I bet I could do the work twice as fast now I know how to ask the horse to do what I want correctly."

"It sounds interesting." Dale motioned the waitress over, and she removed the plates.

"Do you ride?" Beth watched Dale divide the rest of the bottle of wine between them. "If I remember, you were a town kid like I was those hundred years ago."

"I did when I was a child. My grandfather had a farm and a couple of nags that we kids used to hang on and fall off of. I haven't ridden in years. It's an expensive hobby when you're raising a family." He leaned forward to fold his arms on the table. "It looked like you were a fairly accomplished rider when I was lurking in the neighbor's barn."

"I started riding when we lived next to a rancher in Rawlins. I became really good friends with his wife. She was the hired man and had a lot of stock to take care of. I had all kinds of spare time, so I volunteered to help if they would tell me what to do." She leaned forward, her hands accenting her speech. "I started helping them gather cattle, and they taught me a lot. They were real hands. I loved it. I should have been a cowboy driving the herds up from Texas. I didn't mind the dirt or weather or sore muscles. I just enjoyed every minute, even the ones that scared me half to death.

"I bought a young green mare and managed not to kill myself breaking her in, and we moved cattle in the spring and the fall. Oh, I had lots of adventures," she said, her eyes shining with memories as she picked up her napkin and folded it neatly beside her plate. "Getting involved with the horses was really a lifesaver for me." Her eyes became soft and unfocused. "I don't know what I would have done if I hadn't had that interest these last few years." She held up her wine glass and smiled at Dale. "I never met a horse I couldn't like." Beth giggled softly. "Sorry, I do go on when I get started."

Dale gave her a long stare. "In the candlelight you look exactly like you did forty-five years ago, except I think you're prettier." He leaned forward and laid his hand on top of hers.

A slow blush spread over Beth's body from the soles of her feet to the crown of her head. She was suddenly so warm that she felt the need to remove clothing, and she was sure this wasn't a hot flash.

"Good Lord, Dale. I'm almost sixty-four years old. I look like my grandmother." She gently pulled her hand out from under his and started fiddling with her wine glass.

"And I look like my grandfather, come to think of it." Dale held up his glass. "To the both of them, let's have some more wine."

The ride back was quiet and relaxed until Beth got to thinking about saying good-bye. *Oh Lord, how do we do that at this age?*

They stood at her door in the soft spring night. The moon was full, and she could see Dale's face clearly.

"I had a wonderful time, thank you." Now that they were to the sticking point, she was calm.

"So did I. We always did if I remember right." He bent toward her, his questioning eyes staying on hers. She turned her head, so he kissed her on the cheek. "Well," he said, "I better finish those miles. I'll call you soon."

Beth smiled and nodded and watched as he drove away. She didn't go in the house but sat at the table on the deck. Things hadn't changed. Dale was as easy to be with as he was when they spent that spring and summer together before she started dating Rob.

It would be nice to have some male companionship again. She could keep it casual, couldn't she? Dale probably wouldn't want a permanent relationship anyhow. Commitment didn't come easily to men. It wouldn't change her life that much, just enhance it to have someone to laugh with and do things with once in a while. To have someone to walk into a room with instead of being the only single one there. They could just be friends, couldn't they?

A laugh of disbelief echoed faintly from the Worry Nag's closet.

She lay awake half the night, trying to read but mostly staring at the pages and growling at the cat when it tried to curl up against her neck.

*     *     *

It was hard for Beth to wait until a decent hour to call May the next morning. She hoped her friend was back from her trip, as she was bursting to talk to someone about her date with Dale. She wished May was home more, but May traveled extensively, visiting her large family and seeing exotic places that Beth only read about.

"I had dinner with Dale last night," Beth broke into the middle of May's dialogue about her family in Nebraska. "Sorry, I just had to talk to you about my date with Dale. Oh damn, I spilled my coffee. Just a minute."

"A little uptight are we this morning?" May chuckled after Beth mopped up the mess. "Did you have a good time?"

"At first I was really nervous, but about halfway through the evening, I finally relaxed. I talked so much his ears must still be ringing this morning. I don't know how women do this kind of thing. The ones that get remarried several times must have nerves of steel." Beth stood at her kitchen counter and looked unseeingly at her side yard and the birds squabbling around her bird feeder.

"Are you going to go out with him again?" May asked.

"He said he'd call. I guess I will if he does. But is it fair if I don't want to get remarried to date him?"

"You're on the path. Why don't you see where it leads?"

"I need to find you a boyfriend so we would have the same sort of problems."

"Don't bother," May said. "You and I have already had this conversation. I've been through one miserable marriage, and that was one I picked when the market had lots of choices. There aren't very many good ones to start with, and the ones that are available now are the ones nobody wants."

"Oh thanks, that makes me feel so much better. It spooks me because Dale is divorced. It would be better if his wife had died. Oh jeez, that was a rotten thing to say."

"Nope, just realistic, and that's you. Don't worry about finding me another guy. I'm just going to take care of myself from now on," May said.

"That's what I said too. But Dale showed up, and I know I'm going to need to bother you with this. I'll need words of wisdom."

"Anytime," May said. "Don't stress yourself over this."

"That's what I'm always telling you. You're the worrywart."

"You're right. Problem solved. You have the fun. I'll do the worrying."

A sensation of outrage filtered into Beth's mind. Oh dear, the Worry Nag was stirring. Beth brought up an image of her shoulder holding firm against the Nag's door. *Take a vacation,* she thought, *or I will get that big lock for your door. Quit muttering, I'm talking here.*

She pulled her attention back to May. "Enough about me. Did your brother ever ask that woman he was going with to marry him?"

Unable to settle down after her talk with May, Beth decided to do some long overdue cleaning in the kitchen. Sorting through food containers that seemed to multiply in the darkness of the lower kitchen cabinets, Beth's thoughts reflected on her long friendship with May.

*What would I have done without her? She was my best friend when we were young brides. I remember when she finally told me about her psychic abilities. She had sensed I had minor abilities but hadn't said anything.*

*Until I dreamed my close friend died. My dream was so real it didn't fade after I was out of bed. Instead, I had grown more and more upset, so I called and was told my friend had a kidney removed. The surgeons were almost positive the kidney was malignant.*

*It wasn't cancer, just an infected cyst. When I told May about the dream she opened up about her own abilities.*

*The "sight" is passed on through the female line. May was third generation Irish in this country. Until she started school, she thought everyone talked to dead people. She could tell fortunes, read palms, and "seeings" would just come out of the blue. But she had accepted it, learned to deal with it, and only talked about it to those she trusted not to make fun of her.*

*I remember the reading May gave me years ago, when she asked if I knew if any of the men in our little crowd of couples was having health problems because she saw a death there. She foretold it would devastate the whole group. We worried about it for a while, but nothing developed, and we forgot,* Beth mused as she tossed old cottage cheese cartons in the trash. *For some reason, I never imagined it would be Rob. And May doesn't remember what she says when she read the cards; she just reports what pours through her from the other side. But after his death, I realized he was the one she saw. We got it wrong—it wasn't health; it was an accident.*

Beth sighed as she levered herself off the kitchen floor. I'm glad we got it wrong and forgot it. It would have been awful waiting all those years for the shoe to drop.

# CHAPTER 5

"Let's make a pact." Dale called a week after their date. "I haven't spent any time in Denver for years. Have you?"

"Not really. When I'm down there I'm usually visiting family or friends, not sightseeing."

"I suggest we treat ourselves each Saturday to something in Denver. How about it?" When Beth didn't answer right away, he added, "Seeing me once a week won't bother you, will it?"

*Yeah, right*, Beth thought. *I guess I might as well find out.* "We could try and see how it goes. There are a lot of places I've thought about going to but never had the time."

"How about the Denver Zoo for our first excursion? I hear the new Lion House is something," Dale suggested.

Beth smiled to herself as she hung up the phone. *It was nice to have something to look forward to*, she thought as she gave in to Taz's repeated demands for her afternoon treat. The blasted cat could tell time. She put a couple of spoonfuls of the dreadful-smelling mystery contents into the cat's dish and dumped the empty cat-food can into the trash.

"You're a glutton for punishment. I knew you would get involved with this man. I told you so."

*Not again*, Beth thought and gave a heartfelt sigh. "I don't need you to nag me. We are just going to be friends. Besides, I told you I didn't need you anymore. My friend May will do my worrying."

"Ha, she can't hold a candle to me in that department."

Mentally, Beth thumbed her nose at the Nag. "I'm happy. Leave me alone. I'm not going to worry about it, just let things happen."

"You're still a child. A man won't let a relationship just be friends. He'll be hauling you into bed before you know what's happening."

"That's it!" Beth snapped. "I forbid you to bother me. Stay in your room."

"Fine." The Worry Nag wagged a finger at Beth and smirked. "You won't be able to keep me in when things get bad, you'll see. Besides, we have worried about this bad boy before, haven't we?"

*Oh Lord, she's right*, Beth thought as the Nag disappeared into the closet.

\* \* \*

It was a perfect day in May, warm and sunny. The zoo landscaping offered spring flowers: hyacinth, daffodils, and primroses sheltered in the shady flower beds. The bright accents were a treat for the eyes, much appreciated after the drab winter.

The recently redone Lion House was a major improvement over the old setup. Instead of being in cages, where they paced back and forth all day, the lions now roamed in natural settings with access to inside shelter in bad weather. The animals were separated from the humans either by moats or glass.

"Oh, this is so much better," Beth said, watching the lions romping in the sunshine. "I used to get so upset at zoos when I was a kid, seeing everything in cages, so sad." She watched as a half-grown cub crawled over his patient mother, who was trying to enjoy the sun. The cub growled and chewed the mother's ears and tail until the female lost her patience and gave the offending cub a swat. It sat on its haunches, blinked for a few minutes, and then started all over again.

Beth looked up at Dale as he watched the lions. "It's good the animals are too far away to be teased. I remember watching a kid at the San Diego Zoo years ago, who, in spite of the Do not Tease the Animals sign, just kept leaning over the rail to bug a lioness that had a couple of cubs in the cage with her. I was about to go over and tell him to lay off when the lioness stopped her pacing, backed into the bars on the front of the cage, and let fly." Beth giggled.

"The lioness . . ."

"Peed all over him. I had no idea they could spray such a distance. It was a good thing I was standing as far away from the kid as I was because she soaked him. He went bawling off to his mother. Served the brat right, which is what I told the mother when she got upset about her dripping offspring."

Dale grinned. "I can just see you laying into her."

"I wasn't rude, just said her brat was bothering the animals, and if I was the lion, I would have wanted to bite his head off."

"I'll remember not to tease, sounds like it might be dangerous around you." Dale took Beth's arm. "Let's go to Monkey Island."

As they walked past the Giraffe House, they stopped to watch a very young giraffe try to get to his feet. Its antics had them laughing softly as he struggled. He finally managed to rise and teetered on his feet, all four legs spayed out. He froze in that position, his eyes rolling as he looked at his mother.

"He doesn't know how to get out of that predicament." Beth said quietly.

The female giraffe swayed over to her baby and nudged it gently. The calf fell over and, instead of trying to get back up, just put its head down and sighed.

"They move like rocking horses, don't they?" Dale observed.

"Mmm, especially when they're running,"

The calf decided to take a nap rather than risk more experimentation, so Dale and Beth left to seek more action.

Frantic antics on Monkey Island had the watching crowd howling with laughter. Up and down the ropes that served as vines, up and down the trunk of the huge maple tree that stood in the center of the island, the monkeys chased and wrestled one another like children on a major sugar binge.

A freckled-faced boy standing close to Beth asked his mother, "Why do they stay on the island?"

"Watch them," his mother explained. "They don't like the water—they will drink it, but they won't go in it. Maybe they think there are crocodiles in it."

The child looked at the water and shuddered. "Wow, that would keep me on the island too."

Beth smiled at two female monkeys that were sitting on their haunches, hugging each other as they watched the bolder ones. They looked like a couple of timid little girls. "I guess these monkeys haven't learned to tolerate water like the monkeys I read about in the *National Geographic* magazine. They completely changed their behavior."

"Tell me about them," Dale said with a tender look at Beth, who missed it because she was still focused on the monkeys.

"These monkeys live in a pretty frigid winter climate. I can't remember where for sure, but I think maybe on one of the islands off Japan. There are hot springs on the island, and the experts figure one of the tribe probably fell into the pools and realized how good the hot water felt. Now they spend all their time in the water in the winter, except when they feed." She turned toward Dale with a grin. "There was a picture of all these solemn-looking monkeys up to their necks in steaming water with a pile of snow on top of their heads. Learned behavior, the experts called it."

"I do like a hot bath myself, but I don't know about the snow on my head." Dale yawned hugely. "Oops, guess that's a sign it's about time to call it a day."

\*   \*   \*

Their next Saturday was spent at the new Denver Aquarium. It had been built close to the South Platte River, adjacent to the new Elitch Garden Theme Park. The baseball stadium was just a mile or so to the south, and the football stadium was a little west.

They spent a lot more time at the aquarium than they planned, and when they walked to the parking lot late in the afternoon, the sound of traffic roaring along I-25 caused Dale to look at his watch. "Wow, we better get out of here. With all this stuff in one location, the traffic gets nuts in just a half hour."

Fifteen minutes later, they were in the middle lane, heading north; and they both gave a sigh of relief.

"What did you think of the aquarium?" Dale maneuvered around a Datsun that was poking along in the fast lane.

"I enjoyed it. I expected fish, of course, but I certainly didn't expect Bengal tigers! Weren't they the most beautiful things you ever saw with those golden coats and black stripes?"

"All the better to hunt you with, my dear," drawled Dale. "The stripes break up their outlines and help them be almost invisible in the underbrush. They're one of the few cats that will turn into a man-eater."

"I've heard of the ones in India. How awful it must be for a village to have one poaching on their children." Beth shuddered.

"It's usually an old one that is having trouble hunting but not always. And once they get a taste of man flesh, they usually keep at it until they're killed."

"I feel sorry for the wild things. We've invaded their territory to the point where they have nowhere to go. There was a mountain lion that tracked and attacked a woman just outside of Lyons, Colorado, a few years ago, and that has been pretty much unheard of."

"The drought hasn't helped either. Poodles taste better than grass when you crave meat," Dale said grimly.

They shared a comfortable silence for a few miles, Dale driving skillfully through the traffic and Beth watching the passing scenery.

Beth glanced at Dale. "On a more cheerful note, I loved the otters. Did you ever see anything have so much fun in your life, sliding down their tunnels and wrestling with each other?" She smiled to herself. "Such little clowns."

"They were fun to watch, weren't they?" Dale agreed. "I didn't think I would ever get you away from them . . . course I thought that when we were watching the tigers too. You really soak in an experience."

"And you are very patient to let me do it without dragging me away like some of the parents had to do with their kids."

"That's me, patient as Job." Dale pursed his lips and scratched his head. "Okay, that's two things crossed off our list of possibilities. What about next Saturday? We still have Pikes Peak, Cave of the Winds, the Royal Gorge, Air Force Academy, or the Butterfly Pavilion."

Without hesitation, Beth said, "The Butterfly Pavilion. I love it. I was there a few years ago when my grandchildren were small and would love to go again. And we wouldn't have to fight so much traffic because it's in north Denver."

"That's a good idea. We'll do the things on the north end first and work our way south. Maybe I could talk you into a baseball game later in the spring?"

"If you do butterflies for me, which I don't imagine is high on any man's list, I suppose I can sacrifice and do baseball with you. I can always watch the crowd."

"That's my girl," Dale said and looked like a kid with an all-day sucker.

*Oh my*, Beth thought with a start. *Am I?*
She thought she heard a snicker from the Worry Nag.

*     *     *

At the pavilion the next weekend, they found themselves in an atrium full of plants and trees that were alive with butterflies and moths. A new hatch of electric blues had just emerged, and Beth and Dale watched in fascination as the creatures flitted from plant to plant. The butterflies were as wide as Beth's palm.

"Let's just sit on this bench and watch," Beth suggested after they had roamed the whole area. They settled close together on the bench, and she felt Dale's arm drape lightly across her shoulders. She looked up at him and smiled, and he squeezed her shoulder. "Isn't this great? So many different kinds, and did you see that huge gray moth that was in the corner . . ." She froze in midsentence as a butterfly settled on his hair. "Oh, don't move. A butterfly is on your head," she whispered softly. "They are the most incredible blue color."

A blur of blue in front of her face resolved into another of the huge things settling on her shirt front, where it moved its wings gently back and forth. They held their breaths, loath to spoil the moment, but when one tried to land on Dale's nose, Beth's strangled laugh spooked the creatures away. They continued to sit quietly in the thatched bower, and they were again visited by the huge blues.

Beth had four of them on her brightly patterned skirt and blouse, when Dale said softly, "They think you're a flower."

"Probably a cactus flower," Beth joked.

"I'd call you a passion flower," Dale said quietly.

Beth looked away as a shiver ran down her spine. She was enjoying being with him as she always had. They were comfortable together and had shared a few careful kisses, but she was hoping they could just be friends. Dale was mostly keeping it casual, but occasional remarks let Beth know that he wasn't going to let it go on that way forever. She was already "his girl."

She glanced at him and decided silence was probably the best policy, so she just smiled and let the flower talk drop.

On their way back north through the chaos of I-25, they passed the exit to Estes Park.

"Have you ever spent much time in Estes?" Dale was concentrating on his driving as a grubby white Volkswagen in a huge hurry cut back and forth in traffic in front of them.

"Not a lot. It's beautiful up there though. I always liked the old Stanley Hotel. What a view you get from the front veranda. It got pretty shabby for a while, but when it was used as background for a movie, it got a nice facelift, and it looks wonderful again. Oh, what was that movie?"

"About Estes Park?" Dale glanced over at Beth, his brow wrinkled.

"No, it was supposed to be a totally different location, but it was about a huge hotel in the mountains. I think it was called the Overlook Hotel, and a writer and his family agreed to live there during the winter and take care of the place then found that the hotel was full of malevolence."

"Oh, do you mean Stephen King's *The Shining*?"

"Yes! That's it. I read the book years before the movie, and as always, I thought the book was better, but they did a pretty good job of it. Jack Nicholson was in it, I think."

"Yeah, he pulled off the spooky parts pretty well." He glanced over at Beth. "Did you ever stay at the Stanley?"

"Oh no, I just admired the setting. I never got up there much. When I was young, I was always working, and after I married, it seemed like we always had something else to do on the weekends."

The Yukon hummed quietly along the interstate.

"You know"—Dale spaced his words—"we could spend a weekend up there." At Beth's sharp intake of breath, Dale added, "Separate rooms, of course."

After a short silence, Beth offered, "Uhmm, better not, but we could do a day trip, maybe." As Dale opened his mouth, she added, "Would you look at that idiot? Where does he think he can go with all this traffic?"

She was immensely relieved when Dale didn't pursue the subject.

# CHAPTER 6

Dale called the following Friday. "What do you think about dinner at my place tonight instead of our trek into Denver? I'll cook my famous beef stroganoff. It's a masterpiece and not to be missed."

Beth hesitated. "I'm just about to leave to go to Loveland. I have a lot of errands to run, and I really don't know how long they'll take."

"No problem, just come over to the condo when you're done. Stroganoff reheats well."

"I don't know . . . I probably should go on home, do chores . . ."

"The chores will wait," Dale said. "It isn't like it's winter. Your horse is on pasture and won't be kicking the barn down thinking he's starving to death."

"Far knows how to tell time. He'll ignore me for days if I'm not there by four."

"I think he'll live, don't you?"

"Sure, but you don't know how that horse can pout." She sighed. "All right, I'll try to be there as close to six as I can," she promised.

Beth drove west on Prospect toward Dale's condo on Elizabeth Street late that afternoon. She had a headache and a nervous stomach caused by the reoccurring mental image of the Worry Nag, who kept butting into her own reservations to add more reasons she shouldn't spend time at Dale's place.

"You said you don't want to get involved."

"I already am," Beth snapped.

"It isn't neutral territory."

"Neither is my house."

"But you are in control there."

"I know that. Who do you think he is? Jack the Ripper? He's been a perfect gentleman."

"So far. Ladies don't go to a gentleman's house unescorted."

"Go away," Beth snapped. Or . . . you've heard the term *drop-kicked*?" She mentally shoved the Nag into the closet and slammed the door.

She tapped her fingers on the steering wheel. "To be totally honest, I'm not afraid of him. I'm afraid of myself. Now that's a thought I didn't need," she said crossly to the windshield.

Beth almost went home.

Twenty minutes later, she thought Dale looked rugged and very male in his Bronco T-shirt and jeans as he opened the door of his condo. The short-sleeved T-shirt showed off his good chest muscles, and his arms were tanned and toned.

*I don't know why a man's skin doesn't get loose and thin like a woman's does at this age*, Beth thought. *Their hormones keep pumping, I suppose. Not fair. Also they can pee standing up, and we have to have the babies.*

She realized she was holding her breath.

"Hi there," Dale said, ushering her into his condo with a flourish.

They had gone by it one time, but Beth had never been inside, so she looked around with interest. Comfortable-looking maroon leather furniture was grouped on a large navy area rug. A few Western pictures hung on the walls. She walked over to a Bama print. "This is one I haven't seen before. Nice. I have a couple at home."

"I noticed," Dale said. "You have some very nice prints and a couple of originals, I suspect."

"Not the Bamas, but the Cox is an original and the mountain man by Maija. She does chalks as well as anyone, but I have never liked her Indian women. They actually look a lot like her, and she's no Indian. Do you like gallery hopping?"

"Yes, I do, but I never had much time to do it."

"I imagine with coaching and teaching, that pretty much took up your life."

Dale rubbed the back of his neck as he smiled at Beth. "I was lucky to do something I loved. I miss it, but now I'm determined to do the things I always wanted to do."

"The past is past. The time is now." Beth laughed and tried to breathe normally. The headache was still there. "So, what are you interested in doing?"

Dale leaned up against the wall. "I think I would like to learn how to hunt. I'm a good shot at targets but never had the time or money to go on a real hunt. It would be wonderful to go hunting in Alaska for bear or a Dall sheep. I always wanted to learn to play golf. I'd like to travel, and of course, I like sports."

"That's a good thing for a coach to like." Beth didn't know what to do with her hands. "I was raised without a man in the family, and my brother was the baby, so I never really got interested in sports. I liked to play basketball, but that was before girls had sports programs. My husband was good at all sports and loved them. I tried to get into football when we got married but never did learn to like it much."

"You don't like football?" Dale put his hand over his heart and staggered backward.

Beth managed a giggle and felt herself relax slightly. "Well, I have to admit I enjoyed one game. It was at the old Mile High Stadium in Denver. I called a close friend of mine at halftime. She couldn't believe I was enjoying the game, as it was snowing like mad, just miserable." She smiled. "Someone had brought a gallon of mulled wine, and I drank a lot of it. Between my snow machine suit and the wine, it was the best game I ever went to even though we lost, as usual."

"Well, at least you tried. That's the important thing. Some women . . . oh wow, I better pay attention to dinner or we will end up at McDonald's."

Dale puttered in the kitchen, putting the finishing touches on the meal.

"Could I set the table to earn my dinner?" Beth asked as she watched Dale sprinkle croutons on a salad.

"Sure, there are plates in the cupboard to the right and silverware in the drawer underneath."

Having something to do helped Beth's nerves. Her headache began to fade as she listened to Dale hum to himself in the kitchen.

They were soon seated, plates of noodles in a mushroom sour cream sauce steaming gently in front of them. Dale poured nice dry chardonnay into their wine glasses and proposed a toast. "May the meal be fine, enjoy the wine." He picked up his fork. "Dig in, it's getting cold."

Beth didn't have to be asked twice; she was starving. She quickly finished her portion and sat back with a satisfied sigh. Dale motioned toward the wine bottle. She nodded and watched him pour more wine into her glass. "I haven't had stroganoff in years. I love it, and this is excellent." She held up her plate. "If there's any left, may I have just a little more?"

Dale obliged. "I confess it's the only thing I really know how to cook. That's also something I would like to learn to do well. I like good food and have fooled around with cooking a little but not enough to do it well. I mostly grill."

Beth grinned at the ceiling. "You could always take cooking lessons. I got talked into doing a cooking class in France once. Of course the chef didn't speak English, and I don't speak French, so even though one of the French women took pity on me and tried to tell me what he was saying, I could only watch.

"But it was fascinating, even with the language barrier. We were in this huge hotel kitchen with all the cooks and waiters rushing around yelling in French. And when the chef turned us over to the chocolatier, I didn't need to speak the language to understand what he was doing. Dessert in any language is easily understood."

"That really sounds interesting. I like French food, and I have learned to appreciate good wine," Dale said.

"Oh, the local wine in France is wonderful. Each district has its own vineyard, and there aren't any additives to the wine because it's consumed locally. At that low altitude, we could drink a lot of it. By the way, this is a nice chardonnay."

Dale held up the wine bottle with an inquiring quirk of his right eyebrow.

Beth nodded and watched as he carefully poured the pale chardonnay into her glass.

She realized she was beginning to feel a buzz from the wine. They had gone through two bottles, and she was out of practice, more from lack of opportunity than anything else.

"Do you have room for dessert? I didn't really get anything done in that department, but I do have ice cream. Ben & Jerry's to be exact."

"Cherry Garcia by any chance?" Beth looked at Dale with hopeful eyes.

"You better believe it—the best flavor they make, bar none."

She sighed with pleasure. "Me too—like it the best, I mean. But I'm full."

"Later then," Dale agreed.

There was a pause, which hung long enough it began to hum.

"Dishes." Beth got up and began picking up the plates.

"The maid will get them, but you can help me clean off the table." He paused, plate in hand. "Should I make some coffee or would you like some more wine?"

"Wine," said Beth, ignoring the Nag who was banging on the closet of her mind.

The dishes were stacked in the kitchen, and they had moved to the living room couch. Beth looked at Dale, took a sip of her wine, opened her mouth to speak, but hesitated until his eyebrow moved upward in a question.

"Do you have a good relationship with Gloria's mother? I hope it was a friendly divorce." She put up her hand. "None of my business if you don't want to answer."

"I don't mind talking about it," Dale said. He shifted, so his arm was lying on the back of the couch. "It really wasn't anyone's fault. Marian and I got along all right, but there really wasn't a lot of spark to our marriage. I was a pretty dull dog, I think. I was so wrapped up in my coaching I didn't pay enough attention to my family. I wanted a son, and I guess since we didn't have a boy, the kids on the team filled that hole for me. All men want sons, to carry on the name, I guess? Anyway, when Gloria left home, Marian and I had become strangers. While my football team had a winning season, I lost my wife to another guy. I can't say I blame her. We're on speaking terms, but they live out on the West Coast, so I don't see her very often." He looked at Beth. "A story much repeated, isn't it?"

She nodded but was unable to find a reply. She fiddled with her wine glass.

The lights were low and the stereo was playing softly. The music was a soft, slow piece she didn't recognize, but it was what Beth had always considered make-out music. Dale shifted his hand, which was lying on the back of the couch; it was close enough to Beth to just touch her shoulder with his fingers. The hair on her arms stood on end, and she realized she was holding her breath again.

He stood up, gently took her wine glass, and put it on the end table. "Dance," he said softly. She rose and walked into his arms. They moved to the music in perfect unison. They always had danced well together. His arms were warm around her. He held her loosely at first and then slowly gathered her close to his body. She felt like she was melting. Her knees went wobbly.

Dale slipped two fingers under her chin to tip her head back. As he raised Beth's head, she grew so dizzy she thought she might faint. Her mouth opened in a gasp, and his lips met hers. Warm and polite at first, the kiss became more insistent. "Beth," he murmured, his lips moving to her ear.

Her knees completely gave way. He tightened his hold on her body even more to keep her from falling. The pressure on her back curved her body tight against his, and a wave of passion swept over Beth. She brought her hands up into his hair, moaning as his mouth moved to her neck. She was burning. Flames dormant for years flared and consumed her. She realized she was grinding her body against his without any reservation whatsoever.

They moved back to the couch, their hands moving urgently over each other's bodies. Clothing became a hindrance. Dale's hands worked under her shirt, caressed her back, and then moved to her breasts, fingers exploring.

*Hot hands*, she thought dazedly as she pulled at his shirt, wanting skin-to-skin contact.

As he lowered them both flat on the couch, Dale said, "My Beth, you are as lovely as you used to be."

She froze.

"What?" he questioned, looking down at her.

"As I used to be. I forgot for a minute what our relationship used to be." She shoved at him. "Get off me." Dale sat back as Beth levered herself upright. She pulled her shirt back down with shaking hands.

Dale looked at her, his hair mussed. "What do you mean?"

"Don't you remember how you used to disappear? We were so happy together. Then you wouldn't come or call until I would begin to wonder if I had been dreaming you. I almost went crazy that summer trying to figure out what was going on. I didn't want to make you feel like I was chasing you, so I just waited. I couldn't eat. I couldn't sleep. I know I went half crazy missing you."

Beth's eyes were laser hot. "I would finally decide whatever we had was finished. Then you would call and waltz back into my life like nothing had happened. I was too young and insecure to ask you where the hell you'd been. I thought it might drive you away again." She stood up and glared down at him. "And I let you do that to me three different times! And here I am involved with you again." She shoved her hands viciously through her hair. "I must be mad."

"Come back down here." Dale took her wrist, tugged gently. "Look, I don't blame you for feeling like that, but let me explain." He looked up at Beth as she hesitated and then slowly sat back down beside him. He let go of her wrist and sighed. "I got scared. We were young. I found myself so wrapped up in you I couldn't think of anything else. The guys would get on me for letting myself get caught up with one girl when there were so many around. So I'd back off. But I couldn't stay away, and you were so sweet. You kept taking me back. Until that last time."

"You let it go too long. I met Rob. You just finally wore me out, and he had no reservations. He wanted me and made that very clear." She looked away. "Do you remember when you heard about him you called me?"

Dale nodded.

"You told me you had decided to go back to school to become a teacher and would I wait for you. But it was too late. By then what we had together was gone."

"I was a fool. I loved you, but by the time I finally realized it, I'd lost you. I vowed then if I ever got another chance, I wouldn't back away again." Dale leaned toward her.

Beth leaned back. "I'm sorry, Dale, but this time it's going to be me backing off. I don't want this. I'm comfortable in my life now. I take trips on horseback with my friends. I spend a lot of time with my son and his family. I'm financially independent. I can do exactly what I want, and I have been able to do that for a long time, even before Rob died."

She looked at Dale, her eyes troubled. "We had a good marriage. He was a good man. We had the same values. It really was a good match. I was just alone too much because he worked so hard at his job and traveled all the time. We ended up living separate lives, just like you and Marian."

Beth scrubbed her hands back and forth on her thighs. "For the first time in forty years, I'm not lonely anymore. That may sound silly when I am alone, but I'm not waiting for my husband to come home. And when he came home, he was exhausted and didn't want to do anything but eat dinner and fall asleep in front of the TV. All his energy went to the job. Even our social life was part of his job."

Beth's face crumpled. "I was his whole world until we got married. Then it seemed he was always too busy. He always wanted a lot of people around, as he needed people. I only needed him. He was there at the bad times, giving me support, but I needed more attention than I got. I know my husband loved me, and he gave me security and a good life, but I needed him to hug me, to talk to me . . . to . . . to . . ."

Beth dissolved in tears. Dale tried to pull her into his arms, but she pushed him away and cried, drawn up in a ball on the other side of the couch. Her sobs finally slowed to became the exhausted hiccups of a small child. She pulled herself back up into a sitting position and took a long breath.

"Well. That's probably not what you had planned. I'm sorry, I've had too much wine." She wiped the sides of her face with the back of her hand. Her fair skin was flushed, and she avoided Dale's eyes by looking at her lap.

"I'd say you needed to do that. I think you've had a lot of feelings bottled up for a long time," Dale said softly.

"I've done nothing but bawl and whine around for the last three years." Beth's voice was husky with tears. "I should have gotten that out long ago. I thought I had."

"I think you need a hug, come here." Dale moved over to her, and even though Beth protested, he brought her head to his chest and held her gently but firmly. She slowly relaxed as he gently stroked her hair. She closed her eyes, gave a shuddering sigh, and fell asleep.

Dale held her for a long time before gently lowering her onto the couch. He covered her with a spread and sat on the edge of the couch, watching her sleep until he began to yawn continuously. He got up, twitched the spread higher under Beth's chin, turned out most of the lights, and went down the hall to his bedroom.

Beth woke up toward morning, confused. She didn't for a minute or two know where she was. Untangling herself from the cover, she slowly sat up. Things were spinning a little.

She groaned as she remembered the events of the evening. The dance had been a close repeat of the one time, all those years ago, that she had gone to Dale's trailer, wanting to see him after one of his disappearances. Except then they had made love. Had he remembered that night and planned a repeat, hoping for the same ending, or had it just happened?

She stood and walked with an unsteady gait down the hall into his bedroom, where she stood and watched Dale's chest rise and fall.

"This is probably a big mistake," she whispered to herself as she shucked off her clothes and quietly crawled into bed, careful not to wake him. Exhaustion and the wine pulled her back into sleep almost immediately.

*   *   *

*Cold*, Beth thought hazily the next morning. She fumbled behind her back, feeling for covers to warm her shoulders. Her eyes were squinched shut but opened wide when her hand landed on a warm, naked arm. She froze like a rabbit as her brain tried frantically to process information. She was in a strange room, in a strange bed, and whoever was behind her, certainly was not Tazmeralda.

Beth rolled over and stared wide-eyed at Dale, who was staring at her. His hair stood on end in spikes, and his left eyebrow was quirked upward.

"Well, what a nice surprise," he drawled. "You were snoring on my couch in the living room the last time I saw you. How did you wind up in my bed?"

"Said the big bad wolf," Beth whispered. She looked at him for a minute, cleared her throat, and said, "I woke up and was cold. I guess I decided to crawl in here. It must have been the wine. And I do not snore."

"No harm done unless you took advantage of me while I was dreaming of taking advantage of you," Dale said with a wicked grin on his handsome face. The sheet was down to his waist, exposing his broad chest, which was covered with fine hair that reminded Beth of a silver fox coat she once owned.

She blushed clear down to her toes. She stuttered, trying to form a sentence, but stopped as he put out a big hand and gently pinched her chin.

"Seeing you in my bed is the best way to start the day I can think of. How about I make us some fresh squeezed orange juice while you get dressed? Feel free to take a shower if you want."

He pushed the sheet aside and got out of bed. Beth was relieved to see he had a pair of navy cotton briefs on. He opened the closet door and pulled a white terry cloth robe off a hanger and wrapped it around his body.

*He still had nice buns*, Beth thought.

Dale gave her a wink and walked out of the room, leaving Beth staring after him. She flopped back down on the bed and squinted at the ceiling. "Sheesh!" At least she had left her underwear on.

She threw back the sheet, gathered up her scattered clothes, and bolted to the bathroom, locking the door.

Twenty minutes later, she sniffed the air as she walked into the kitchen. Her reddish hair was still damp, close and sleek to her head. Her face, scrubbed clear of makeup, looked young and defenseless. "I'd kill for a cup of the coffee I smell."

The kitchen was compact, but a breakfast nook in the corner offered a small table, where two plates and silverware sat on red-and-white checked place mats.

Dale looked at her out of the corner of his eye while he put butter in a skillet. "I thought I would scramble us some eggs to go with the orange juice. Are you hungry?"

"Ravenous," Beth said, smiling.

As she finished the last crust of toast, Beth looked up at Dale and then glanced away. "I really made a fool of myself last night. I don't drink much anymore. That was way too much wine." She sat back in her chair. "I didn't mean to get so emotional."

"Forget it. You've been through a lot. I think you needed to unload on someone. I bet you've been doing just fine to all appearances, and everyone thinks you're over your husband's death, right?"

Beth looked down at the table, pushed her plate aside. She leaned on her elbows and frowned at Dale. "I guess some of our friends think I didn't care that much about Rob because I have just gotten on with my life. I don't cry about it. But I've never cried easily. He was about the only one that could make me cry . . . oh damn, there I go again." Beth angrily wiped a tear from her left eye.

"Do you know how green your eyes get when you cry?" Dale said softly.

Beth looked at him. There was naked need in his eyes. It scared her to death.

She pushed back from the table, scraping the chair legs across the floor. "I can't do this. Thanks for breakfast, but I've got to go home and do chores. Oh damn, purse, keys." She found her purse on the floor next to the couch and fumbled with the lock on the front door.

"Oh Lord, my car's been parked here overnight. That's just great." She turned to face Dale, who had followed her to the door. "Thank you for dinner."

"I'll call you," he said.

"I don't think it's a good idea."

"I'll call you." He leaned against the door jamb, still in his robe, and smiled at her, relaxed and confident, which further irritated Beth.

"I can't promise I'll go out with you again," she said, backing down the sidewalk.

"I'll call you. I'm not going to disappear again, Beth. I promise you."

# CHAPTER 7

*I'm going to wear the carpet out*, Beth thought as she paced back and forth in her living room. She couldn't settle on anything this morning. She hadn't done chores, had breakfast, or fed the cat. The view was not comforting.

The Worry Nag was silent, but she was out of the closet. Beth had a vision of the Nag pretending to sweep the floor, all the time smiling with an edged sweetness and mouthing silent words that Beth could read as if they were spoken out loud.

The phone rang. Just before the machine would have picked up the message, Beth grabbed it off the base.

"Hello, Dale."

"Hi." Dale hesitated; she could hear him breathing. "Did you get my calls? I called a couple of times."

"Yes." Uncomfortable, Beth didn't know what to say.

"Oh. Look, Beth, I know you're embarrassed about the other night, but don't be. After all, nothing happened."

"Your daughter doesn't know that if she noticed my car. Tell me she didn't notice my car."

Another hesitation. "She did . . ."

"Oh great. What did she say?"

"She wasn't very happy. In fact she was very upset. She doesn't want me to get involved with someone new. I have to say it kind of surprised me, but I told her I was involved, and I wanted the two of you to meet. Would you meet her?"

Beth didn't respond.

"Would you meet her? Please."

"I don't think so, Dale. I just can't handle that kind of complication. You know I've been hesitant to get seriously involved with you from the start, and a resentful daughter is not going to make things easier."

"We can work things out."

"Things," Beth said so slowly the word came out with a hiss. "I'm not sure where you want to take this."

"I want to spend the rest of my life with you, Beth. I want to marry you and grow old with you. I hadn't planned to ask you over the phone, but now that it's come up . . ."

Beth took in a sharp breath. "Oh, Dale, I enjoy being with you, but I don't want to get married again. I really didn't mean to lead you on. I hoped we could just be friends. There are so many women out there that would jump at a chance to get married again but not me. I think it's better you don't call me anymore if that's what you want."

The silence from his end of the line hurt her ears.

"I'm sorry," Beth said in a small voice and gently hung up.

Dale hadn't called since, and Beth was relieved, but after a few days, she realized she really missed him. Her life had a hole in it again.

She was pacing again midmorning, three days after his call, trying to ignore the Worry Nag, who was doing a silent jig in front of her closet door with her finger held against her lips.

*Music.* Beth decided that's what she needed; it always helped elevate her moods. She turned the radio to a Western station, went into the kitchen, and began washing the few dishes left from breakfast. As she scrubbed hard at a crusty skillet, LeeAnn Womack finished a song Beth was only half listening to and then started singing, "I hope you dance."

Beth's hands stilled in the soapy water as the words to the song caught her attention. Her breath caught in her throat as she listened closely. LeeAnn might have been singing directly to her.

*God forbid love ever leaves you empty handed . . .*
*Whenever one door closes, I hope one more opens . . .*
*And when you get the choice to sit it out or dance, I hope you dance . . .*
*I hope you dance . . . I hope you dance . . .*

"Oh God, how I miss Rob's arms around me," Beth whimpered softly. They had done a lot of dancing during their marriage, as it was one thing Beth insisted they do. Reluctant at first, Rob had learned to enjoy the music and developed his own style. At one of the bank's black-tie dinners, Rob's boss had remarked that they seemed to float around the floor. Beth had always felt that dancing with a life partner was the closest thing to making love.

*Never settle for the line of least resistance . . .*

*Lovin' might be a mistake, but it's worth makin' . . .*

*Don't back away from life is what she means*, Beth thought. *Isn't that what I'm doing with Dale? Backing away from a new life? Am I afraid he will leave me again, or is it just being unwilling to start over, to change?*

Beth finished the dishes lost in thought and got on with her day. She rode with Nancy for four hours on the canal, so she should have been tired, but she spent the night staring at the ceiling. Sleeping was getting to be almost as hard as it had been right after Rob died, and twice she had to forbid the Worry Nag against invading what little sleep she did get.

Two days later, Beth snatched the phone off its base and dialed Dale's number.

"Hi, it's me. Beth." Her hand clutched the phone so hard it hurt.

There was a short silence. "Well, this is a surprise. I thought you didn't want to have anything to do with me," Dale said.

"I didn't . . . don't . . . but I can't seem to be able to get you out of my head." Beth sighed. "I'm making a mess of this. This isn't easy for me."

"I know." His voice was soft. "I'm glad you called. I've had a talk with my daughter. I'm not going to be alone the rest of my life because of her resentment."

"After I told you not to call me anymore?"

"I'm not giving up, Beth. I think we can have what we missed the first time. I feel we were meant to be together, and we don't have time to waste either. I don't feel alive unless I'm spending time with you."

"Me either," Beth mumbled.

"What?"

"I said me either."

There was a long pause, neither of them knowing what to say.

Dale cleared his throat. "Mmm. So what's the next move?"

"You wanted me to meet your daughter. I guess that would be something we should try. Where? She would feel I was invading your territory if I came to your condo, wouldn't she? We could do it out here if you want. I could make lunch."

"If you don't mind, your place might be better. A public place might be awkward if there is a blow up. When?"

"Next Saturday? It will take that much time to get myself talked into it and figure out how to cook a meal for company again. I don't think one of my frozen dinners would be acceptable, do you?"

"Probably not," Dale said. "Gloria is a pretty good cook and will be looking to be critical."

"Oh, thanks, that makes me feel so relaxed about the whole thing." Beth groaned, "It will probably be worse than being looked over by a prospective mother-in-law. But I'm tough, I'll survive. I think."

"I'll check with Gloria to make sure she doesn't have to work Saturday. Thank you, Beth. It means more than I can say that you called me." Dale's voice sounded husky.

"It's probably another mistake, but if I don't take the chance, I can't dance," Beth said.

"Huh?"

"Never mind, Dale. It's one of those deep, dark female things. See you Saturday and hope for a miracle."

"And don't you say a word," she snapped at the Nag, who popped out of her closet the moment Beth hung up. "I'm through dodging this second chance. Get used to it."

# CHAPTER 8

Saturday was a beautiful day, but Beth hardly noticed as she worked to get the luncheon set up. It had been a long time since she cooked for company. Meals for twenty or more used to be no big deal; she did it all the time. Those days were long gone. *Concentrate, concentrate, this had to be just right.*

She managed to avoid cutting her fingers and only dropped one bowl as she hurried through the last-minute details. It was an old one but a favorite. *No matter,* she told herself as she cleaned up the shards.

Dale's blue SUV came down her lane at eleven-thirty. *Right on time,* she thought, pushing at her hair. Taking a deep breath, Beth imagined she'd be less nervous having dinner with the governor. Politicians usually played nice.

She walked out the front door onto the east deck and watched as Dale and a tall, very thin woman with dark hair walked toward her. Dale's daughter would be attractive in normal circumstances, but right now she was so sullen she looked like a teenage boy forced to go to a dance with his sister.

"Hi," Dale said, taking Beth by the arm and giving it a gentle squeeze. "This is my daughter, Gloria. Gloria, Beth Waterford."

Gloria nodded. Unsmiling, she looked Beth up and down, just below the point of total rudeness.

*Hostile,* Beth thought. *She's here not because she wants to be but because she feels she has no choice. I guess I don't either if I'm going to be involved with Dale.*

"I'm glad to meet you, Gloria. Dale has told me a lot about you." Beth managed to dredge up a smile.

It wasn't returned.

*This is going to be a rough row*, Beth thought. *Gloria looked as happy to be here as someone about to be interviewed by the Spanish Inquisition.*

"I thought we'd eat outside on the west deck," she continued. "It shouldn't be too hot in the shade."

Beth led them through the living room and out the sliding doors onto the deck, which ran the full length of the house. Deep eaves gave protection from the sun, and a green wrought-iron table with four chairs just outside the doors looked inviting.

"Sit down," Beth urged her guests.

They all took a chair. Dale rambled on about how clear the mountains were today and how he enjoyed the view until he ran out of adjectives.

Gloria barely glanced at the view. She focused mainly on her father.

"Would you like some iced tea, Gloria?" Beth offered.

"No." Gloria barely looked at Beth as she spoke. Her voice was low and flat.

"I would," Dale said and added as Beth got up to go back into the house, "Let me help." They walked back into the kitchen, and he said, "I'm sorry, I've been on the verge of stopping the car and giving her a well-deserved spanking most of the way here."

"Let's just pretend she's a child having a tantrum. The best thing to do with a cranky kid is to ignore him. Usually, they eventually quit." Beth slid her arm around Dale's waist and gave him a squeeze.

"Thanks, I needed that," he said, the smile lines around his eyes deepening.

Beth served pasta salad with her special bran muffins and had Ben & Jerry's Cherry Garcia ice cream for dessert. The meal was consumed in strained silence, except for almost desperate bursts of conversation from Beth or Dale.

"Dale tells me you're a nurse. What kind of nursing do you do?"

"Trauma," Gloria replied, looking at the mountains.

"I imagine emergency room nursing would be exhausting." Beth ventured hopefully in that direction.

"Yes."

Rather than kick Gloria, Beth gave up for a moment. Dale's efforts were not any more effective, and Beth could see he was having a hard time keeping his temper. The muscles in his jaw were clenched. *I hope he doesn't crack a tooth*, Beth thought. *I would like to take Gloria over my knee and give her that before-mentioned spanking, but she isn't a child, even though she is certainly acting like one.* Sighing, she gave up the effort to visit for the moment.

They finished the ice cream and sat in silence. As Beth searched for something else to say to keep Dale from the explosion she felt was coming, she noticed Far Horizon ambling along the fence line. His head came up when he noticed them on the deck. He stopped and nickered softly, ears pointed toward them.

"Is that your horse?" Gloria asked as she got up from her chair and stepped to the railing of the deck.

Beth glanced at Dale, hope in her eyes. "Yep, that's Far Horizon. He's the only horse I have on the place now, but there are horses on the other side of the fence to visit with, so that helps."

"Doesn't he like being by himself?"

"Horses are herd animals. They're not happy alone." Beth smiled at her. "Do you like horses?"

"My grandpa had some. Do you remember, Dad, when you used to take me out to his place when I was little?"

"Sure. He had an old mare that let you climb all over her." Dale looked at Beth. "Could I take her down to meet Far?"

Beth nodded and got out of her chair. "Let me cut up an apple for you. He would roll over and play dead if he knew there was a treat coming."

She picked up the plates and took them into the kitchen, returning in a few minutes with a large apple cut into quarters. She handed it to Gloria.

"Are you coming?" Dale asked.

Beth wiped her hands on the towel she had draped over her shoulder. "Why don't the two of you visit with him, and I'll clean off the table before we attract flies. Take your time."

She watched the two of them as they walked over to the horse. *Maybe Far can be the catalyst to her accepting me*, she thought as Far Horizon delicately picked an apple quarter off Gloria's palm. Beth smiled and went back inside the house.

By the time she had the few chores in the kitchen done, Gloria and Dale were back in the house. "It's getting hot out there," Dale said.

"I try to be back in the house by ten when I'm riding during the summer. I have trouble with the heat," Beth said.

"Where do you ride?" Gloria asked.

"On the canal just down the road. I can cross a couple of fields and be right there. It's really nice not to have to trailer every time I want to ride out. Would you like to come and ride with me someday if I could borrow a horse for you?"

"Maybe," Gloria said.

It was a relief to Beth when Dale and Gloria left half an hour later.

She slammed the dishes into the dishwasher and decided to straighten her living room to work off her frustration. *Thank goodness for Far Horizon. That was the only positive reaction I saw*, she thought as she furiously dusted her bookshelves. She doesn't want to share her father with me. It wouldn't matter if I was the Queen of Sheba and gave Gloria the keys to King Solomon's mines; she still wouldn't want to let me in.

She stared unseeingly at the book she held in her hand. The whole luncheon had been futile. Well, she had tried.

Beth shrugged, jammed the book untidily back into the crowded shelf, and decided to take a bath.

As she was undressing, she summoned the image of the Worry Nag's closet and politely knocked on the door. It opened slowly as the Nag peered out at Beth with a look of surprise.

"You and I need to talk," Beth stated as she peeled off her T-shirt.

The Nag came through her door and stood with her hands clasped in front of her.

"We're going to negotiate a truce," Beth said, wrapping her robe around her as she marched into the bathroom. "You were right. I'm going to be doing a lot of worrying with this relationship. I can see that. The daughter is a jewel, isn't she?"

The Nag nodded, grinning.

"Could I get you to only come out if things get really bad and not bother me when I am just fretting about stuff? Would that be possible?"

The Nag shrugged her bony shoulders and reluctantly nodded her head.

Beth gave a sigh of relief. "That's a yes?"

The Nag nodded again.

"Well, why don't you say so?"

The Nag whisked into the closet and returned shortly with a sign, all the letters underlined.

Beth squinted; the area around the Nag's closet was poorly lit. "You told me not to talk," she read slowly. Laughing, she turned the water on in the tub. "All right, when you're right, you're right."

Chin high, the Nag walked back into her closet and closed the door.

Candles flickered softly on the edge of the tub as Beth soaked and tried to unknot both mind and body. There were so many issues she and Dale had to deal with before she could feel comfortable going down the road to marriage. The daughter was a major chuckhole and then the other issues—where would they live, money, her son who was not aware of Dale yet.

They hadn't been to bed yet. Dale surely wasn't going to be content with that much longer; neither was she for that matter, if she was perfectly honest. *I don't even know if I can let myself be with a man*, she thought, her spirits glum. My body isn't that good anymore. Rob was so proud of my figure. I didn't have the sense to realize how good it was until it disappeared. Well, most of it—my breasts haven't completely fallen to my waist. I'm sure not going to walk around naked like we used to. Can I forget how Rob looked, or will I be always comparing the two of them? The rangy build to the stocky, not much body hair to a pelt, bald to a nice head of hair. Won't he be doing the same thing?

Beth stayed in the tub until the water cooled and then got into her pajamas, took out her diamond ear studs, and washed her face. Looking in the mirror, she put moisturizer on her skin and looked critically at the lines that were slowly creeping across her features. If Dale just wanted a trophy wife, he would surely look for someone younger. Somehow, that comforted her. She slid between the sheets, thinking about the conversation with May the day before when she went into Greeley. She had stopped after running errands for tea and some advice.

"It's going to work out, have faith." May had smiled at Beth. "This man is right for you and will be good for you."

"I had a dream that we had an argument about Dale." Beth frowned at her cup of tea.

"Rob is upset that Dale has come into your life."

"I thought it was just my insecurities. He really isn't happy about it?"

"He complained at length. In fact I had to tell him to go away." May shrugged and added, "If I tell them to go away, they must leave."

"That isn't fair. I told him years ago if something happened to me I wanted him to remarry. I even had someone picked out for him." Beth stabbed the piece of cheesecake she was toying with. "Surely he would want me to be happy?"

"He'll have to get over it if you stay involved with Dale. The dead don't like change any more than the living, and you were his for a very long time." May poured Beth more tea.

"Well, damn him. That makes me mad." Beth's face flushed with anger.

May just smiled. "Good, you need to concentrate on how you feel. The dead have no power over us. They can only watch."

*Rob had always wanted things his own way,* Beth thought as she slid deeper under the covers. "You have no say over me anymore," she growled. She turned onto her right side and drifted into sleep.

# Chapter 9

"I met your daughter. You need to meet my son," Beth said to Dale as they finished a dinner of steak, salad, and garlic bread along with the last of a bottle of merlot. They sat side by side on her west deck, waiting for the sun to go down, watching the robins on their late worm hunt.

"All right. Wow, look at that sunset."

Beth's attention shifted away from the skyline to Dale. "Did I tell you about the time I saw the sun go sideways when I was in Alaska?"

Dale snorted. "Sideways? I know it stays light or dark up there for long periods, but I never heard of the sun going sideways."

Beth sat up straighter in her chair and gave him a look. "Well, I hadn't either, but I swear to you I saw it happen. We watched the sun go down behind Mount McKinley while we were sitting on our hotel's patio. Even though the sun had just gone down, it was eleven-thirty in the evening." Beth looked at Dale.

He nodded. "Uh-huh, and . . ."

"And the sun came back up from behind a peak that was just east of McKinley about fifteen minutes after it went down. We couldn't believe it, but that's what happened. At that time of year, the sun is down for such a short period of time the rotation of the earth makes it appear to go sideways. It really never got dark, just got what I'd call twilight. It was weird."

"Well, live and learn." Dale stretched his hands over his head and yawned. "Were you with a tour?"

"Yes."

Dale yawned again.

"Stop that," Beth said and then broke into a huge yawn herself.

Beth's cat was on her lap, giving Dale the evil eye.

He leaned over his chair arm and tried to stroke Taz's head. The cat held her ground but hissed at him. He pulled his hand back and looked glumly at Beth. "She doesn't seem to be taking to me very fast."

"Maybe she's been talking to your daughter." Beth gave Dale a crooked smile as she stroked Tazmeralda. "Cats are independent. It has to be their idea. If you act like you don't like them, they get determined that you will. Reverse psychology, I think you call it. Be nice," Beth added to Taz, who continued to glare at Dale.

Dale shifted his attention from the cat to Beth. "How do you think your son will react to you having a man in your life?"

Beth leaned back in her chair and looked up at the sky. The stars were struggling out one at a time.

"He's a loving person, and he wants me to be happy. He told me shortly after Rob died he wouldn't mind if I found someone else. Unless you act like Gloria, I think he will approve."

"Ha ha," Dale laughed in funeral tones.

He swiveled his chair so they were sitting knee to knee. Taz gave him one last drop-dead look and jumped down on the deck. Dale picked up Beth's hand and started stroking her fingers.

"Stop that," Beth said and pulled her hand away.

"Why? You know you can hardly keep your hands off me."

Beth frowned at him. "That's another problem. I don't know if I can . . . well, I don't know how I'm going to feel . . ." She shifted in her seat. "I . . ."

"You don't know if you can go to bed with me," Dale stated, his face impassive.

Relieved to have her thought in the open, Beth nodded. Neither one said anything for a full five minutes.

"I want to," Beth said slowly. "But I haven't been with a man other than my husband since I was nineteen years old. Can you understand how I feel?" She looked down at her lap. "I'm scared," she said so softly Dale could hardly hear her. "It wouldn't be so hard if I hadn't loved . . ." Her throat closed with an audible click, and she fluttered her hands helplessly.

Dale captured her hands, brought them to his lips, kissed them, and placed her hands on her knees, keeping his on top. His hands were big and warm. It had been so long since Beth had anyone touch her. She sighed and relaxed slightly.

Dale gave her hands a squeeze and slowly straightened up. He looked off into the night. "I'm nervous too. Can I measure up to your husband? When we get to the bed part, was he a better lover? Are you thinking about him when you are with me? I guess I shouldn't be jealous of a dead man, but I come pretty close sometimes." Dale sighed. "All the trepidation isn't on your side, my dear."

"I might as well tell you another thing that keeps me backing away from you." Beth shifted in her seat and drew her hands away. She wrapped her arms around her body. "I buried one man. I don't know if I could stand to do it again."

"Why do you think you would?"

"Women outlive men. I always figured I would outlive Rob, planned on it. I'm a realist if I'm anything, and it's a fact that most women outlive their men."

"I don't plan on dying, Beth."

She stood up, walked over to the deck rail, and then turned to look at Dale. "Neither did Rob. We could have a few years together, and then I could lose you to a heart attack or another accident." She shivered and turned her back to him.

Dale got out of his chair, came up behind Beth, wrapped his arms around her, and pulled her gently against his body. His warm breath on her neck made some of the stiffness leave her, but she was still tense. He rubbed her arms, staring out into the night.

"That's perfectly true, my love. Or I could lose you in one of the many ways life has of tearing couples apart." He turned her in his arms and smiled down at her. "Or we could both live to be ninety. That gives us almost thirty years."

Beth gave him a faint smile. "I know that in my mind, but my heart is full of fear."

"It will work out, Beth. We just have to live it a day at a time."

She sighed. "That's how I got through the last three years. You're right, but if . . ."

"Let's not worry about the long term. We have enough short-term things to get through. How about we get back to sleeping together?"

Beth stared at him.

"I suggest we get drunk." Dale grinned. "We came very close the night you were at my place, and it didn't seem so hard, did it?"

Beth smiled and shook her head.

"Why don't we do this," Dale said. "Let's not worry about it. Nature has a way of working out these things on her own schedule. I don't think it's very romantic to set a date for a seduction, do you?"

Beth huffed out a nervous laugh. "No, I just wait until I get swept off my feet?"

"Right. Why don't we practice just a little right now?"

Dale picked her up, swung around in a circle, and sat back down with her on his lap. "We don't need to rush this. It won't be the easiest thing I have ever done. To wait. But I want it to be good for both of us."

He kissed her ear as she settled back against his body, and they sat together in the soft night air, grateful for each other's company.

*   *   *

Beth called her son the next evening.

"Steve?" Beth sat at the small desk off the kitchen, cell phone at her right ear, jiggling her leg nervously.

"Hi, Mom. What's going on? I haven't heard much from you, keep meaning to call. Is everything all right?"

Her son's deep voice always gave Beth pleasure, although at times it was slightly painful since he sounded so much like his father.

"I'm fine, love. In fact things are interesting down here. I've met a man. There was a pause. "Well, say something," she added, rattled by the resulting silence.

"Aha, so who is it?"

"I used to go with Dale before I met your father. He showed up about three months ago and just keeps coming around even though I've tried not to get involved with him."

"Tried . . . that means you are, right?"

Beth sighed. "I guess so. I think you should meet him. When can you come down? We could come up, but it might be better if we all met at my place. What do you think? What would work better for you?" Beth felt she was chattering like a monkey.

"Let me check with Liz."

There was a short muffled conversation while Beth chewed her lower lip.

"We'll come down next weekend. Don't worry, Mom. You remember what I said after Dad died?"

"Yes, but you need to meet him. I need an objective opinion."

"Your opinion is the important one." Steve paused. "The only thing that is important to me is if he makes you happy. You deserve it."

Beth could hear the love in his voice, and she felt tears blur her eyes. He had always been such a joy to her from the moment he was born. Her friend May told her that both she and Steve were old souls and had been together in many previous lives.

"Thank you, love. I appreciate that. We're comfortable together, and it's nice to have someone to do things with, but his daughter is having a struggle accepting me," Beth said.

"Then she must be nuts. Don't worry about it, Mom. Unless he beats you, I'm sure I'll be fine with it."

"If he tried, he would only do it once." Beth giggled nervously. "See you soon then."

She sat by the phone, thinking how lucky she was to have a son that was so compassionate. Steve had always been concerned about other people, more than he was about himself.

She called Dale and told him Steve and his family would be down the following weekend. "Should we ask your daughter to come out too?"

Dale hesitated for a couple of beats. "Let's just keep it your son and his family and us and get everyone together later. I tried to talk to Gloria about how rude she was to you when you had us out to lunch, and she just ignored me. So I've let it be. Let's let your son have a shot at me. I guess it's my turn to be nervous."

"That was my very thought," Beth crowed with delight. "But I think you two will get along fine, and my grandbabies will probably climb all over you. Well, the youngest anyway. She was only two when Rob died. The older one remembers her grandpa, so she might have more trouble. But they're good girls."

She drew in a breath. "It just now dawned on me, you aren't a grandpa. Do you enjoy kids?" She hurriedly added, "You must if you taught and coached all those years."

"I really do, all ages. That is one of the things I miss the most being retired. I'll wear your granddaughters out for you."

"Now remember, these are girls. They probably aren't into football." Beth laughed. "Although the younger one is going to be like me, I think, a real tomboy, so you might be able to talk her into it."

They enjoyed a long loving phone conversation, which left Beth feeling good about the coming weekend.

# CHAPTER 10

Saturday morning, the sun was out, the wind down, with the temperature predicted to be almost seventy-five degrees. Beth and Dale had cleaned off both decks, put out the rest of the deck furniture, and were drinking coffee at the dining room table.

"They're here," she said, seeing Steve's truck come down the lane. They started for the door, but Beth pulled Dale back and gave him a quick kiss on the cheek. "For strength," she said, going on through the door. She hurried down the deck steps and ran, her arms open to capture the two small girls ejecting from the pickup.

Dale held back, watching Beth hug her granddaughters, who were swarming up one side and down the other of her. Her son was tall and lean, at least six foot three, balding, with one of those faces you just naturally trust. The daughter-in-law was pretty with dark hair and fabulous eyes. The flurry of hugs and kisses dwindled down, and Beth turned to Dale, motioning him to join them.

"Dale, this is my son, Steve Hart, his wife, Liz, and my granddaughters, Jacklyn and Carrie. Everybody this is Dale Runnington."

There was a short silence while everyone looked at Dale.

He waited, smiling, feeling naked.

The two girls decided to ignore him and looked at Beth.

"Grandma, we saw a rabbit *mished* on the road," the smaller one said.

"Not *mished*, stupid—*mashed*," the older one said, rolling her eyes.

Steve watched his mother, who was concentrating on the girls, shook his head, walked forward, and stuck his hand out to Dale. They exchanged a hearty handshake and then looked each other over.

*They look like two Neanderthals sniffing each other out over the women,* Beth thought as she watched out of the corner of her eye. She had a hard time stifling a laugh. "Girls, I put some carrots in the shed for you to feed Far, and here he comes."

The girls scampered off, chattering like magpies.

Beth put her arm around her daughter-in-law's waist and said, "Let's let the guys do manly things, and you come and get settled in and tell me how you like your new part-time job."

By late afternoon, full of hearty barbeque, the men had consumed enough beer to be relaxed and were talking football and tools.

The little girls were tearing up and down the lane on small pink bikes, yelling like Comanche Indians.

Tazmeralda was hiding in the lilac hedge.

Beth and Liz were in the kitchen, cleaning up.

"Remember what you've been saying for three years?" Liz gave Beth a lazy smile. You weren't going to get involved with a man. Didn't need one, didn't want one, they were too much trouble."

"I know," Beth said, putting dishes in the dishwasher. "You would think I would listen to myself, wouldn't you? I had no intention of doing this, and here I am, almost against my will."

"You don't have to get involved with him if you don't want to, you know." Liz opened the refrigerator door and put the leftover salad away. She leaned against the counter and looked at Beth. "Don't get pushed into anything. Make sure it's what you want."

Beth sighed. "I keep telling him no, and he keeps calling, and when I tell him not to and he doesn't, then I call him. It's almost as bad as high school. I think he's getting to be a habit. And maybe that's the best way to do it."

"Have you been to bed with him yet?" Liz gave her mother-in-law a wicked grin.

"Liz, for heaven's sake!" Beth felt her face flush.

"Is that a yes or a no? Never mind, none of my business." Liz laughed, gave her mother-in-law a hug. "I think he's nice," she said and changed the subject.

Dale stayed until just before it was bedtime for the girls. Beth started the bedtime ritual, knowing there would be protests, but the girls were worn out from climbing trees and racing around in the pasture, pretending to be horses.

"Grandma, is that man your boyfriend?" Jacklyn, the ten-year-old stared at Beth with a frown, her head on her pillow as Beth tucked eight-year-old Carrie into bed and gave her such a big smacking kiss that Carrie giggled.

Beth tucked the cover under Carrie's chin. She sat beside Jacklyn and gently stroked the girl's brown-gold hair. "I don't know what you would call Dale at my age, honey. He isn't a boy, that's for sure. Maybe a special friend?"

The frown still lingered. Jacklyn could remember Rob. "Aren't you married to Grandpa?"

"I was when he was alive, but now that he's dead, I'm a widow, and I'm not married to anyone."

"Like, how did you meet this guy?"

Beth hesitated a moment. "Well, he used to be my boyfriend when I was nineteen, not all that much older than you are. And I really liked him. I was gone on him, as we used to say. But I married your grandpa instead."

"Why?"

*Oh, the why stage*, Beth thought. Jacklyn used to use that word every time she opened her mouth. It looked like she was still at it. Beth smiled wryly. "Dale didn't want to get married back then. I met your grandpa, and he did, and he just swept me off my feet."

Carrie giggled and scooted deeper under her covers.

"That's right, just picked me up and swung me like I used to swing you both before you got so big." Beth blew out a big sigh. "I was very happy with your grandpa, but I've been lonely since he died. Now Dale is in my life again, and this time he does want to marry me."

Beth pulled the sheet toward Jacklyn's chin. She fiddled with the hem of her T-shirt as she looked at her granddaughters. "What would you girls think if I got remarried?"

"Would you still love us, Grandma?" The little one was sitting up in bed now with a frown on her face to match her sister's.

"Oh my, yes!" Beth smiled. "I will always love you, whether I'm married or not, as long as I live. I will love you and watch over you all of your lives. After I'm gone, you will feel me at your shoulder whenever you're sad or in danger. I will be your guardian angel."

"Like on TV?" Carrie cocked her head like a bright little chickadee.

"Just like that. Never doubt it."

"I don't want you to die, Grandma." Jacklyn's sober face stared up at Beth as she adjusted the pillow behind the girl's head.

Beth leaned over to place her hand on the child's chest. "We all die, my love. We have to so those that are born have a place. You see how many people are down here where I live?"

Jacklyn nodded, her eyes fixed on her grandmother's face.

"If everyone lived forever, we would get so crowded there would be no space, so we live as long as the Lord allows and then we go on."

"Did it hurt Grandpa to die?"

The question hit Beth right between the eyes. *Oh, let me deal with this right,* she prayed.

She hesitated for a moment. "You know what it's like when you blow out a candle on your birthday cake?"

Jacklyn nodded.

"Well . . . that's what it was like for your grandpa. God blew him out just like a candle. He was gone, just like that, and I don't think he felt a thing."

The child thought for a moment, nodded, and snuggled deeper under her covers. Beth got up, kissed the girls again, and stood by the door. "Get to sleep. Far Horizon will be waiting for you in the morning."

She left the door ajar. *I hope that helped her,* Beth thought. *You never can tell with kids; their thoughts are much deeper than we think at this age.*

She moved down the hall into the living room, where Steve and Liz were watching TV. She plopped down on the couch next to Taz, who glanced sleepily up at her. "Well, what do you think?" Beth slid her sandals off and wiggled her toes.

"I like him, Mom," Steve said slowly. "He seems sensible, easy to visit with, and he assured me that he isn't trying to rush you into anything or is after you for your money."

"Ha, he sure isn't letting me drift away either. As for the money, we really haven't even discussed that yet. I will need to talk to a lawyer if this goes much further. He has a nice condo and seems to be comfortable enough. What do you think, Liz?"

"He's nice looking, always a plus. He was good with the girls when they finally got over being shy, and I think he's serious about you. So go for it, and I hope he gives you the attention you deserve."

"The girls asked me about him and if I would love them if I married Dale. I hope I reassured them. Dale loves kids, and he has no grandkids, as his daughter has never married."

Steve shifted in the recliner and leaned forward. "What about the daughter?"

"She is less than thrilled, but Dale has more or less told her she'd better get used to it or else. I really think he means it."

Liz scowled. "He'd better. You'll have a mess if he doesn't."

"That's why none of this is going to happen in a hurry. We'll see how he handles Gloria. If he's all talk and doesn't stick up for me, there isn't going to be any us."

Steve stretched his long arms out in front of his body. "I hope it all works out, Mom. You've been alone a long time, and I would sure worry a lot less about you if you had a man around."

"I know, love. You've all been so good about checking on me, but I know how busy you are with your own lives. You don't need to be worrying about me too. I hope it will all work out, but I'm just taking it a day at a time." A huge yawn surfaced unexpectedly, and she smiled at her son and daughter-in-law. "Boy, I'm for bed. I'm pooped. Being courted is hard work for someone my age. I guess I'd better get my beauty sleep."

Beth got off the couch, kissed Steve and Liz, and gathered up her sandals. "I'll see you in the morning. Sleep in if you can."

Taz followed Beth down the hall, her tail twitching back and forth like a metronome.

# CHAPTER 11

It was a week after Steve's visit, and Beth and Dale had fallen into the habit of morning telephone visits.

"So what kind of hard dirty work are you dreaming up, woman? You said yesterday you had to start your late spring cleanup. I'm available for a modest fee as usual. Just a couple of kisses will do it."

Beth giggled and considered. "I've got to get started on the south yard. I leave that until last, but my handyman has turned into a house painter, so he isn't available this year."

"Want some help?"

"Well, yeah, I guess so. How are you on raking? My back won't stand that very long, and I've got piles of trash to gather."

"My back's still good, so I'd be glad to help out."

"That'll be great. That's my last big spring push, and I've been putting it off."

Beth had a hearty breakfast of eggs, sausage, and hash browns ready to put on the table when Dale arrived early the next day.

"Wow." Dale goggled as she dished up the meal and handed it to him. "I may founder on this and be no help at all."

Beth grabbed the full plate back from him, marched over to her garbage pail, and cocked her head.

"Hey, hey, I was only kidding, woman. Whew. I'll have to remember. You have no sense of humor in the morning."

Beth gave him back his plate. "Not until after my second cup of coffee, and I only had one so far." She pecked him on the cheek.

They ate hastily, opened the shed, packed rakes to her side yard, and began to tackle the debris piled against her lilac hedge. It looked like the neighbor's entire cornfield had blown into the lilac bushes when the fields were plowed last fall. The corn shucks, combined with leaves from the big cottonwood in the west yard, provided enough trash to use most of a roll of extra-large garbage bags. Only stopping for a brief lunch, they were both getting tired by midafternoon as they finished cleaning up the huge pile of leaves the wind had blown into the patio outside the walk-out basement doors.

"Let's put the trash in the dumpster and quit, or I won't be able to walk tomorrow," Beth said as she stretched her back. "I always overdo it. I just can't realize I can't do the whole thing in one day."

Dale groaned. "Thank God, woman. I was about to lie down and die. You're a real slave driver. I fear I may never be the same."

Dale staggered magnificently as they went into the house.

*I love a man with a sense of humor*, Beth thought. *It adds so much to life.* Her muscles gave a twinge, and she flinched.

"I think we deserve a drink. It will loosen up those abused muscles. What will you have? Wine? Or I have Jack Daniels, which is my poison of choice," she said.

"Jack Daniels, please," Dale said. He started to sit down on the couch and looked at his jeans. "I'm too dirty to sit down."

"Don't worry about it. I picked that couch to not show dirt," Beth said. "Ice and water?" When Dale nodded, she went into the office to the small wet bar, returning with generous amounts of Jack Daniels in square glasses.

They clinked glasses and watched each other over the rims as they took hearty swallows.

"I see you take yours neat," Dale said as he watched Beth exhale a long breath.

She nodded. "I learned that in Wyoming, when we gathered cattle in the fall. The water system at the summer headquarters was a beaver pond with a ditch to the cabin. But the beaver didn't like sharing, so they would dam the ditch up every morning. We would come back after a long day, filthy and thirsty and be out of water. I don't think there is anything worse than that. There is little you can do without water. Can't wash, can't drink, cook, do dishes, you name it. Don would go tear out the dam, but it would be hours before we would have water again."

She twirled the glass slowly, deep in her memories. "The propane refrigerator had such a small freezer we saved the ice for more important things than a drink. I learned to rough it working with them, and it got rough at times, in lots of ways." Beth downed her two fingers of Jack Daniels and headed back to the bar for a refill while Dale sipped his slowly.

As she came back out of the office, she glanced at the unique grandfather clock that hung suspended on the wall. The pendulums were almost to the bottom of their chains. "Oops, I'd better wind the clock," Beth said as she sat her drink on the top of the stereo unit.

A full-length, curved piece of glass covered the innards of the clock. Carefully, Beth stretched her right arm up to pick a key off the top. As her fingers touched the key, she doubled over with a muffled yell.

"Oh damn, I did it again." Beth looked up at Dale as he rushed to her side, looking completely baffled. Holding on to him for balance, she said, "My shoulder's in a spasm. Pull my arm up, will you? Gently, gently," she groaned as Dale tugged too hard. "Try it again," she said, tears running down her face. Her face contorted as he tried again. "Stop. No good, no good."

"What can I do?" Confusion and concern lined Dale's face. "Call the doctor?"

Beth panted with pain. "No, but if you massage my back and shoulder, maybe we can get it to relax. I'll lie down on the floor."

Dale straddled her and started rubbing her shoulders and back. "I think it would be better if I had some lotion or something and we got your shirt off," he said after a minute or two without results.

Beth got up and led him into her bedroom. Groaning, she slowly crawled onto the end of the bed and let him pull her shirt off. She rolled over facedown. "There's lotion in the master bath on the counter by the sink," she said.

Dale rushed into the bathroom, came back with the lotion, and put some on his hands.

She yelped as he put the cold lotion on her back.

"Sorry, sorry," he apologized. "I should have warmed that up first."

Beth groaned as he started massaging her back, concentrating on her right shoulder blade area, where he could see the muscles twitching. Beth fought to concentrate, not to fight the spasms—staying tight only made things worse. Slowly the heat from Dale's hands began to soothe and lengthen the muscles; relief came like a benediction.

Beth became aware of Dale's body against hers as the pain receded. He had climbed onto the bed and straddled her again so he could get the right angle to work her shoulders. His legs were gripping her hips and his pelvis was against her buttocks.

If he was relaxing her, it was very apparent she wasn't relaxing him. Big warm palms stroked up and down her back, which had always been the most sensitive area of Beth's body. Warmth containing small tingles of pleasure spread clear to her toes. Spasms of pleasure at her very center replaced the pain. Oh God, it felt so good to have his hands on her. Dale dug his thumbs in gently close to her spine. Beth squeaked.

"Did I hurt you?" He bent down across her shoulder so his face was beside hers.

"No, I'm just a little sensitive there."

"Sorry, your muscles seem to be more relaxed. Do you want me to keep going?" His eyes were full of warm concern. He really did care for her.

"Yes." Beth hesitated, looking sideways at him, and then added with a sigh, "All over."

Dale's mouth dropped open slightly and then rearranged itself into a grin. "Are you saying what I think you're saying?"

Beth's voice was husky as she purred, "Get off me, you big lug."

Dale rolled off. They lay side by side, staring at each other.

Beth ran her finger over his full bottom lip and smiled as she watched his eyes widen and darken. "You remember when we talked about waiting until it felt right that night on the deck?" Her finger teased his lip, gently back and forth.

Dale nodded dumbly.

Beth's arms went around Dale, and she snugged herself into his body and sighed. "It's time."

*   *   *

*And the rest is history,* Beth thought the next day, grinning to herself as she and Nancy rode through an early morning, everything gilded with gold. It was fitting; she was still glowing from within. *I think I surprised him,* Beth sniggered to herself. She had been the aggressor at the start, busily stripping him while he stared at her nonplussed. When she started tugging at his zipper with her tongue between her teeth, he put his hand over hers. She glanced up at him with a frown.

"Beth, are you sure?"

She stared at him and then grew a slow wicked grin that made him catch his breath.

"You already asked that. So . . . do I have to do all the work here? I've been waiting and waiting for you to get with it and you . . ." The rest of her sentence was smothered by his mouth. His arms went around her so hard her teeth clicked together.

How wondrous was the closeness between man and woman. It had been tender and wonderful; she hadn't thought of Rob at all. She hadn't realized just how much she missed the closeness and release of loving. She had sobbed with gratitude afterward, as she had never expected to feel that way again. All her fears had been for nothing; any awkwardness stemmed from lack of practice. They laughed wildly as they touched and tasted and surrendered to the passion they had suppressed for so long.

Beth hated to send Dale home, but she was a little uncomfortable about having him stay. Dale seemed to sense it and relieved her of the decision by saying he needed to get home.

*I imagine Gloria would notice if he stays out all night,* Beth thought as she rode through the bright morning. And she wasn't very keen to have her neighbors notice that Dale had not left, if she was totally honest.

Far Horizon stumbled and jerked Beth back to the present. The women were riding along the big irrigation canal that meandered through the neighboring fields. It was a perfect training situation for the horses. The waste ditches from the fields ended at the canal road in places. When the farmers irrigated, the ditches burbled loudly along the road, helping the horses get used to the noise of moving water.

The corn grew higher than the horses could see over in late summer. It hid rustling monsters that surely favored horse meat. Rusty ghosts of long outdated machinery lurked in the weeds, causing many a nervous equine glance. The riders could make a two-hour circle, perfect to keep the horses in condition between day trips. At the same time, it built trust between mounts and riders.

Beth supposed the fields would gradually turn into several acre places like her own, and the wild world would disappear. She would miss the encounters with the animals. The canal provided water and cover for the ducks and geese and their young. She had seen foxes, coyotes, skunks, and even a young golden eagle. It had been hopping on the ground, unable to turn loose of a rabbit it clutched in its claws as it watched the riders approach. They had ridden a wide circle around it not to panic the youngster.

"A penny for your thoughts," Nancy said as her gelding caught up with Far Horizon and slowed to match his walk. "You aren't on this plane today. What are you thinking about?"

"Things," Beth said, grinning.

"What things? It wouldn't have anything to do with that yummy-looking guy that seems to be hanging around your place lately, would it? His name might be Dale?"

Beth gave her a startled look and then shrugged her shoulders. "I should have known you guys would be keeping track of who was going in and out. You've always watched my place like a hawk."

"As you do ours. That's what good neighbors do. We aren't meaning to be nosy. We just care about you."

"I know that. Yeah, it does have something to do with Dale. I think I have met someone that may . . . well, who knows?"

"Ah, aren't you the one that always says a man is too much trouble, you have a full life the way it is? Are you thinking marriage? You aren't going to do anything in a hurry, are you?"

"Oh Lord, no. He would have to sign off on a list of things I won't do. It's about two legal pages long."

"Like what?" Nancy was intrigued.

Beth snorted. "Well, he would have to understand I'm not going to pick up after him, do all the cooking unless I want to. If I want to go do things with my women friends, I will, and he'll just have to deal with that. My family is very important to me and here a lot. I don't want to move off this place."

She blew a long breath and continued. "Let's see, we would have to have an understanding about money and lots of other things. I only iron a couple times a year, so he would have to do wash and wear. Ironed, starched shirts are out. If I feel like being lazy and staying in bed to read a book and eat crackers, I will. I don't know that he will be willing to agree to everything I don't want to do. And if he agreed and then didn't do them, where would I be?"

"At least you're thinking about those things instead of being head over heels without a thought in your head except being with a man."

"I never understood women who would rather put up with a jerk than be single. I guess some women just can't stand to be alone."

"There're worse things, that's for sure, although I can't imagine life without Len," Nancy said with a little shiver.

"Let's hope you never have to learn." Beth squinted at the sun. "We better turn around and head home. It's getting hot."

Far Horizon thought that was a good idea.

# Chapter 12

If being in love meant having no time to yourself then Beth decided she must be in love. Her best intentions of slowing things down in her relationship with Dale never seemed to work. Spring had turned into full summer, and he was occupying more and more of her time. The Saturday time together gradually expanded to an almost everyday occurrence. Determined to take a day to herself, Beth found that Dale would manage to wheedle himself into the barn or yard work, or she would call him and find herself agreeing to meet him for dinner. They went to plays and musicals, sometimes just for drives, and still managed to get more work done around her place than had been done in years.

If she managed a day alone, it didn't produce much, as she found herself thinking of Dale instead of focusing on the important things she needed to be doing. It was really pathetic, Beth thought as she toiled at the big roll top desk in her office. She hadn't paid her bills, and the to-do piles were getting out of hand.

The phone rang just as she sealed the envelope for the water bill. She shuffled hurriedly through the piles of papers to find the receiver.

"Hey," Nancy said. "I know you're busy with your new man and all, but we need to be doing some planning for the horse camp. It's in two weeks, remember?"

"Lord, I had forgotten all about it. The first part of July has just flown by." Beth squinted at her calendar on the wall and flipped the month of June over. She shifted the phone to her other ear. "Well, we have been riding most mornings, so the horses are in condition and so is our equipment. The motel reservations are made. I think we're in pretty good shape."

"Good thing," Nancy joked. "You are still planning on going? Len was wondering if you were going to go, as you have been, ahem, somewhat otherwise occupied."

"Oh, knock it off. You know I wouldn't miss our yearly escape. I better tell Dale, however."

"Do you suppose he'll be able to survive without you?" Nancy was enjoying herself.

"He has no choice. He can go to a football game."

"Beth, they do not play football in the summer."

"Oh. It seems to me that they play year-round."

Nancy laughed. "Len and I know how little you like sports. I have always appreciated the fact that you don't make fun of our obsession."

"Well, everyone should have a passion. It just happens to be at the end of my list or, more truthfully, completely off my list.

"It's probably on your waste-of-time list," Nancy said.

"I'd have to admit that. But Dale knows all about it. I confessed to the sin of disliking football early in the game, when he was telling me about how much he enjoyed coaching. I think he has forgiven me by now. I'm sure there is something he dislikes just as much, but up to now I haven't heard about it. Mmm, he may be secretly jealous of Far."

\* \* \*

Beth told Dale about the horse trip the next day. They were at the nursery, loading fertilizer for her pine trees. He had come to help her with the yard again, offering to provide the muscle to pick up the fertilizer and stack it in her shed. He finished loading the last sack into the back of her Yukon and straightened with a groan, wiping sweat from his neck with a handkerchief.

"A whole week? Where do you go?"

"Chugwater, Wyoming. That's where my trainer lives. We relearn what we forgot during the winter. The group got into cattle working last year, and we will be doing a lot of that this summer. We always have a great time. It rained a couple of afternoons last year, but we just cowboyed up and went on with it. They needed the rain so bad we didn't even care if we got wet."

Lunch was a stop at Burger King. Beth glanced at Dale between bites of her hamburger and said, "You're thinking so hard I can almost hear you."

He ate a few more fries, studied her seriously. "Could I come to the clinic?"

Beth chewed reflectively, swallowed, and said slowly, "I think the clinic is full. They keep it to a low number so they can give us a lot of attention. Why?"

"I just had a thought." He took a swig of his Coke and continued, "Do you remember Gloria's interest in your horse?" When Beth nodded, he added, "Maybe, just maybe, it might be a way to get her involved with the both of us without it seeming like we are trying to force her. Would you find out if there's room for us? Could your trainer provide a couple of nags for us beginners? I know Gloria is about ready to take some time off." He ate a few more fries. "She really did love to ride when she was a kid. I don't know what her skill level would be, but she wouldn't be a beginner. I'm close but do know one end of the animal from the other."

Beth hesitated. Dale put a hand over hers and added, "I really don't want to intrude on your trip, but it might help."

"I'm not sure it would work, but maybe . . . I'll check with Amy. Sometimes she does have cancellations. If she does, it might be worth a try." She swallowed the rest of her hamburger, eyed Dale's potatoes. "Can I steal a few of your fries?"

*   *   *

When Beth told Nancy that Dale and his daughter were going to come to the clinic, Nancy was less than enthusiastic. "Are you sure this is a good idea? You won't have your full attention on the matter at hand. It's good for Amy to fill those two cancellations, but I'm surprised the daughter agreed."

"Dale says that she wasn't interested, but he talked her into it." Beth looked at her friend with a grimace. "I'm not too enthused either, but it just worked out that there was room, so we decided to try to make some headway with Gloria."

"It won't be the same," Nancy said sadly. "This is our special time together. Don't get me wrong. I've got nothing against Dale. He seems like a nice guy, what little I've be around him. But you'll be making calf eyes at your boyfriend while the daughter will be looking daggers at you. And I'll be caught in the middle. Nuts." She tugged her hat brim down toward her eyebrows and swatted at a mosquito.

They were riding on the canal again, alternating between trotting and walking the geldings. Both the women's horses were beautiful under saddle, muscles tight and hides gleaming.

"I'm going to concentrate on the clinic, not Dale," Beth said firmly. "Not to change the subject, but it sure feels good to be in shape again. I hate it when I lay off riding too long. It makes me sore until I get toughened up again." She stood in her stirrups and rubbed her rear end thoughtfully. "Buns of steel, ready for anything."

"Okay, I get the hint, change the subject. I'll let it go and hope for the best." Nancy laughed and added slyly, "I bet Dale appreciates your steel buns. You look really good. You've lost weight. Is it being in love?"

"I overeat when I'm unhappy. Lately I really don't care if I eat at all, so it must be love." Beth laughed and nudged Far Horizon into a lope. "Let's make time. I have a lot to do."

*   *   *

Two days before the clinic, Beth took a break from her packing and called Dale. "How do you want to work the trip to Chugwater. Do you want to follow us or what?"

"Why don't you just give me the directions? We'll come up Monday morning. It isn't hard to find from the way you talked. Are you going up Sunday night?"

Beth sighed. "No, my friend gets up at four thirty, so she would rather go Monday morning. Nancy has been up so long by the time I get out of bed she feels like six is the middle of the day. We'll have everything packed Sunday night so all we have to do is load the horses and make sure Taz is in the house. We should be at Amy's by eight-thirty. Things are supposed to start at nine, but it always runs a little late, so don't push it if you get a late start."

"Are you sure the trainer's horses will be all right for us?" Dale sounded a little nervous.

"I asked Amy for old Sweet Face for you and specified Killer for Gloria," Beth joked. "Seriously, you'll be on well-broke horses. Amy doesn't want an accident any more than you do." She sighed. "This better help our problem with Gloria. The clinic is a special deal for my riding group."

There was a short silence.

Dale cleared his throat. "I hope you don't mind me butting into your time with your women friends, but I thought it might be a way to change things with my somewhat stubborn daughter."

"If she gets too nasty, there's always a rope and a tree." Beth stared out the window and watched Far Horizon as he rolled in the pea gravel of the loafing area. The gelding got to his feet and shook himself briskly. She cleared her throat. "Seriously, Dale, I decided it's worth a try. I really want her to accept us because it won't be pleasant if she doesn't."

"She understands this is going to happen—us I mean, with or without her approval."

"As long as you stand by me, we can work it out one way or another. But if our families can work us against each other . . . it'll be a nightmare."

"Not going to happen. I promise you," Dale assured her.

"You'd better keep that promise. That kind of thing ruined my sister's third marriage. Well, it was part of it, but the fact her husband wouldn't stand up for his wife against his kids was the final straw."

"I understand. We cleave to each other like the Bible says," Dale said in somber tones. "What's *cleave*? I've often wondered." He thought for a moment. "Well," Dale mused, "probably they take a big knife . . ."

"Ow, enough!" Beth shuddered.

"See you in three days. It will be our first big adventure together," Dale said.

"I hope we don't wish we had taken a cruise."

Beth called May the next morning to let her know she was leaving. They hadn't done much together since Dale had come on the scene. Beth missed her friend. *Must not lose my women friends over this guy*, she thought as she waited for May to pick up her phone.

"This trip was planned, but he goes with you, doesn't he? And one other?" May paused and added, "A woman?"

"Yes," Beth said. "His daughter is going with us."

"She does not like you," May stated. "She will be a lot of trouble to you. She has a black heart, one that will not share. But I still see happiness for you."

"I hope so, May, I hope so with all my mind and soul. It's gone so far now that it will kill me if it falls apart. Wish me luck."

"Maybe the daughter will fall off her horse and break her neck."

Shocked at her friend's vehement remark, Beth said, "I should be so lucky. But I better watch out for Dale. I think Gloria would rather see him dead than with me. How's that for wanting your parent to be happy?" She sighed. "Whatever happens will happen, but I think I need a miracle."

Sunday night, the Yukon packed, the last item checked off her list, Beth was in her bathroom getting ready for bed. While she was brushing her teeth, she glanced at her wedding ring and tugged it off her finger. It really needed a good cleaning, she decided. Dumping it into a jar of ring cleaner, she swished it around, rinsed, and dried it. It was a beautiful piece of jewelry, a marquise diamond centered on a wide gold band. Admiring its glitter, Beth regarded it thoughtfully. A ring was like a brand. Her hand looked naked without the wedding band, but it didn't feel right to put it back on. Although Dale had not brought up the fact she wore her wedding band, its presence suddenly seemed wrong. Rob's claim was no longer valid.

In her bedroom, she placed it in her jewel case, slowly sliding the drawer shut on the fire of the freshly cleaned diamond.

*You won't be happy about this either, my old love, but our life together is over.*

# CHAPTER 13

Beth eyed Nancy the next morning as her friend heaved her suitcase into the Yukon. "It's not fair. You always make me feel like an unmade bed. You look so bright eyed, your makeup is perfect, you even manage to look good at the end of the day while I look like I've been wandering in the desert for a week."

Nancy' response to Beth's complaint was a sweet smile. Beth gave it up and brushed her forearm across her brow. "Wow, it's heating up fast."

"It feels like a scorcher. We'll have to pour water in and over us to keep from falling out of the saddle." Nancy put a small cooler behind the passenger seat. "I'm sure glad you hooked up the trailer last night."

"It's nice the horses loaded easily. Remember what a time you used to have getting Mista into the trailer? It wouldn't be much fun in this heat."

"I thought we would never get it through her head there were no monsters lurking in there" Nancy dumped her purse on the dash, looked at Beth. "Are we ready?"

Beth rechecked the trailer hitch. "Looks like I did it right. Are the tires up on your side?" When Nancy nodded, the women climbed into the Yukon and buckled up.

"Let's get this show on the road," Beth said. "Yee ha!"

The pasture grasses were baked blonde as the Yukon rolled north on Highway 85 through the small towns of Pierce and Nunn. The Nunn water tower had an addition to the Watch Nunn Grow sign. Some wit had added the word *weeds*. Traffic was light, the wind down, so the Yukon managed the steady climb in elevation easily as they drove toward the Cheyenne Ridge.

"Len looked already lonesome as we pulled out of your driveway," Beth said. "Men sure don't like to be on their own."

"Len doesn't. We've always spent all of our free time with each other. Now that we're both retired, it's been wonderful." Nancy pulled a small package of hand wipes out of her purse, briskly wiped her hands clean.

Beth glanced over at her friend. "I always looked forward to it being just the two of us when retirement came, but it was hard on Rob. I think he was lonely. He started doing all our errands. He would leave to go to town to pick up a couple of things and be gone all day. It finally dawned on me he needed to be with people. He did go on fishing and golfing trips with two old buddies of his. He always worked hard, so he deserved to play, and the way it worked out, I'm glad he got to do as much as he did." She bit her lip. "He only had five years." She shrugged her shoulders, shifted her hands to a new grip on the steering wheel. "A lot better than dying in harness, don't you think?"

Nancy reached over, patted Beth on the shoulder. After a short silence, she asked, "What about Dale? Does he have friends he runs around with?"

"He doesn't seem to. He moved here from Sterling once he got divorced. Small towns don't offer much for single people. Most people are drawn to bright lights and crowds, I guess."

"Except for you." Nancy grinned, stretched. "Now are we going to stop in Cheyenne for that latte I'm dying for? Nothing but cowboy coffee from that point on."

\*     \*     \*

The small town of Chugwater hugs the side of Interstate 25 about thirty miles north of Cheyenne in a valley carved by the Chug River. Walled by bluffs east and west, the valley is an irrigated oasis of refreshing green in the heat of early August.

The LaPlat Ranch, a mile east of town, featured a nice ranch-style home with the ranch outbuildings nestled among huge cottonwood trees close to a century in age. Cattle and horses grazed in the pastures surrounding the large barn and adjoining corrals.

Most of the other riders had come in the night before, and they were well settled in the choice spots close to the barn. Beth's two-horse trailer looked like a bug next to the large sleek rigs containing sleeping quarters and tack rooms. She pulled alongside the last rig in the row, turned the key off, and stretched. "We have a long walk to the barn."

"I don't imagine it will hurt us any except maybe by the end of the day. Let's try not to stagger." Nancy beamed. "I love it here. It's the highlight of my year."

During the process of unloading, finding pens for the horses, greeting friends, Beth forgot all about Dale and his daughter. She finished situating Far Horizon in his pen and had just latched the gate when someone touched her on the shoulder. She turned to see Dale and Gloria standing behind her.

"Hey, you made it." Beth gave Dale a swift hug, turned to Gloria. *She's tight as a watch spring,* Beth thought as she greeted Dale's daughter. "Let me introduce you to the rest of the group. Gloria, this is my neighbor, Nancy Delagon."

The riders were all women, dressed in jeans, riding boots, and T-shirts. Dale smiled at one T-shirt that had a picture of a glorious woman outfitted in jeans, chaps, Western shirt, blouse, and boots. She stood with her hip cocked, head lifted, her pretty face belligerent. A rope dangled from her shoulder. The caption said, "I don't do coffee!" The owner of the shirt probably didn't make the coffee either.

"I guess I'm the token male?" Dale inquired.

Beth grinned at him. "Close, but Amy's husband, Mark, shares in the training, so there'll be two of you. It'll be fine. We're so busy learning nobody pays much attention to anything else."

She put on her wide straw hat. "Let's introduce you to our trainers so we can find out what horses they want you to use. I imagine Amy and Mark are in the barn." One of the other women nodded. Beth added, "Coming, Nancy?"

Nancy shook her head. "I'll catch up with you later. I want to go visit with Sue and Marcy."

Beth led the way to the barn. As the three stepped through the wide door, the shade felt like a benediction. A tack room full of racked saddles was on the left and a feed room on the right. Several kittens played on the worn wooden floor, bright scraps of color. There were two feed bunks on each side of the barn and several stalls toward the back of the building. An open sliding door at the back pulled a breeze through the interior.

A woman came out from behind the palomino horse on the far left stall, and Beth heard Dale give a soft *wow* under his breath.

"What every cowgirl wants to look like, our trainer, Amy LaPlat." Beth gave the tall, willowy woman a tight hug, turned to reach toward Dale and Gloria. "This is my friend Dale Runnington and his daughter, Gloria. Gloria is a nurse," she added as Amy was shaking hands with Dale.

Amy turned to Gloria. "That's good news. I hope we won't need you, but it's reassuring to know we have a professional with us if something goes wrong." She gave Gloria a swift appraisal. "I think I have the stirrups set about right for you on Rio's saddle. Come meet him." She led Gloria over to the palomino.

"Pull your eyes back in their sockets, you dog." Beth looked at Dale with her eyebrow quirked. "You're drooling."

Dale just shook his head. "Yessum. Wow, she's got a million-dollar smile. What's her husband look like?"

"He kind of resembles the Marlboro Man. I guess you could call them the Marlboro couple. They're both that good-looking."

Amy backed the gelding out of the stall and handed the reins to Gloria. "Why don't you take him out to the arena and get acquainted with him while I get your dad set up? Just go out the back of the barn, and you'll see it. Most of the other riders are already out there."

Gloria nodded and left leading the horse.

Amy moved to the seal brown gelding tied in the adjoining stall. "Dale, I've put you on Buddy. He's a gentle guy with impeccable manners. He'll take good care of you. Why don't you follow your daughter outside? Just be sure to check the chinches—those two suck in air when you're saddling them." Amy held the reins out to Dale.

Dale took the reins, tipped his straw hat to the women, and left.

Amy watched Dale until he was out of earshot. "Well now, he's nice. I'm glad for you. The daughter doesn't say much."

"He thought you were nice too, and no, the daughter doesn't say much. Doesn't like much either." A kitten that looked like a cross between a Siamese and a Manx wobbled over to Beth and decided to scrabble its way up her leg. She bent over and worked to remove the tiny claws out of her jeans. "Like I explained, we're hoping being in a neutral setting will get her used to the idea of us being together and give her some pleasure at the same time. The only positive response I have ever seen from her was her reaction to Far. They aren't going to be as advanced as the rest of us, so I hope that doesn't cause a problem."

"Will can work with them if they need extra attention."

"Will? I don't think I know him." Beth cuddled the kitten under her chin, and it set up a raspy purr, its eyes closed in ecstasy.

"We hired him as day help this spring. So far, he's working out well. It sure has been wonderful to have an extra pair of hands around here. Don't worry about Gloria and Dale, just enjoy yourself." Amy plucked a bridle off a peg, pulled a pair of gloves out of her back pocket.

"I leave them in your capable hands." Beth put the kitten down and smiled at her friend. "I'm just going to let the chips fall where they may, as the saying goes. If it doesn't work out, at least we tried, and Gloria can go hang. I guess I'd better get ready, or I'll be holding everything up."

As she saddled Far Horizon in his outside pen, Beth watched Dale and Gloria walk and trot their horses in the arena. *They don't look too bad*, she thought. Gloria had a good seat; Dale handled his horse all right, although he didn't look as relaxed as Gloria.

The rest of the riders were already warming up their horses, so Beth hurried to finish saddling. She joined the group as a handsome, long-legged man rode into the center of the arena, adjusting his microphone, which gave a loud whine until the volume was right.

His deep voice cut through the chatter. "Well, ladies, here we are again. Luckily the wind is down, so let's make the most of it. I'm riding a green-broke mare. Her name is Clemmy. Form a circle around us, and since we have a couple of new people, let's introduce ourselves. I'm Amy's husband, Mark. My wife is the expert, so if we have any hard questions, she's the one to ask."

Amy, sitting on her stud horse, Chinka, waved and blew Mark a kiss, which got an appreciative laugh from the group.

Mark grinned back at his wife, his attractive face creasing into deep laugh lines. He sported a mustache going from blonde to gray. Tugging his light-colored felt hat a bit closer to his eyebrows, he reined his horse to face Dale. "Why don't you tell us who you are and what you want to get out of the clinic."

Dale looked around at the group of women, who were watching him with interest. "I'm Dale Runnington, a friend of Beth's. I'm interested in improving my horse skills, which are pretty pathetic. Mainly, I don't want to fall off." He looked at his daughter and nodded.

Gloria shrugged, looked at Mark. "I'm his daughter, Gloria Runnington. I haven't ridden for years so I'll have lots to relearn." She looked at the woman next to her.

"Hi, Dale and Gloria. I'm Jane and mostly interested in improving my cow work this year. This pretty bay mare's name is Fancy."

Much the same message was repeated by each of the women as they went around the circle. There was Sue, mounted on a chestnut quarter horse mare; Marcy and Nancy on paint mares; and Rhonda on a black gelding. Beth, Susan, and Becky had gray geldings; and Mary, who was the shortest woman in the group, was mounted on the tallest horse, a rangy red roan gelding. His name was Tall Man.

A horse and rider came through the gate into the arena. Amy said, "I want to introduce Will Meyer. Will is helping us this summer, and he is riding Romeo." Will took off his hat, bowed from the saddle, and flashed a shy smile at the group. He was a tall lean man, who looked to be about forty-five. Romeo was a seal brown gelding with a white strip down his nose and white socks.

"All right then," Mark announced. "Walk your horses out, and we'll see what kind of mood they're in today. We'll tune them up this morning. Work on any problems that stand out. Remember, there is no such thing as a dumb question. Let's all circle to the left."

The riders rode around the large arena, working at different speeds, turning and backing and letting the horses get used to each other. There were a few squeals and kicks, mostly between the mares, but the horses soon settled down. When the trainers spotted weak spots in either horse or rider, they would ask if anyone else was having the same problem and either work it as a group or one of the trainers would concentrate on the problem while the other two worked the group on something else.

When Amy called for the lunch break, the riders were all eager to escape the heat and dust.

"Oh boy, am I glad to get off that horse," Dale groaned to Beth as she walked Far Horizon past Buddy's small pen. "Do I unsaddle him during the lunch break?"

Beth stopped, hooked her arms over the top rail of the pen. "I don't. Take his bridle off and just loosen the chinch some so he can relax and eat. You looked pretty good out there."

"I sure have a lot to learn, but it was interesting to see how they teach. This soft-feel stuff and loose rein is something different from what I learned. The trainers sure throw a lot of stuff at you."

"This group has ridden together for several years, so we are all about the same skill level. Don't try to absorb it all, just work on what is giving you the most trouble. I'll go put Far Horizon up and come back. Be sure Buddy has hay and water."

Gloria's horse was in a pen down on the other end of the barnyard. She walked toward Beth and Dale, brushing at the wisps of hay on her jeans, looking hot and tired.

They walked together toward the ranch house, where lunch was set up in the garage to protect the diners against the usual Wyoming wind. So far it was just a breeze that had helped the riders and horses stay a bit cooler. Chugwater was famous for its wind, which could blow paint off a wall when it got determined.

"Are you hungry, Gloria?" Beth asked as she rolled her shirt sleeves off her wrists.

"Yes." Gloria glanced at Beth and Dale, averted her face, and picked up speed to walk ahead. Her posture was rigid.

Dale and Beth looked at each other. Beth shrugged and said in a low voice, "I guess it was too much to expect a change in one morning."

Dale nodded glumly.

"I think we better ignore each other at lunch. I want to visit with my friends anyway. I haven't seen some of them since the clinic last year."

They joined the other riders for the hearty lunch waiting on a long table. Beth was more interested in something to drink than eating but knew she would need energy for the afternoon. She filled her plate with a hamburger, beans, and potato salad and went to sit with Nancy and the rest of her friends.

"I hear that Dale is yours." Sue grinned at Beth as she chewed vigorously. "Too bad, isn't it, Marcy?"

Marcy nodded. "He's really nice looking. Where did you meet him?"

"We used to date before I met Rob. He just showed up at my place one day. Hey, what can I say? He just wouldn't give up."

"Lucky you," Rhonda said wistfully.

Beth smiled at her, wishing her friend could find someone to replace the fiancé she had lost years ago in an auto accident shortly before their wedding day. It had been a long painful pull for Rhonda, but her interest in horses had helped her get through it. *As it did me*, Beth thought. *Horses are surely a gift from God.*

"Yes, I surely am lucky." She patted Rhonda on the hand. "I hope the same for you someday."

Rhonda shrugged. "It's been so long I have just about given up."

"Don't. I felt the same way, and all of a sudden it happened. When I was least expecting it. Never when I was in a situation where I thought something might develop."

"Well, I'll keep hoping for a while then." Rhonda bit off a healthy bite of hamburger bun. "Then I'll just give up and get fat." The two women grinned at each other and concentrated on their lunch.

"What's with the daughter?" Sue, blunt as always, eyed Beth over a brownie. "She seems about as friendly as a cottonmouth."

Beth pushed her plate back and sighed. "She doesn't seem to like the fact that her dad is involved with me. Dale thought maybe this would be a way to get her thinking about something else, maybe get her to change her mind."

"Huh," Sue said, unconvinced.

Beth wasn't too convinced herself so far. *But I will have patience*, she vowed to herself as she helped herself to a brownie and groaned with pleasure. "I won't be able to get back on my horse after this." She chewed in bliss as she watched the crowd.

The noise level was high as conversation centered on the morning's work and plans for the afternoon. The ranch dogs were making the rounds, looking for handouts and affection from anyone. There were four of them, an old Saint Bernard, a couple of mixed mutts, and a dachshund who didn't seem to fit in as a ranch dog. Mark had given it to Amy when she had back surgery to give her something to take care of while she was healing. It was difficult for Amy to just relax. The puppy had helped a lot.

Mark, Will, and Dale were sitting together, a male bastion against the females. They seemed to be getting along, laughing at each other's jokes. Amy was sitting on the other side of the table with her friend Barbara from Chugwater, who catered for the clinics.

Gloria sat by Barbara. Dale's daughter didn't join in much, just listened and answered when spoken to. Beth noticed Gloria get up and leave while most were just getting a second drink. She was already in the arena when the rest of the group arrived back at the barn.

*     *     *

"Let's split up and work in groups this afternoon." Amy was taking the afternoon session. "Those who want to rope and have done it before, work with Mark, those that haven't roped and want to can work with Will, and those that want to work in the round pen cutting cattle, work with me. When we warm up in the morning, if the horses have their heads on straight, we will ride out." She smiled at the cheer that went up. "Okay, gang, let's cowboy up!"

Beth, Nancy, Marcy, and Sue helped Amy run four steers into the round pen and took turns cutting. Beth glanced at the arena as she waited for her turn. Dale and Gloria were learning to make loops in their lariats with Will while the other riders were using the roping dummies. Rusty from a long winter, there were lots of misses accompanied by high-spirited banter from the participants.

"Beth, you're next," Amy shouted. Beth rode into the round pen, where she forgot everything except the thrill of working Far Horizon on cattle. He liked it and was doing well with a steer that was willing to move. One steer had been too lazy, the other one wild as a March hare, but this one was just right, trotting briskly around the pen, giving Far and Beth time to react well. The steer shut down and swung his head toward them. Beth stopped Far Horizon slightly ahead of the steer, and as the steer turned, it was as if Far was pulled along right with him without Beth having to do anything but think the turn.

"Perfect!" Amy grinned at Beth. "Put your hand on his neck so he will know you're done. It's a good time to quit and let someone else try."

Beth joined Dale on the outside of the round pen. She was glad she had been concentrating so hard she hadn't noticed he was watching. She was so pumped up she could hardly sit still. "Did you see me? Oh man, what a high!"

"I'm impressed," Dale said. "You and Far were really something to watch. He likes it, doesn't he?" Dale leaned forward to rest his arms across his saddle horn.

"He loves it. I wish I were still in Rawlins working cattle with my rancher friends. He would make so much more progress if we were putting in eight-hour days like I used to. The old saying, 'Wet blankets make good horses' is totally true." Beth pulled her water bottle out of its holder and poured it over her shoulders after taking a drink. "Wow," she gasped, "I'm so hot I could melt." She looked at Dale. "How're you doing? Did you enjoy the roping?"

"Yeah, but after a while my shoulder started getting sore, and I wanted to watch you cut."

"That's my problem with roping, my shoulder won't take it. I didn't think I would ever learn to build a loop, but I did. I can rope something that's standing still, but I like my thumbs."

"Thumbs?" Dale stepped down from the saddle, walked over to Beth and Far, and put his hand on her leg.

"When you dally in a hurry, you can wrap your thumb in with the rope. When the steer hits the end of the rope, your thumb is removed from your hand in a particularly nasty way," Beth said as she smiled down at Dale.

Dale gulped. "I won't plan on a long roping career then." He glanced over to the other side of the arena. "Gloria is sticking with it. She seems to like roping." They watched as Gloria built a loop and started swinging it, doing well until her speed slowed and the rope settled over her shoulders. She made a face; Will walked over and started talking to her.

Beth turned Far so her back was to Gloria. She didn't want Gloria to think she was watching her. "I hope she's enjoying herself. It's hard work. A lot of people aren't willing to put forth the effort."

"Gloria's a worker. If she's interested in something, she'll stick with it." Dale glanced back at Gloria just as her loop settled over the horns of the roping dummy. She whooped and turned to laugh at Will. "Well, I'd say she's having fun. She doesn't laugh much." He watched his daughter for a few more moments and then turned back to Beth. "What happens after we finish here this afternoon?"

"What do you mean?"

"Do I get to see you tonight? Maybe you have a muscle spasm that will need to be massaged?" He leered at her.

Beth raised an eyebrow. "Hey, behave yourself, you mug. I think it best we don't spend a lot of time with each other. Remember, this is to ease Gloria into accepting us. It isn't to ignore her while you and I are being all snuggly. I want to spend time with my women friends anyway. So let's keep it casual."

"No adoring looks and sighs of frustration?" Dale looked as pitiful as possible.

"Stop it, you idiot. In fact, we've probably spent enough time together right now. Go tell your daughter how well she's doing. Let's try to make this a wonderful experience for her. If we have to sacrifice some of our time together, it won't kill us."

"Speak for yourself, woman. I'm feeling really deprived already, or is it depraved?"

Beth pushed her stirrup toward him, shaking her head. "Probably both. Have fun." She walked Far back over to the round pen just in time to see Nancy make a perfectly smooth turn, her horse flowing with the steer as it tried to escape. "Beautiful," she yelled, settling into her saddle to soak up every possible scrap of the experience.

"Let's call it a day," Amy said about three-thirty. "We don't want to kill you right off the bat. I know some of you need to get back to the motel to get unpacked. Dinner and breakfast are on your own, and we will see you at nine in the morning."

There was a lot of groaning and laughter as the riders unsaddled their horses and put them in their individual pens with enough hay and water for them to last the night. A good rider tended to his horse before he considered his own needs.

\*    \*    \*

All of the riders were camping at the ranch, except Gloria, Dale, Nancy, and Beth. Nancy wasn't much of a camper, and although Beth had done a lot of it when she was younger, using a tent in the Chugwater winds was courting disaster. Nancy and Beth always stayed at the only tourist accommodation, imaginarily named the Chugwater Motel. It was clean and had a restaurant attached, and the women had become regular summer guests over the last few years.

"What do we do for dinner?" Dale asked Beth as the four of them headed toward their vehicles.

"The motel restaurant is good. There really isn't any other choice, as the soda fountain on Main Street isn't open in the evening. We may see you at the restaurant if we decide to eat a meal. Right now all I want is a hot shower and rest. Nancy brought some snacks, so we may just do that. Maybe we can meet for breakfast. They start serving at six. Nancy will be waiting at the door, won't you, Nancy? I told Dale how early you get up."

"It's a date, Nancy. I'm an early riser too," Dale said.

"Beth tends to hug her pillow and groan in the morning, so we can probably eat, go feed the horses, and be back before she is ready." Nancy ducked as Beth took a swing at her.

"What about you, Gloria? You're probably used to all hours working as a nurse. And how did you like the first day?" Beth smiled as she looked at Gloria, who was pulling off her ball cap.

"It was all right and I don't eat breakfast." Gloria got into her father's SUV and shut the door. There was a short silence. Beth gestured to Nancy, smiled at Dale, and the women got into the Yukon.

"Boy, she just won't give an inch, will she?" Nancy frowned at Dale's vehicle as he drove away.

Beth said, "I don't really care right now, and I'm not going to make much of an effort other than to be polite. She'll have to come around herself. It won't do any good to try to make her like me. But she will. How can she resist?" She put her rig in gear, and the women laughed and talked about the thrill of working the cattle while they drove to the motel, got checked in, and unpacked.

"Do you want the shower first or can I have it?" Nancy started stripping out of her dirty clothes.

"Be my guest, but don't hog all the water. I'm physically incapable of doing anything more strenuous than breathe in and out right now." Beth flopped onto the bed.

By the time Beth had her shower, the friends agreed to just have a snack out of the cooler. By eight o'clock, they were fast asleep.

# CHAPTER 14

The next morning, Nancy and Beth were up with the sun. They drove out to the ranch, threw hay to their horses, including Dale and Gloria's, and went back to the motel to eat.

Dale and Gloria were sitting at a table as Beth and Nancy entered. Dale stood up and said, "Join us, we just got some coffee." He picked a piece of hay off Beth's shoulder as she settled into the chair he pulled away from the table for her. "You have hay left over from yesterday."

Nancy laughed as Beth looked at the wisp of hay with a grimace. "I tried to get her to take a shower last night, but I thought she changed her clothes." She smiled sweetly at Beth's mock glare. "We were already out to the ranch so we could feed the horses. We fed yours too. Maybe we can take turns going out in the morning so we all won't have to go."

"Thanks, I didn't even think about that," Dale said.

They all ordered a good breakfast, except Gloria who just ordered toast. Beth started to tell her she better eat so she would have strength for the morning but bit her tongue and said nothing.

Gloria fiddled with her toast while the rest ate their eggs, sausage, and hash browns with good appetite and little conversation.

"So now what?" Dale asked after they paid their bill.

"We like to go out about an hour early to get the horses cleaned up and saddled so we aren't rushed," Nancy said. "We can warm up in the arena if we want or we sometimes help Amy and Mark with their chores so we can get started earlier. With Will around, it will help things go faster for them in the mornings and at night too. They have so much to do after we are through."

"Sounds like a plan. We'll see you out there," Dale said.

As Beth slathered sunblock on her nose back in her room, she hoped Gloria had enough sense to do the same. *She doesn't have much protection with just that ball cap, but she won't appreciate me bringing it up, I'm sure,* she thought. *Anyway, I'm not her mother.* She made a face at the mirror, looked at Nancy, who was carefully putting on a layer of lipstick. "That's it, make me look dowdy."

Nancy grinned and offered the lipstick to Beth.

"Oh no, I just eat it off." She pulled a tube of lip protector out of her jean pocket. "I'm for protection, not perfection."

Nancy blew a raspberry at Beth as they gathered up their gloves and hats.

\*    \*    \*

They left ahead of Dale and Gloria. It was a beautiful summer morning with a slight breeze ruffling the grass in the pastures. There wasn't a cloud to mar the perfect blue dome of the sky, although Beth hoped some would form to shield them from the afternoon heat.

"Good morning," Mark said into the microphone when everyone was gathered in the arena again. "How are your muscles? A little sore?" He laughed as they all groaned. "Amy and I think you're all doing well enough to ride out of the arena and gather a few steers. Then we will do some team penning today. How does that sound?" He smiled at the enthusiastic response from the riders.

While they were gathered at the gate leading out of the ranch, Mark gave them the rules for group riding. No loping off without asking permission. If someone's horse started acting up, everyone shut down. If a horse had to pee, everyone waited. "Let's stay safe, particularly as this is the first time out. I think all our horses are pretty settled, but this is the first day out, so we're going to take it easy. And we work cattle slow, none of this whooping and running them like you see in the films."

"Why not?" Gloria queried.

"Cattle are mostly sold on gain, a set price per pound. Running takes off weight . . ."

"I get it."

The group ambled through the meadow just outside the arena, and all went well until they came to the first irrigation ditch. All the horses crossed quietly except for Mary's gelding. He balked and would not cross.

Steve called the other riders back so the horse would not get more upset. The two trainers worked with Mary while the other riders watched.

"I thought all of you were pretty accomplished riders. She can't get her horse to cross that little ditch?" Gloria shook her head. "Nobody else had any trouble."

"Mary's gelding is only a three-year-old. He probably never encountered a ditch before. Horses have no depth perception. He can't tell if that ditch is two inches or a mile deep." Beth leaned back in the saddle, a hand on Far Horizon's rump as she watched Mary's gelding. He wanted to join the other horses but was fearful of the new experience. "Most of us went through the same experience a few years back when this group was just starting Amy's clinics."

"Who's that?" Dale was looking at a mounted figure coming fast from the north.

Gloria and Beth turned their horses toward the oncoming pair.

"I think that's Will," Gloria said. "But what's he riding?"

A strident bray split the air.

"That's a mule, and it looks like things are out of control," Beth said. "Hey, gang, heads up," she yelled at the group.

The riders scattered, trying to get out of the way as the mule charged through them, braying at the top of his lungs. Beth and Gloria reined to the side, but Dale's horse began to give him trouble. Mary's horse forgot about the ditch, turned tail, and headed for the arena, just ahead of the mule. Mary managed to stay in the saddle but was unable to slow the big gelding. Off balance when Buddy stepped smartly sideways to keep the receding animals in sight, Dale tumbled to the ground with a thud.

Beth was off her horse and running toward him while the rest of the crew was still staring openmouthed. She slowed as she approached so she wouldn't spook Buddy, but he just stood looking down at Dale as though he was wondering why his rider was on the ground.

"Are you all right?" She knelt beside him.

Dale gasped for breath. "Got the wind knocked out of me," he wheezed.

Gloria ran up. "Dad, are you all right?" She dropped to her knees beside her father.

"He's fine, give him a minute," Beth said quietly.

"Oh, so now you're a nurse too?" Gloria put her hand possessively on her father's shoulder.

"No, just been dumped quite a few times." Beth sighed and got to her feet. "I'll leave him in your hands." She walked over to Far Horizon, picked up the reins, mounted, and rode toward Amy, who was just coming back from the arena.

"Is he all right?" Amy reined in her stud horse, Chinka, and they sat watching while Gloria tried to get Dale to stay on the ground.

"Just shook up, the ground is soft. I'm surprised Buddy reacted the way he did."

"He's probably never seen a mule. I asked Will to take him out, bad timing on the return. My fault."

"Is Will all right? How about Mary?"

"They're both fine. The gelding ended up in a dead heat with the mule, so he's been exposed." Amy snickered. She watched as Dale slowly got up. "Steve's helping Will get the mule unsaddled. They'll be here in a few minutes." She picked up her reins. "Would you gather the others up and tell them we'll be leaving in a couple of minutes if Dale's willing?"

Beth nodded.

"I'm going to ask Gloria if she will wait for Will and ride with him. He's going to be on a green horse, and after all, she is a nurse." Amy gave Beth a sly wink and rode off.

Dale was game to go, so the riders checked chinches and rode off again, this time detouring around the ditch. Amy assured Mary the ditch would be no problem to a tired gelding, anxious to get back to the barn.

Instead of going cross-country, the riders stayed on the two-track road that wound through the ranch. They rode north until they passed through two wire gates. Then Amy headed them east, where the terrain had the horses climbing hills and crossing washes, all the time working toward the big sandstone buttes.

"Switch positions as we go, lead, then fall back and work your horses around the brush and the rocks. Use your legs instead of the reins. Don't just ride along," Amy instructed.

Gloria seemed pleased to be riding with Will. Beth and Dale gradually managed to ride together.

"Is it safe, you think?" Beth looked sideways at Dale.

"I think your trainer is a sly wench. Gloria is so puffed up she's responsible for Will, I doubt she will give me a thought." Dale shifted in his saddle with a groan.

"Are you all right, hon? You're probably going to be a little stiff tomorrow."

"I'll live. I can't believe how fast I was on the ground. Just shows how bad a rider I am."

"Not really. Buddy's a cow horse. He can turn right out from under you if you aren't balanced. It's happened to all of us. I'm just glad you didn't get bucked off." Beth glanced back over at Gloria.

"I'm sorry she was so nasty. I didn't have my breath or I would have stood up for you."

"No apologies. Remember, I'm a big girl. If she gets in my face too many times, I will just deck her." Beth grinned at the thought.

"Be my guest, darling," Dale replied as they came to the top of a hill. "Aha, critters. That must be the herd."

The riders spread out behind the steers to move them west until they hit the two-track road. They turned the herd south and pushed them toward the ranch, an hour away.

It was slow going, hot, and dusty. The cattle were reluctant to move in the heat, they had to be urged along constantly, and it was noon before they got them back to the ranch.

They left the cattle to settle in while they went for lunch. Beth sat with Nancy and the rest of her friends. She noticed that Will went to sit beside Gloria. Dale, Amy, and Mark were deep in conversation. Beth hoped that she wasn't the subject, but Amy winked at her once, so it was a distinct possibility.

Everyone was eager to try team penning, so they didn't linger over the food.

Will and Mark ran a dozen steers into the arena and let them settle at the north end while Amy gave instructions. There would be three riders on each team. Two of the riders stayed away from the herd while the other cut three steers out and headed them away from the other animals, toward the other team members. All three would work the cattle across the arena to a small pen that was set up at the opposite end. They had to get all three steers in the pen and hold them in the open pen for a count of ten. Sounded easy, but it wasn't.

The afternoon blew by as the riders struggled to make the steers do what the riders wanted. The steers proceeded to do just the opposite. Steers like to hang out with steers, so the ones that were cut out tried every trick in the book to make it back to the bunch. They would separate and go every direction except toward the small pen set up opposite from the herd. There was lots of shouted advice from the watching riders to add to the confusion.

All the riders had their turn, except Dale and Gloria. Amy asked Will to be the third rider of the group, and he motioned for Gloria to go in and get the animals. She did a good job cutting them away from the herd. Using Will's suggestions, they managed to get the steers all in the pen, which got them a lot of appreciative applause, as nobody's team had managed it all afternoon. Dale waved his hat, bowed from the saddle, and Gloria even smiled.

The day burned hot without the hoped-for cloud cover. The riders were overheated and dirty when Amy released them at four-thirty.

As they walked toward their vehicles, Dale pulled Beth back and said quietly, "I haven't had a chance to talk to you since breakfast. What about dinner tonight?"

"All right, I think we have left each other alone enough. If Gloria is upset, it's her problem. I missed you. See you about six."

*   *   *

"I'm just too pooped to care about eating," Nancy said when Beth got out of the shower. "Go enjoy your lover boy. I'm going to read a little bit and pass out. That was a hard day, but we all did well, don't you think?"

Beth patted Nancy on the shoulder as she passed the bed. "I'm really proud of you. Remember after your first clinic, how frustrated you were? I had to coax you into doing another one, and here you are doing team penning."

Nancy smiled as she nodded. "I had no idea how much I had to learn."

"We'll never live long enough to know it all, but trying keeps us young," Beth said as she went to the door. "Sure you don't want me to bring anything back for you?"

"Four pieces of that good apple pie with ice cream," Nancy said, smiling at the ceiling as she lolled on her bed. "On second thought"—she pinched her thigh and grimaced—"I'll just pass. And thanks for the compliment, it means a lot. Go to your lover man. I'll just lay here and feel deserted for maybe two minutes." She heaved a huge yawn and waved Beth out of the room.

Beth was relieved to find Dale by himself when she got to the restaurant. It would be a real relief not to have Gloria dampening their evening, she thought as she watched Dale chatting with the waitress. He was like Rob that way, always wanting to know people while she kept more to herself.

"Gloria didn't feel too well, too much sun I think," Dale replied to Beth's inquiry.

"I think she's going to find that she needs to eat more. I hope she's putting on sunblock. You too," Beth said as she reached over to gently tap his nose. "You look like a bloody steak."

"I really thought I had enough tan not to really worry about it. The back of my neck is sore too. You would think a cowboy hat would be enough."

"Gloria doesn't have anything but that ball cap?" Beth held her glass of ice water to her neck, enjoying the coolness. She felt withered from the day's heat.

"Nope, she doesn't like hats. I had a tough time getting her to bring that," Dale said.

"I don't like hats either, but for the sake of my skin, I wear the biggest brim I can find and just endure terminal hat hair." She ignored Dale's amused snort. "Back to Gloria, the little building sitting at the side of the driveway at the house is Amy's tack shop. If we can get her in there, maybe she could find something she likes. I got my hat from Amy. It's the only one I have ever had that was the right size for me because I have a small head."

"Those are pretty expensive, aren't they?" Dale asked, nodding to the waitress as she put his salad in front of him. He ate a couple of bites musing. "Gloria has her birthday in a couple of days, come to think of it. I haven't bought her anything. Maybe that should be her present."

The waitress brought their dinner, and the couple turned their attention to the meal. Halfway through her spaghetti, Beth realized she was practically gobbling her food, but one look at the way Dale was inhaling his steak made her realize he was just as ravenous. They finished in companionable silence.

"Do you think Gloria is having a good time?" Beth pushed her plate away and wiped her hands on her napkin. "I really didn't pay much attention. I get so focused when I'm riding I don't notice much else."

"It's hard to tell with her. She has always kept to herself so much, being an only child. I think I mentioned she didn't get along well with her mother. She was heavy as a girl, and Marion used to criticize her all the time for that. I don't think she has a very good self-image of herself even though she has been thin for a long time. She has locked herself up so she doesn't get hurt again."

"Again? She was involved with someone seriously?"

Dale pushed his plate away to the side of the table and bent a little closer to Beth. "She was involved with a doctor when she was in nurses training. She thought they were going to be married, even had her dress picked out. He dumped her. I thought, for a while, it was going to kill Gloria. She has never allowed herself to get involved again, devotes all her time to her nursing career. It makes me sad, but you can't talk to her about it."

Beth put her hand on his. "I'm glad you told me about all that. It makes me understand her a little better. It may help me be more patient."

"I'm not going to be too patient, woman. Time is slipping away from us." Dale drew Beth to her feet. "I feel that you need a good kissing almost immediately."

"Shush, you fool." Beth was glad the only other diners were on the counter stools with their backs to the rest of the room.

They went out of the restaurant with their arms around each other. "Where do we go?" he asked as they stopped in the lobby. "For the kissing," he added at her puzzled look. "Is there a broom closet? A real dark bar would be nice . . . no? Darn." He snugged her against his side. "Since we're all on the first floor, let's go see what's on the second."

They went up the stairs and sat at the very back of an area that looked like it was used to hold receptions. Dale pulled Beth onto his lap and proceeded to give her a very thorough kissing and handling until he had Beth rosy and flustered and hungry for him.

"Damn," he said, absently stroking her hip. "I wish we could go to my room, but it is probably not a good idea to have Gloria see you come out of my room, and with our luck . . ."

"We can't go to mine, so I guess we will just have to grin and bear it, although my grin is kinda lopsided right now." Beth sighed and climbed off Dale's lap. "Tomorrow is going to be another long day. We better get to our separate cold beds."

They parted reluctantly. Beth was relieved that Nancy was asleep, snoring gently. She didn't even stir as Beth tiptoed around the room, getting ready for bed.

# CHAPTER 15

"Today we're going to gather the rest of our cattle," Mark announced the next morning as the riders gathered together in the center of the arena after warming up their horses. "There are three hundred steers scattered around the hills to the east and north of here, on past the pasture we gathered yesterday. We'll split up in groups to go gather, move them back to the ranch and into the pasture to the west. And remember tonight there will be a catered dinner and drinks at the exclusive LaPlat garage."

The riders chatted cheerfully with each other as they moved north toward the bluffs and their new adventure. Mark sent Beth, Gloria, and Dale east. They rode through grass that was dry and brittle from the summer heat and lack of rain. The hills were dotted with clumps of sagebrush, cactus, yucca plants, and numerous anthills. They rode slowly, mindful of the heat. It would be a long day for both horse and human.

Two hours later they came to a stop at the east fence line. Giving their horses a breather, they looked west and down into the deep cut a creek had made through the bench the riders had been traveling on. It meandered in big lazy loops, willows growing close to the water. A large number of cattle were scattered along the creek bottom as far as they could see.

"How do we get down there?" Dale swallowed nervously as he looked down the steep rocky hill.

Beth leaned forward, absently stroking her horse's neck. "We'll go down slow and easy on a zigzag path. Don't worry, the horses know how to do it. Just give them their heads and they will follow mine down." She gave Dale and Gloria a reassuring smile and started slowly down, her horse kicking rocks loose as he picked his way along.

Beth could hear hooves scattering rocks behind her as she rode slowly down the hill. When she got to the bottom, she turned Far around. Dale was right behind her but Gloria was still at the top. Her horse was trying to follow, but Gloria was reining him back. He was getting upset.

Dale looked up the hill. "I thought she was behind me, but I was so busy trying to tell myself I wasn't scared I didn't realize she wasn't coming. Man, that's steep."

"She's going to get hurt if she doesn't let her horse join ours. I'll go get her." Beth nudged her reluctant horse back up the hill.

Far was blowing hard by the time he reached the top. Beth reined him in beside Gloria's horse and just sat, not saying anything. Gloria's horse calmed down immediately with company.

After Far Horizon's breathing evened out, Beth said, "I remember the first time I came down this hill. I was with Amy. When I saw how steep it was, it scared me to death. But I thought if she can do it, I can do it. I was on one of her seasoned horses, so I knew he would take care of me. You're riding Rio, the same one I was that day."

She glanced at Gloria. "I'm going back down. Give me about four horse lengths and then let your horse follow. Just stay in the center of your saddle. If you can't do it then I'll send your dad back up and you both follow along the ridgeline. If you see any other steers, try to bring them along with you."

Gloria gave a sharp nod without looking at Beth.

Beth started back down. There was no sound but her horse scattering stones as he made his way across the face of the hill until she heard Gloria's horse coming behind her. When they reached the bottom, she gave Gloria a smile and a nod and said, "Let's go get those steers."

The steers were reluctant to move. They had to harry them out of the willows and then block them from going back. The penning work in the arena helped them figure out how to do it, and Beth was confident they hadn't left any behind as they pushed their steers west.

It took all day to gather and move the steers back to the ranch and into the new pasture. Back at the corrals, there wasn't much conversation as the riders unsaddled and gave their tired horses food and water. Beth was the last one through the outside corral gate. She put her arm through

Nancy's and announced to the group at large. "Last one to the bar gets to do the dishes." Nobody wasted time cleaning up.

"Oh boy, does a stiff drink help the body," Dale said to Beth. "It has feeling again, at least in some parts. There's one part that will be forever numb." He looked so mournful Beth laughed.

"Such a tragedy. I will have to find myself another man." Beth looked around the garage. "Let's see. Mark is taken. That leaves Will. Who is where? Aha, there! Oh no, he's taken by your daughter!"

Will and Gloria were standing close together, talking. He suddenly threw back his head and laughed loudly.

"My lord, he sounds like a donkey braying," Dale said incredulously.

"It's infectious though. You can't hear him and not laugh. I guess I'm stuck with you." Beth grinned. "I think I need another drink for my old bones."

They headed back to the bar, cheerfully elbowing their way through the crowd.

The meal was marvelous—hamburgers cooked on the grill to order, several salads, baked beans, plus a wonderful moist chocolate cake.

Beth ate with her friends again.

"Is progress being made with the daughter?" Sue looked longingly at the chocolate cake. "I swear I saw her smile a couple of times as we were pushing the steers toward the ranch, but I may have been delusional." Her hand wavered over the largest piece of cake.

Marcy slapped at Sue's hand. "You said you weren't going to have desert tonight."

"But its chocolate!" Sue had a whine that always broke the women up. "Wasting chocolate is a sin."

"Amen," Nancy said and pinched the largest piece right out from under Sue's hand. Sue ran her hand through her dark hair, going to salt and pepper, and gave Nancy a mock glare. Her complaints about her weight and her fight with her sweet tooth were a constant thread through the friend's conversations.

After she finished her meal, Beth wandered around, visiting until she reached Amy. "Would you do me a favor? Mention your tack shop and invite them to shop after lunch? You usually do it later on, but I want to get Gloria in there, if I can, before Friday. It's her birthday, and she really needs a better hat. Do you have any similar to mine?"

The plot was in motion. Amy announced the tack shop was open. Beth asked Nancy to try to get Gloria into the shop. "I know better than to try to do it myself, but maybe if it's someone else's suggestion, it might work."

Nancy, who qualified as a master shopper, worked with consummate skill as she cut off Gloria, who was leaving early to go back to the barn, and steered her into the tack shop. Beth stayed in the garage, visiting with Sue and Marcy, who were still consumed with curiosity about her relationship with Dale.

"Is this thing with Dale getting serious?" Sue was not one to beat around the bush.

"It looks like it's going that direction. It's sure not something I was expecting at this stage of my life."

"I hope we don't lose you to a man." Marcy's blonde good looks were a foil to Sue's darker coloring. "Just joking, but hey, we have a great group going."

They all looked at Beth, who shrugged helplessly.

The team penning that afternoon produced better results as the riders relaxed into the program. Gloria's horse had done a lot of cattle work, and she had enough sense to let the horse take over when things got sticky, so she was doing well. It seemed she and Will were always next to each other.

"Do I sense a budding romance?" Nancy nodded toward Gloria and Will, who were working with Sue to move three reluctant steers in the right direction.

Beth leaned forward and adjusted her horse's brow band. "I certainly hope so. It might do a lot for her disposition."

"It has for yours. Hey, don't glare at me. I was just kidding." Nancy grinned. "I'm real happy for you. Dale is a nice guy."

"Thanks, I think so too. I guess I might as well admit I'm hooked." Beth sighed. "Line and sinker," she added as she watched Dale, Sue, and Mark move their three steers into position.

"Oh, by the way, I had Gloria try on hats," Nancy said. "She found one she liked. I had Amy put it back for her."

"I owe you one," Beth said.

"Okay, I get first shower tonight."

"That's a deal." Beth laughed.

She told Dale about the hat that evening. They were in the upper level conference room that had become their place.

"How do we do it?" He nuzzled at her neck.

Beth was sitting on his lap. He tried to kiss her, but she ducked and said, "Hold on, Dale. We need to get this settled." She shook her finger at him. "I'll go early and pick up the hat. You can give it to her before we start riding. Let's not say anything about me being involved. She needs the hat, but I don't think she would wear it if she thought I had anything to do with it."

"You're probably right. Thanks for setting things up. Let me show you how grateful I am. Oh come on, I need a few more kisses to have strength enough to go to bed," Dale said as Beth pushed herself away and got to her feet.

"I'm beat. It's going to be another long day tomorrow." Beth put up her hand as Dale opened his mouth to protest. "Don't whine, love. You'll sound like Taz telling me she needs her wet cat food when I have her on a diet."

Dale laughed so hard he almost choked.

# CHAPTER 16

Beth called Amy to make arrangements to pick up the hat. The next morning she made sure she and Nancy left the motel before Dale and Gloria. She put the hat in her vehicle in a bag for Dale and was already working in the arena when they arrived.

When Gloria came into the arena on Rio, she had the hat on and smiled when she received compliments from several of the women.

The day flew by as the riders improved by the hour. At the end of the afternoon, Amy and Mark announced that tomorrow they would do a day ride. "We all need a change of pace. The horses get as tired of the arena as we do," Amy said. "We'll do a four-hour ride, have a sandwich out on the trail, then those that want to can do arena work after we get back."

After they got the horses bedded down for the night, Nancy, Beth, Gloria, and Dale walked to their rigs. While Nancy rummaged in the Yukon, Beth said to Gloria, "That hat looks nice on you. It keeps your pretty face out of the sun."

Gloria looked startled and then said, "Dad gave it to me for my birthday. It's Friday."

"Well, we should give you a birthday party," Beth said without thinking.

"Don't you dare," Gloria spat. She jumped into the pickup and yelled to Dale, who was talking to Nancy. "Let's go, Dad. Now!"

\* \* \*

"Well, that went the wrong way again." Beth sighed as they drove back to the motel. "I guess I'm better off just not talking to her at all."

"Don't you get the urge to slap her upside the head?" Nancy was disgusted and showing it.

"More like beat her whole body with a big stick," Beth muttered.

Nancy peeled off her gloves and threw them on the dash. "Well, since that probably isn't going to happen, what do we do for dinner? I'm not hungry. Should we just snack?"

"That sounds like a good idea to me. Let's just hole up in our room and let the other two fend for themselves tonight."

Dale came to their door about eight o'clock. "I wanted to see if you were all right since we didn't see you at dinner."

Beth stepped out into the hall. "I'm tired and disgusted. I don't seem to be making any headway with Gloria. She isn't going to accept me, and at this point, I could care less."

Dale put his arm around Beth's waist. "Why don't we go upstairs and talk about it, or we could go to my room. Gloria and Will went into Wheatland for dinner."

Beth pulled away. "Oh good, their romance is going well, is it? How nice for them." She glared at Dale. "I don't want to talk about it. I'm going to bed." She turned toward the door but whirled back sharply. "And I would appreciate it if you would stay away from me tomorrow. Let me enjoy a ride with my friends and not worry that I am too close to you or some other little stupid thing that will offend your daughter. We aren't even married, and she is causing us all kinds of trouble."

"You know it won't matter to me."

"I don't want to talk about it. This just isn't working."

Beth slammed the door, sat on the bed, and ran her hands through her hair. She looked at Nancy, who was pretending to be reading in bed. "I know you probably heard all that. You told me having them here probably wouldn't work out. I thought I should at least give it a shot, but I'm getting sick of the whole mess. It's too bad we don't have some Ben & Jerry's Cherry Garcia ice cream so I could eat the whole pint. At least it would make me feel better."

"How about some dark chocolate?" Nancy bent over the side of the bed and pulled two large candy bars out of her goody bag.

"I love you, friend. I do, I do," Beth said gratefully. She pulled down the wrapper on the candy bar, took a big bite, sighed, and looked toward the ceiling. "That must be what heaven would be like if it was a taste."

"Don't you think you were a little rough on Dale?" Nancy licked her lips as she savored the chocolate. "He's only trying to get her to accept you. It's really not his fault she is so bone stubborn about your relationship. Bringing her here still might help."

Beth licked her finger. "I probably am being a bitch, but right now that's how I feel." She got off the bed and dropped the wrapper in the wastebasket. "Maybe a day away from both of them will improve my mood. "Do you have any more chocolate?"

By the time Beth showered and got into her pajamas, Nancy was asleep.

*   *   *

Instead of going for breakfast the next morning, they ate some fruit from their cooler and managed to avoid seeing Gloria or Dale until everyone was in the arena.

The riders did groundwork to get themselves and their mounts focused before they set out for the hills. Nancy and Beth rode toward the back of the group of riders. Gloria and Dale were toward the front, as both their horses were fast walkers.

"Dale sure looked glum this morning. I feel sorry for him," Nancy said midmorning as they worked the horses down a sandy draw. "Notice that Will is riding with Gloria?"

"I forgot to tell you Will took her out to dinner last night. He seems like a nice guy."

"Other than that laugh." Nancy shuddered.

"Rob had a very distinctive laugh too. I always knew where he was in a crowd when he laughed. Do you think I will ever get over thinking of him?"

"When you have someone else to think about. If Dale is right for you and he isn't going to let his daughter stand in your way, why are you?"

Surprised, Beth looked over at Nancy, who smiled gently and added, "Think about it."

Beth watched Gloria and Will, who seemed to be having a great time, while Dale was just riding along, looking away from the group. *He's lonely,* Beth thought. *Oh, I know how that feels. To have no one to share things with, to be the only single in a room full of people. He is offering me a chance to be part of a pair again. Am I going to let that chance go without a fight?* She chewed at her bottom lip for a while and then straightened up in the saddle. *All right, Gloria, the gloves are off,* she decided and squared her shoulders. *I'll give it my all, and if it doesn't work out, at least I gave it my best shot.*

Beth caught up with Nancy, who had pulled ahead and was visiting with Sue. Her two friends looked over as she approached and reined Far Horizon alongside their mounts.

"Nancy, if you don't mind, I think I'll take your advice, and to hell with Gloria. I'm going to spend the rest of the day with my man. Thanks, girlfriend," she added as she nudged Far Horizon into a trot.

"Go, cowgirl," Sue hollered.

Beth gained on Dale until she was even with his gelding. He was so lost in thought he didn't notice her for a few seconds.

Beth nudged Far Horizon closer to Dale's horse. "Do you want some company?"

He looked up and grimaced. "I've been missing you. I'm sorry . . ."

"I am too. I can be a bearcat when I get tired. It's a fact to remember for the future, my dear." Beth leaned toward him, looked him straight in the eyes. "I have decided your daughter is just going to have to deal with the fact of us. If she blows up, she has been mad the whole time anyway, so what have we got to lose?" Beth took a deep breath and gave Dale a toothy smile. "Care to have lunch with an old broad that thinks you're sexy as hell?"

Both horses and riders were grateful for a break by the time the group reached Chug Creek. Old corrals set back from the road made an interesting contrast to the willows along the water. It was a nice place for a picnic.

Dale and Beth sat close together on a log. They ate and laughed and ignored everyone else.

"How can you eat those?" Dale watched Beth open a can of sardines. "I can't stand the things."

"They're good for you," Beth popped a sardine in her mouth.

Dale gagged.

"I'm not crazy about them. The only ones I can stand are the mustard ones, and I burp them the rest of the afternoon. But they pack well and don't go bad in the heat, so I figure it's a good time to eat them because they're good for your bones. Also, the horses don't have their noses in my face while I'm eating because they don't like them either." She took a cracker and scooped another sardine out of the can and popped it into her mouth. "Yum."

Dale shook his head. He carefully unwrapped and bit into his ham sandwich, glancing around at the rest of the riders who were sprawled in whatever shade they could find. There was no place to tie the horses, so each rider was trying to fend his horse off long enough to eat. Beth had pulled a bandana full of oats out of her saddle bag and tied it to Far Horizon's *bosal*. He munched contentedly, his eyes half closed.

After the group ate, they wandered around the corrals and along the creek. Sue discovered a big snapping turtle when she went looking for a place to wet the weeds. Discussion flew back and forth about the animals they had seen during the ride. A lone coyote traveling up one of the draws and an eagle that flew over them. It was carrying something, probably a rabbit, home for its nestlings. A huge bee's nest hung just under the lip of one of the buttes, secure from any marauders.

Beth could hear Will's laugh but didn't bother to locate him. She gave her complete attention to Dale.

Forty minutes after they dismounted, the group was ready to head back to the ranch.

As they packed up the remains of their lunch, Beth said to Dale, "I'm plotting here. Both our horses can out walk the others. If we get far enough ahead, we can be off by ourselves. I know the way so Amy won't worry about us."

He nodded.

They were both stiff from riding almost three hours. With his long legs, Dale managed to get on his horse, but Beth had to put Far Horizon downhill from her on a slope before she could pull herself back onto the saddle.

"I don't feel old riding until I can't get a toe in my stirrup to get on my horse. It used to only happen when I had a tall horse, but now it would probably happen with a burro." She laughed and turned Far Horizon's head to the south.

The two horses took off in the long swinging walk all horses excel at when they are headed back to the barn. They were in the front of the group, soon pulled ahead, and gradually moved away from the other riders.

The road followed Chug Creek, so the going was easy. They rode in silence, caught up in the rhythm of their horses and the continuous ripple of noise from the creek. As they came around a bend in the road, they saw a fawn, so young it still had its spots, standing in the tall grass close to the creek. It saw them, dropped down, flattened out, and the grass hid it from sight.

"That's another advantage to being ahead of the group. We women can be a chatty bunch. It scares off all the critters," Beth said.

"Why do they call it Chug Creek?" Dale took off his hat, wiped his face and hat band with a bandana. His hair was sopping wet.

"When I was a kid I thought it was because they had warm springs around here and they made that kind of sound, but according to the museum in Chugwater, the Indians ran buffalo off the cliffs into the creek. *Chug* was the sound the buffalo made when they hit the water. The Indians thought this was as nice a place as the white man. There are still teepee rings in the area, one just on the hill behind the ranch. There's lot of history in this valley. This dirt road was used by the stage route that came through this part of the country."

She looked back over her shoulder. "When we go around this next bend, let's put the horses into a trot and make some time. We can get back to the ranch before the others."

"What did you have in mind when we get back?"

"Nothing but a cold drink of water and some shade." She batted her eyelashes.

"Aha," he snorted. "I can think of other things."

They let their horses move into a trot, riding side by side in comfortable silence until they reined the horses back to a walk about a mile from the ranch to give the animals a chance to cool down.

"It's hard to realize that tomorrow is the last day," Beth said.

"What will we do tomorrow? More of the same?"

"The last morning we usually do a two-hour ride up to the top of the bluffs. It's quite an experience scrambling up the trails."

"Oh great, that sounds relaxing." Dale frowned.

"Just hang on and let your horse do the work, hon. It's worth it." Beth waved her arm toward the north. "The view is fantastic. You can see clear to Laramie Peak, which, if I remember right, is the highest mountain in Wyoming.

"By the time we get back to the ranch we're starving, so we eat a quick lunch, and it's time to pack up and go home. For anyone that wants to do more shopping, Amy has her tack shop open so people can browse before they leave. She has some really nifty things in there. I almost always get into trouble." She grinned at Dale. "Yes, I do occasionally shop."

Beth shifted in the saddle. "There will be some riders that will want to work in the arena when we get back from this ride. Nancy and I usually poop out, go take a nap, and clean up so we can enjoy our last evening without looking like we've been rode hard and put away wet." She grinned at Dale's chuckle.

They were back at the ranch by this time, the other riders still not in sight. Dale and Beth dismounted in the shade under a huge cottonwood. They looped the reins over their saddle horns and let the horses go for the water tank.

Dale pulled Beth into his arms and kissed her soundly. She pulled slightly away from him but left her arms around his neck. "This is a nice addition to a good ride. I think I might just make a habit of this. I like it." She leaned on him. "You have a nice seat, by the way."

"Beg pardon?" Dale looked down at her with a frown.

"I meant the way you sit a horse, not your buns, my dear—although they are not bad for a man of your advanced years."

"I could say the same for yours," he said as he slid his hands down and cupped her buttocks.

"Oops, here come the troops. What on earth will they think, a couple of seniors groping each other? Unhand me, sir." Giggling, Beth pried herself out of his arms and went to get her horse. They were busily unsaddling when the rest of the group made it to the barn.

"Anybody that still has some energy and wants to do some cattle work can do so," Amy said. "Or feel free to rest and get ready for our last night. We have a wonderful dinner planned." She got off her horse and let it drink at the water tank while most of the other riders headed for the arena.

Beth walked over to Amy and hugged her. "What a great ride. We really enjoyed it. I'm sure you noticed we took off once we got far enough ahead not to stir up the other horses. We saw a fawn shortly after we left the group. It was nice to get away by ourselves too."

"How's it going with Gloria? I noticed you were sitting with Dale at lunch, and Gloria was too busy with Will to notice. Or if she did, she didn't care." Amy recaptured her long hair back into a sloppy braid. "I'm a mess. I hope I have time to clean up before dinner. We have a bunch of gung-ho cow workers."

"I decided Gloria can go hang. Nothing I try to do works, so I'm not working at it anymore. I may sit on Dale's lap all evening just to really stir her up. But I'm going to slack off this afternoon, go take a nap. Grandma's tired. I think Nancy probably will too."

"No problem, you've hung in there all week. You guys enjoy your break." Amy looked toward the arena. "Better go, the natives are getting restless." She swung easily onto her saddle and left at a trot.

Dale joined Beth as she was throwing hay to Far Horizon, who had been hanging his head over the fence, asking her why she was so slow about it.

"Are you sticking to your plan?" Dale watched Far as he spread the hay around, looking for the best tidbits.

"Yep, I feel hot, tired, and just a little old. I hear a soak in the tub and a nice nap calling my name."

"I think I'll hang around a little longer. Maybe I can get Mark to work with me on cutting, for which I have no talent."

Beth brushed as much of the hay off her clothes as she could and then kissed Dale on the cheek. "See you at dinner then. I need to check with Nancy, then I'm out of here."

Nancy decided she had enough energy to do some more arena work, and Dale offered to take her back to the motel. Beth hurried to her vehicle and left.

\*　　\*　　\*

It felt good to be alone. Back in the room, Beth drew a nice hot bath and settled in for a soak. Steam curled around her face, and she drew in the moist air. Her skin sucked up moisture like a sponge after the long day of wind and sun. She closed her eyes and sighed.

"You're dreaming if you think Gloria has changed in her feelings toward you."

Beth sat up so abruptly water slopped out of the tub onto the floor. "How did you get out? I wasn't worrying, you shouldn't be out. What about our deal?"

The Worry Nag gave a chuckle that sounded more like a growl. "Maybe on the surface you weren't, but underneath—ha!" She leered at Beth's mental scowl and swaggered back toward the closet, swinging her scrawny hips. "Just remember I told you so when everything goes south."

*That sure spoiled my relaxing bath,* Beth thought resentfully as she grabbed the soap and furiously washed. *Good thing for the Nag I can't actually get hold of her. I'd scrub her to death.* She muttered under her breath as she mopped up the floor, cleaned her face, and dried her hair. *All right, I'm through thinking about the Nag,* she thought as she put on clean underwear. *She had her say, doesn't mean she's right.*

Totally exhausted, she crawled into bed. When Nancy came back, it barely registered. She did hear her friend throw back the covers to her bed but dozed off again until she woke to the alarm that always-structured Nancy had set.

After much yawning, the two friends chattered while they put on their makeup and worked to erase the damage a week of hat hair had established. Beth began to get into a party mood. The turquoise shirt she pulled off its hanger had rhinestones sprinkled across the fabric. "I feel like a little sparkle tonight," she said, tucking the shirt into black jeans. "Wow, feels like I lost an ounce or two."

"We clean up pretty good, don't we?" Nancy wore a black vest over a red checked shirt and blue jeans. A black belt with lots of silver and red boots completed her ensemble. "Don't add 'for our age' or I will deck you. Don't you hate that? My doctor is always telling me what good shape I am in and then spoils it by adding 'for your age.'"

"Doctors," Beth sniffed as she bent over to get her boots on her feet. She stood up, stomped the boots in place as she looked into the mirror. She fluffed her newly conditioned hair and shrugged. "That's as good as it gets." She smiled at her friend. "Let's go, the bar should be open by now. It's party time!"

# CHAPTER 17

Before they went to the party, the women drove to the barn to check on their horses. Far Horizon was standing in a corner of his pen, eyes half shut, belly full.

Nancy gave her horse some water and then came to Beth, wiping her hands on her jeans. "I think we're the last ones here. Are you ready?"

"You know, I'm going to stay down here for a while. Take my rig on up to the house. I'll walk up in a little bit."

Nancy looked at Beth. "Are you all right?"

"I just have a little thinking going on."

Nancy gave Beth a gentle pat and drove away.

Beth sat on the cement steps at the side of the barn with a kitten curled on her lap and listened to the sounds of a summer evening. She could hear the honking cries of the blue herons that roosted in the big cottonwood trees. They looked too large and awkward to perch in the tree tops, but they built their nests and raised their chicks at the ranch every year.

The sun was low, painting the valley in shades of gold. A slight warm breeze kept the mosquitoes hiding in the grass.

It was a relief to be by herself. She was not used to being around people all the time. She lingered, watching the sky paint its farewell to the day using all the colors ever imagined.

The kitten purred, vibrating its tiny body. She stroked it gently, her thoughts scattered. How she had enjoyed herself here with her friends over the years. Learning and laughing, building wonderful friendships she would not want to lose. Without a man, a woman has much more time on her hands to do as she pleases.

Now there was Dale. He would change her life again if they decided to stay together. Things would be different with him than they were with her husband. She needed to be very sure she didn't compare them. *I don't want to make the same mistakes I made with Rob,* she mused. *I didn't realize how many ways he showed his love without speaking it until he died. I hope I can be wiser in a second marriage in many directions than I was in my first. I won't have the excuse that I was young this time. I want to be less critical, more open, not as self-centered.*

*Maybe we can have more fun,* she thought. *There won't be the pressures of work, children, and parents. We can concentrate on each other.*

*But you will have a man around all the time. How well will you deal with that? Remember the wives you knew that went back to work to get away from their retired husbands?* She sighed.

The worry closet opened a crack.

*Don't even think about it, Nag!* Beth slammed the door in her mind shut. Hard.

It was time to go to the party.

The kitten was reluctant to lose Beth's soft lap; she had to detach it claw by claw. Placing the tiny cat gently on the ground, she walked over to Far Horizon's pen. He looked up from his pile of hay, cocked an ear at her, and strolled over for attention. She stroked his elegant head, murmuring endearments. "I hope I can still ride when I'm in my seventies. Let's grow old together, old man." She worked her fingers around the gelding's ears. Arabs have long lives. Far was in good shape, so hopefully she would never have to buy another horse. She tugged his lower lip gently. He nudged her arm and then turned away to finish his hay.

Beth walked slowly through the twilight to the house.

The party was in full swing when she reached the garage. Beth pushed through the noisy crowd and got herself a margarita. She sipped it, nodding and smiling at people, watching the social dancing without joining in. *She was waiting for Dale,* she realized. While she was still a part of this group, his presence in her life had changed the way she reacted to her friends.

"Earth to Beth," said Nancy, approaching with a very large margarita clutched in her hand. "Are you receiving or still out in space? You look like you're a million miles away. Is your radar sweeping for an object named Dale?" Nancy eyed the crowd. "Where is he anyway? Gloria is here with Will."

"I don't know, but I feel the need for another margarita," Beth said.

"Brilliant," Nancy agreed. They headed to the bar, visiting as they snaked through the crush.

A short time later, Beth frowned down at her glass; it was empty again. Should she have another drink? It would be easy; she was standing right by the bar. While she considered, a large pair of black boots edged into her line of vision. They stopped when they nudged her toes. *Big feet—therefore, male*, she thought. The aftershave was familiar. It made her want to rub herself all over the owner's body. A smile made its way across her face as she raised her head to see Dale watching her.

"Are those any good?" He pointed at her margarita.

"Oh yeah," Beth purred with a satisfied grin.

Dale quirked an eyebrow at her as he poured green liquid from the large pitcher that sat on the plank bar table into a very large paper cup. He took a swallow. "Whew," he wheezed, "that will dull the pains of the average cowboy." He took a more cautious sip. "Medicinal, that's what this is."

Beth snagged him by the arm to tow him over to one of the tables covered with paper cloths in a red handkerchief design. They sat side by side, hips snugged together, drinking and watching the crowd, not speaking, just enjoying being together.

Will's laugh brayed through the crowd. Having him as a direction finder would simplify avoiding Gloria. *She isn't going to spoil my evening, no way, no sir*, Beth vowed silently.

"I'll get the steaks," Dale said when the call for the rare ones came. Beth got the baked potatoes and salad. Their hunger satisfied, they worked on a couple more margaritas. The noise level was so high visiting was almost impossible, so they sat quietly, elbows avoiding the debris of the meal.

Beth leaned against Dale, half asleep from the food, drink, and exercise until he reached over, took her by the chin, and looked into her eyes.

"Let me take you back to the motel. Will picked Gloria up tonight. Since he lives at the ranch, I think they will probably stay here until the party quits."

Beth stared at him, said nothing—just stared until he blinked at her, unsure of her mood. He relaxed as she began to smile.

"Are you trying to ruin my reputation?"

"I guess so. Do you care?" Now it was his turn to stare.

*I guess this is what they mean by sexual tension*, Beth thought. She longed for the closeness they enjoyed before they came to Chugwater. They shouldn't, but fueled with recklessness from the margaritas, Beth nodded. "Let's go."

Without another word, they got up and walked out of the garage. If anyone said good-bye to them, they never heard it. They walked over to Dale's SUV, got into it, slammed the doors, and sat there for a moment.

"Your place or mine?" Dale stared straight ahead, fingers drumming the steering wheel.

Beth giggled. "Yours, I guess, Nancy might . . . oops, Nancy. I need to let her know I'm leaving." She opened the car door. "Be right back."

Dale watched as Beth walked a somewhat unsteady line back into the garage. She was gone long enough that he considered going after her, but she reappeared and made her way back to the SUV, grinning like a Cheshire cat.

"What took you so long?"

"I had to find her first. She was with Sue and Marcy."

"What did you tell them?" Dale peered nervously toward the garage door.

"I told them I wanted to make love to my man. They all thought it was a great idea."

Dale's eyes widened.

Beth giggled. "I really told them I was going to go back to the motel with you because we wanted to be alone."

Dale gaped at her. "You might as well have said we were going to . . ."

"Yes, I know, but we're all adults, a little over the age of consent if the truth be known. Nancy goes to bed so early she won't be able to stay awake too much longer, but she said she could manage another hour. So we can use my room and won't have to worry about Gloria. What are you wasting time for?"

Dale didn't.

*       *       *

Sometime later, Beth yawned, stretched, and looked up at Dale. She was cradled in his arms, enjoying the lovely afterglow of sex. "That should help my complexion, don't you think?"

Dale looked at her completely baffled. "Say again?"

"Don't you remember the saying when we were teenagers that if you had a bad complexion sex would clear it up?" Beth wiggled even closer to Dale and threw her leg over his.

Dale laughed. "I must have missed that one somewhere along the line. We weren't as worried about our complexions as we were about things lower down." His smile faded as he smoothed a finger down her nose. "You know I love you, Beth."

"Ah, you just love me for my fabulous body." Beth crossed her eyes, looking at his finger on the end of her nose.

They laughed, kissed, and cuddled until Beth, looking around the room said, "Oh man, we have clothes strewn everywhere. We better get dressed because Nancy will probably be showing up anytime. Getting caught naked is going to be embarrassing."

They cut it a little fine. Dale was looking for a sock when they heard Nancy saying loudly outside the door, "Thanks for bringing me home, Sue. See you in the morning." She made a lot of noise trying to get her key in the lock.

Dale still couldn't find his sock, so he finally jammed his bare foot into his boot. When Nancy came in, Dale and Beth were sitting on the bed, trying to look innocent. Dale was having a hard time of it. His face was beet red.

"Hey, Nancy," Beth said. "Is the party still in full swing? How come Sue brought you back?"

"You forgot to leave the keys," Nancy said. "As for the party, it kind of got broken up."

"Broken up?" Dale and Beth said together.

Nancy put one hand on her hip. "I hate to say this, Dale, but your daughter threw a fit and ruined the party. Someone made the comment that it was wonderful to see Beth in love and what a nice guy Dale was. Everyone agreed they were so happy for both of you. Gloria heard and went ballistic."

"Oh Lord, what did she do?" Dale asked.

"She was screaming that Beth was never going to get her hooks in her dad and a lot of stuff I don't care to repeat. She's pretty drunk."

Nancy sat down in the only chair. Beth and Dale stared at her from the bed.

"Will tried to calm her down, but she turned on him, said some pretty ugly things, so he gave up and went back to his trailer. She's walking back to the motel. She won't let anyone pick her up. Sue and I tried."

"I better go get her," Dale said. He got up, kissed Beth, and left.

Beth sat on the bed, staring at the door, bent over with her head in her hands. "Oh crap, what a mess. I knew this would happen. Dale keeps saying it doesn't matter, but it does to Gloria."

Nancy went over to the bed, put her arm around Beth. "It will be all right."

Beth looked at the floor. "I'm really beginning to doubt it."

*     *     *

Beth stared at the ceiling for hours until she dozed off late into the night. Sunlight peeking through the blinds woke her early.

When she heard Nancy get out of bed, she pretended to be asleep.

"Wake up, Beth." Nancy shook her. "You need to see this." She handed Beth an envelope and watched as Beth read the single page. "Is it from Dale?"

Beth crumpled the letter in her hand. "Yes, he took Gloria home last night. From the letter they must have had a hell of a fight. She refused to go back to the ranch this morning and apologize, so he felt it might be good to just get her out of here."

"He should have dragged her back there, made her apologize for ruining the party, and then horsewhipped her. I imagine he was just as anxious to get out of here as she was after what she pulled last night. If it was my kid I'd be embarrassed to death and would have made sure she apologized, but when the kid is Gloria's age, I don't know if it would do any good. I'm sure glad we don't have to deal with any horses because of them," Nancy growled.

"It embarrasses me too, but I have to go apologize to Amy. I don't want to cut you short on the morning ride either, so we'll stay until noon like we usually do." Beth looked glumly at her friend.

"Atta girl." Nancy gave Beth a big hug. "Now how are we going to get to the ranch? Your vehicle is there."

"I should have put Gloria on Growler," Amy grumbled when she came to rescue the stranded women. "He would have dumped her on her head on the nearest rock."

"I'm so sorry about the whole mess, Amy," Beth said.

"She's the one that should apologize, so I don't want to hear any more about it."

Everyone else felt the same way. The matter was dropped, and the group saddled up for the morning ride. It was one of the highlights of the clinic.

Beth rode with her friends to the top of the bluffs. The spectacular view of Laramie Peak, crowning the horizon at over ten thousand feet, normally enthralled her. Today it barely registered.

As Far Horizon's hooves slid over the sandstone ledges on the way back down the steep trail, her mind considered what happened between Dale and his daughter and how it would affect her relationship with him. Gloria couldn't care much about her father to take his possible happiness and stomp all over it like she had been doing.

Far Horizon slid close to the edge on one particularly wicked ledge, and Beth realized she better pay attention to what was going on, or they both could get hurt.

She was relieved when they could load the horses and leave. She drove wrapped in silence. The only sound in the vehicle was the low murmur from the radio. But in Beth's mind, the Worry Nag was out of the closet and yammering away.

"I told you so, I told you so, what did I tell you?" The Nag's face was triumphant.

"You're repeating yourself. Get in the closet before I drop-kick you back in there. I'm in no mood to listen to you."

"The daughter will not let you have her father. You're whistling into the wind."

"Please go away. I'm too exhausted to argue with you."

The Nag retreated, sticking out her tongue as she swung the door shut.

Nancy turned the sound down as they approached Cheyenne. "Do you want to talk?"

"I don't know. What is there to say, really?" Beth gave a weary shrug. "It turned out badly, but I suppose it could have been worse."

"True. I think it caught us off guard, don't you?"

"Off guard? How?" Beth glanced over at Nancy.

"Well, Gloria and Will were getting along like gangbusters, and we hadn't had much real friction since she flared up about the birthday party. I really thought it had gone fairly smooth, so I was surprised when she blew last night." Nancy hesitated. "I feel somewhat responsible."

"Why?"

"If your friends, including me, had kept their big mouths shut about you and Dale . . ."

"It's not your fault. Most of the bunch didn't know I was having problems with her, so it was natural for you to talk behind our backs when I tottered off." Beth offered Nancy a small wry grin. "If I had behaved properly, it might not have happened."

"Well . . . it's done," Nancy muttered.

"Yeah, Dale and I will just have to deal with it one way or another."

They drove on through the afternoon toward the consequences of the night before.

# CHAPTER 18

With a grunt, Beth dropped her heavy duffel bag in the hall leading to her bedroom. Taking a deep breath, she shuffled wearily to the blinking answering machine. The message was from Dale, asking her to call as soon as she got in. Her feelings were mixed—disgust at Gloria, sorrow for Dale. As miserable as her day had been, his must have been far worse.

She unpacked slowly until she realized she was stalling. *All right, girl, ignoring the problem won't make it go away*, she thought and dialed his number. "Dale, it's your abandoned woman," she said when he answered.

"I'm so sorry, darling. Can you stand to see my face? I'll come on out if it's all right with you?" He sounded tired.

"All right, I'm almost unpacked. We can go into the Chinese place in Ault for dinner. I don't have anything in the house to fix."

"Why don't I pick up something and bring it out?"

Beth sighed as she ran her hand through her hair. "That would be lovely. I'm tired."

She hung up, walked into her bathroom, and looked at herself in the mirror. She looked every bit her age. A long hot shower and blowing her hair dry helped her feel more human. She didn't bother with makeup, except darkening her eyebrows. *I look like a corpse without my eyebrows*, she thought as she pulled on a pair of shorts and a yellow T-shirt.

Dale arrived with a sack of food that had Beth salivating. He kissed her tenderly.

"I bring gifts of food to nourish body and soul," he said as he unpacked fried rice, sesame chicken, and garlic shrimp along with paper plates and plastic forks.

"Do we want wine or hot tea to drink?"

"Better do wine to settle my nerves." He grimaced as Beth brought the glasses. "How about we just relax and enjoy the food before we talk about this mess?"

Beth nodded, and they gave the food the attention it deserved. Together they cleaned up, took their wine into the living room, and settled on the couch.

"Oh, I feel so much better, thanks." Beth sighed as she put her feet up on the footstool. "I was hungry."

Dale sat his wine glass down on the side table and took her hand. "Beth, I'm so sorry for what happened. I'm just glad that we weren't there when Gloria had her fit, or I don't know what I would have done. I'm sure it was hard for you to face everyone this morning."

"It was a little embarrassing, but everyone was very kind about it. I apologized to Amy and Mark. Amy, God bless her, said it would probably be one of their more memorable windup parties."

"I should have made Gloria stay and apologize, but she wouldn't have. She was just completely unreasonable. I never knew she could be this way. It doesn't matter what I say. She just refuses to listen or consider anybody's viewpoint but her own." Dale scrubbed at the back of his neck and rolled his shoulders.

"And that is?" Beth asked.

"She seems to feel if I'm involved with you, it leaves her alone. And no matter how much I tell her it won't, she's convinced we'll cut her out of our life completely."

Beth looked at him. "So what are you going to do?" She realized she was holding her breath.

"As far as I'm concerned, this changes nothing. I told you, I'm not giving you up this time. She will come around eventually."

"And if she doesn't?"

"Then I guess I've lost a daughter." Dale looked away and took a deep breath. "And I told her that," he said, exhaustion shadowing his eyes.

Beth put her hand on his leg and squeezed it gently. His sadness hurt her heart. He turned toward her with a groan, and they sat close together as the room grew dark. Beth absently massaged the back of his neck. It wouldn't help the hurt, but it made her feel better to be doing something. "I'm sorry. I didn't want this to happen."

"I know," Dale said glumly. "It tears me up inside to listen to her when she gets so hysterical. But I want to be happy. We deserve to be happy. I want her to be happy too. I had hoped maybe she and Will . . ."

"I suppose she will blame me for that too." Beth sighed and dropped her hand onto her lap.

"Probably, if he doesn't call—and why would he after he saw the fit she threw? It would scare anybody off."

"Not me, buddy. If you're going to stand up to your daughter, I'm yours for life. But it won't make me happy if you lose Gloria because of me."

"I know," Dale said again. "We'll just hope she comes to her senses."

Beth drew in a big breath. "So now what?"

"How soon can we be married?"

Beth pulled away a little, took hold of Dale's chin, and gently pulled his head around until he was facing her. She cocked her head, looking intently at him with a crooked little smile. "That depends on what happens when you propose."

"I did," Dale said. His forehead crinkled in a puzzled frown.

"When?"

"Over the phone, months ago. Don't you remember?"

Beth shook her head. "I didn't consider that a proposal, just a ploy." She moved until she was nose to nose with him. "I've never had one."

"What do you mean you never had a proposal? You've been married before."

"Rob never actually asked me. He asked my mother if it was all right if he married me. And that was it. And I was young and dumb then, and now I'm old and smart. So I want a proper proposal this time. Don't you think I deserve one?" Beth put a whine into her voice and pounded gently on his chest. "I want one, I want one."

"Okay, okay, you got it. Quit bruising me. I'm going to be an abused husband, I can see it now."

"Probably." Beth smothered a laugh and then leaned back a little and looked at him with soft green eyes. "Now that I've put my point across, I just want to be quiet and close. The future will take care of itself."

They sat thigh to thigh in the dark, watching a sunset of screaming red accented with heavy dark gray clouds.

*　　*　　*

The next afternoon, Beth was working in her shed when she saw a UPS delivery truck drive into her yard. *My vitamins, just in time*, Beth thought and yelled at the driver, who was headed for her front door.

"Beth Waterford?" The young man looked at a clipboard as she approached him.

"Yep, that's me." She tried not to stare at his legs. The shorts he wore displayed elaborate tattoos that swirled around his legs to his ankles.

He smiled at her, walked back to the truck, and brought out a long white florist box.

"It must be your birthday," he remarked as he handed her the box.

"No, no occasion I can think of. Thanks."

Hurrying into the house, she tore open the box. With shaking hands, she carefully peeled apart layers of damp paper colored a soft spring green. A dozen velvety yellow roses, their stems nestled snugly into a vial of water, stunned her. There was a note that said, "To My Best Girl." Gathering the flowers carefully into her arms, she watered them with happy tears.

Nancy noticed the roses when she came the next day to bring back a borrowed cake pan. She also handed Beth a man's sock. "I think this must be Dale's. I found it in my dirty clothes bag when I unpacked."

Beth blushed and fiddled with the sock while Nancy walked over to the table and smelled the flowers. "Are these from the alleged sock owner?" She turned from the flowers and raised a questioning eyebrow at Beth.

"Yep." Beth stood with her hands behind her back. Her eyes were shinning, and she looked young and happy.

"An apology?"

"An invitation."

"To what?" Nancy was burning to know.

"Oh, to a proposal." Beth hugged herself and spun in a little circle. "My first!" She had to tell the story all over again as she poured large glasses of iced tea.

"So what's he going to do?" Nancy pried. "Come on, don't keep me in suspense."

Beth laughed. "He won't tell me, says it will be at one of his favorite places."

"A football stadium?"

"That joke's getting worn out, Nancy. I really have no idea."

"Come on, tell me all. You know I can't stand not knowing all the details."

Beth shrugged. "All I know is he is going to propose this weekend." She giggled gleefully. "It's kind of romantic. I guess you never get too old to appreciate that."

"No, I don't think we do." Nancy glanced absently at her watch. "Oh shoot, I've got to go." She headed for the front door, Beth following along. "Maybe with all this romance in the air, it will inspire Len. Wave some of it over our way." She gave Beth a wistful look. "Let me know what happens. I'm so happy for you." She hugged Beth and left.

*Where will he propose?* Beth wondered as she drifted through the house. She dumped dirty clothes in the washer without adding water, made half the king-sized bed before wandering off. The chores in the shed were forgotten as she dreamed up scenarios with violin music and a bended knee. She absently slammed Taz's tail in the door. It took nearly all day for the cat to quit glaring at her and allow Beth to pick her up. She found herself daydreaming, staring at the ceiling while she was supposed to be paying bills.

A proper proposal after all these years, Rob had just casually asked her one night as he drove them back to her mother's house if she didn't think they should get married. She had nodded just as casually. It had seemed perfectly adequate at the time. When Dale brought marriage up, her insistence on a proposal had surprised her almost as much as it did Dale. Why had she made such a point of it?

She called May.

"I'm sorry I didn't get back to you sooner. I've been busy getting back in the groove after being in Wyoming."

"So how did it go?"

"It was difficult with Dale's daughter being her wonderful self, but we managed to get through it." After a short pause, Beth said, "He wants to marry me."

"Ah, I told you it would happen. I'm so glad for you both." May drew in a sharp breath. "You did accept?"

"Not yet. I insisted on a proper romantic proposal, which he has promised will be delivered shortly, this weekend in fact."

"Was your husband romantic at all?"

"When we were dating, he was very much so, but after we got married . . . you know to be honest he was not so much romantic as he did things for me. He gave me surprise birthday parties and once a trip to Hawaii. I took all winter clothes because he told me we were going to San Francisco. I guess that's romantic, isn't it? He was sparing with romantic talk, and I had to train him to kiss me hello and good-bye, but that's the way he was raised. His family was not at all demonstrative." She hesitated for a moment. "Maybe I'm being silly about this proposal thing."

"Perhaps you are testing Dale," May said. "Since Gloria is still being difficult, you might have needed reassurance that he would concede to your wishes. Do you feel he has to prove himself?"

"I don't know," Beth groaned. "Maybe I still feel we're rushing things. Rob and I went together almost a year. I got in a fight with my mother and moved away from home, had to change jobs, and I broke my ankle during that period of time, and we went through it together without a problem. It just felt right."

"And does it feel right with Dale?"

"Yes, but it's all happened so fast. I just don't want to make a mistake."

"Just because you get engaged, you don't have to get married right away. If it isn't right, you will feel it. You are not a stupid woman, and you are not looking for someone to take care of you. That is what gets so many women in trouble," May counseled. "That and not being able to be alone and you know how to handle that."

Beth felt better after talking to May as she always did, and she tried her best to stuff the little frizzles of doubt that bubbled into her mind into a sack marked "go away" in big neon letters. She threw the sack into the closet with the Worry Nag and slammed the door.

\*   \*   \*

She could get no more information from Dale other than she didn't need a change of underwear, that jeans and a nice shirt would be appropriate. She was so nervous Saturday morning as she put on her makeup that she had to redo her eyebrows twice.

Dale was relaxed and cheerful when he picked her up, which made Beth a little irritated with him as she felt like she was stepping up on a horse she knew was going to buck her off.

Dale headed north on Highway 85.

"Where are we going?"

"No questions, just relax and enjoy the ride." Dale smiled sweetly at her and turned the radio up.

The SUV ran down the highway, retracing the same route Nancy and Beth had taken when they went to the clinic. Dale stopped in Cheyenne to get lattes and then headed north on I-25 toward Chugwater.

"Dale . . ."

He just shook his head.

Beth sighed. *All right*, she thought. *Be a good girl, don't spoil his surprise.* She sat back and listened to the radio. Tired from a busy week, it wasn't long before Beth nodded off. The vehicle slowing woke her up. They were at the turnoff for Chugwater. Dale took it and headed for the LaPlat Ranch. When Beth looked at him, he just smiled and put his finger to his lips.

Beth felt like a child trying to wait for Christmas. She was completely mystified but bit down on her lip and obediently kept silent. It wasn't polite to spoil surprises.

As Dale turned into the entrance to the ranch, he said, "We just need to find Amy and Mark. I have to ask them something and then we we'll be on our way. They said they would be at the barn."

"Hello," Dale yelled as they stepped through the barn entrance.

"Come on up, we're in the hay loft," Mark hollered.

"You first," Dale motioned Beth to go ahead of him. They carefully mounted the steep steps to the loft.

As Beth's eyes came level with the loft floor, she saw Mark and Amy standing in front of a pile of hay bales that were head high. Amy and Mark walked toward them as Beth clambered up the rest of the steps. Giving them both a hug, she said, "I didn't know I'd be seeing you again so soon. Mr. Mystery didn't tell me where we were going."

"Oh, really. What are you up to, Dale?" Amy smiled at Beth, who was looking back and forth at her friends and Dale with a puzzled frown.

"Dale said he had to ask you something, Amy," Beth said.

Beth's son, Steve, came from behind the hay bales, followed by his wife and children. "I think it's something he wants to ask you, Mom, not Amy."

"Close your mouth, dear." Dale put his arm around Beth as Nancy and Len and Sue and Marcy and more of her friends came out from behind the bales.

Beth was incapable of speech as she kissed her son and family. She turned to Dale and sputtered, "But you said we were going to one of your favorite places."

"I lied. I really meant one of your favorite places. You come here all the time, right? You consider these people as family and friends, right?"

Beth nodded.

Dale pulled her toward a lone bale of hay and asked her to sit down. Her friends and family made a circle around the hay bale as Beth focused on Dale. He got down on one knee and cleared his throat. He reached in his pocket, pulled out a black velvet box, and held it in his hand. He hesitated, leaned forward to whisper in her ear, "Forgive me for not doing this forty years ago."

Dale straightened back up, took her left hand in his. "Beth Waterford . . . I loved you as a young man. I have the chance to love you again as an old man. Will you love me again as you loved me once before? Please, in front of God, your son, and these witnesses, marry me. I ask you to be my wife."

He opened the box and handed it to Beth.

Everyone was silent, caught in the event unfolding in front of them. Beth's hands shook so hard she almost dropped the ring as she took it out of the box. She could hardly see the slim circle of garnets for the tears filling her eyes. She gave Dale a watery smile and slipped the ring on her finger. "Dale Runnington, I loved you once, and I find, to my surprise, I have a chance to love you again. So I will love you and marry you and spend the rest of my life with you." She kissed him and whispered, "Thank you for the best proposal I ever hoped to have."

Dale pulled her to her feet, slipped an arm around her waist, and they stood together as the dust motes danced in the light of the old barn loft, lost in each other and the moment. Beth's son let the silence grow until Beth looked over at the group waiting for them. He came toward them and said, "I wish you wisdom, happiness, and good health." He kissed his mother, hugged Dale, and then stepped back as Beth's granddaughters came forward and shyly placed flower garlands around Beth and Dale's necks. Steve and Liz repeated their good wishes and then waved the rest of the crowd forward.

A bar was quickly set up, food appeared from many coolers, Western music flowed from a boom box, and the noise level began to rise. Beth's friends were delighted with her happiness and the chance to share in her special moment. Congratulations swirled around the happy couple like bees around a flower bed.

Grinning, Nancy said, "Well, you are going to do what you said you wouldn't do ever since Rob died. I'm glad for you, and I think that nice man will make you very happy. He called me and wanted to make sure he didn't leave anyone out for this party."

"May isn't here," Beth said as she looked the crowd over.

"She is on another of her trips, relatives I think. She will call you as soon as she gets back." Nancy hugged Beth fiercely and whispered, "Did you talk to Dale about your won't-do-this-anymore list?" At Beth's look of total incomprehension, Nancy added, "You know, no more football games in subzero weather, wash-and-wear clothes, only cook when you want to stuff."

The puzzled look on Beth's face faded and she snickered. "I think I've got him wrapped around my ring finger."

"Better have him sign off on it just to be sure he understands the program. It's my duty to pick up these little details you might forget in all this bliss. Be happy, my dear friend. You deserve it."

It took a while for Beth to work her way back to Amy. "Thank you so much for helping Dale out. I know how busy you are. How did you manage to pull this together so fast?"

"Dale did all the work, cleaned out the barn, did all the calling. We didn't have to do much but provide the space. How can you say no to a man that drove all the way up here the day after camp to apologize for his daughter's behavior, then asked for help to make one of my special people happy?" She smiled at Beth. "He loves you very much, and I think you will be really good for each other. Now go enjoy your engagement party."

Beth certainly did.

The ride home was almost as quiet as the ride up had been. The radio was low, the silence comfortable. The headlights cut through the night, which enclosed the SUV like a womb. Beth turned her new ring on her finger, watching the light from the dash refract from the dark garnets. "Did you know that garnets are my birthstone?"

"I did," Dale replied. "I looked it up after I double-checked your birth date with Steve. If you would rather have diamonds, we can exchange it."

"Oh no," Beth said. "This is beautiful. I love garnets." She sighed. "I will never forget this day. To even get Steve and his family here. You just blew me away."

"Good, I wanted it to be special for you, and the idea just popped into my head. You have a great family and special friends, and they all jumped at the chance to share in my proposal. They think a great deal of you, my lady."

"I'm so happy I don't know what to do with myself."

Dale laughed. "I know what to do. I need to know when shall we get married and where?"

"Dale, there is something we need to talk about before we make plans."

"What?" he said, glancing at her.

Beth looked down at her hands and sighed. "Well, you see, I have this list."

# CHAPTER 19

Three days after Dale's proposal, Beth concentrated on mowing her yard, the big Dixon mower moving quickly over the large area. *If the lawn would only all stay the same length*, she thought. But trash grasses always grew taller than the desirable grass, making the lush green surface uneven. Her face was masked against the dust and pollen she was allergic to, and she had ear protectors on over a sun visor. It was mid\afternoon and the sun was hot.

It would be so nice to have a man to help out with all the work around her place, especially her man. They had decided Dale was going to move into her place and either sell or rent his condo.

They had also decided they wanted to be married by a justice of the peace in Fort Collins and then go to Estes Park for a honeymoon. No date had been set because Beth was dragging her feet a little.

The apprehensions she still felt allowed the Nag to weasel her way out of the worry closet to pester her as she tried to concentrate on the job at hand.

With her finger wagging at Beth, the Nag started in. "You need more time. You don't know this man."

"I knew him and loved him years ago. I love him now, so we're already through all that."

"How do you know he isn't after your money?"

"He doesn't know I have money."

"Ha. All he has to do is look at this place."

"He doesn't know it's paid for. We never discussed money, but he seems to be all right."

"Many things are not as they seem. Men are not to be trusted."

"Who asked you? Get back where you belong." Beth mentally shoved the Nag back into the closet. *I'd better get a lock for that door. The Nag is not keeping to our bargain,* she thought and sighed.

And yet she had to admit, the hurry bothered her. She understood Dale's point about not wasting time but still . . . she wished she could reclaim the calm she had sheltered in before her first wedding. She had been lost in a happy fog, the only one in the wedding party that hadn't been on the edge of hysterics. But that ease eluded her this time.

*The Nag is right. I knew Rob a lot better than I do Dale,* she mused, mowing around trees in her pine grove. *But still, in many ways, we did it on faith just like I'll be doing with Dale. Do we ever really know anyone completely?*

Weaving the mower back and forth under the pines and managing to avoid the one sprinkler that stuck up just a little high, she pondered the problems she had ignored when she married the first time.

*When we left the church after the ceremony, we had no place to live, no money, and no job. Rob had two years of college to finish, and we just jumped off the edge and got married in spite of it all.*

This time a job was not necessary. They had a place to live, time to play. Everything should be wonderful unless they lost their health. There was Gloria, but Beth was convinced by now that Dale meant it when he said Beth would come first.

Her mind went around and around, like thread around a spool. *Didn't you swear you would not let life drift by you anymore?* she thought as she finished mowing the yard and moved to the lane to mow the grass on the sides of the black top. She had to lift the mowing deck and then settled back into the hypnotic movement of the machine.

By the time she reached the end of the lane and started mowing her way back to the house, she was thinking about the timing for this second wedding. *If we wait two more weeks, it will be five months since Dale showed up on my doorstep. That's half as much time as I went with Rob, but I'll only have half as much time to be married to Dale. Maybe it's a sign.*

She finished the lane and trundled the mower across the parking area to the shed and turned it off. She pulled the ear protectors off her head and groaned as she climbed carefully off the mower. It was tempting to leave the lawn mower and go take a shower, but she forced herself to clean off the deck and refill the gas tank before she went into the house.

*　*　*

The phone rang just as she finished dressing.

"How's my almost bride? Sitting around eating chocolate and reading romance novels I bet."

Beth snorted into the receiver. "This almost bride was hot and dirty until just a little bit ago. I mowed the yard and the pine grove and the lane. I know you said you couldn't wait to get your hands on the Dixon mower. I'll be glad to turn it over to you. I bet it will start every time you look at it instead of playing the dead battery bit like it loves to do with me." She stretched her neck. "So what did you do today?"

"I talked to a realtor and put the condo on the market. He feels it will sell quickly. I hope he's right. It would be great if it sold before we get married, wouldn't it?"

"Yep, one less thing to take care of. There is plenty out here to keep us both busy." Beth hesitated. "What did Gloria say?"

"We aren't speaking since I told her I asked you to marry me and was going to move out here. She just walked away. It's her choice." His voice held both anger and regret.

"I'm sorry," Beth said slowly. "But this is the last time I'm going to say I'm sorry about your daughter. It will just have to be understood."

"It is, darling. I know you didn't want it to be this way." Dale hesitated. "Have you decided on a date yet?"

"I was thinking that two more weeks would make it five months since you showed up and started pestering me. Are you sure we aren't pushing it too hard?"

"Not really. All I want to do is be with you, so why not do it as a married couple? Or I guess we could live together as significant others, but I'm not really comfortable with that. Are you?"

"No, I wasn't brought up that way. I would feel we were living in sin. I know a lot of people our age are doing it, but no. I guess the thing that bothers me the most is I don't know what makes you upset. You know I get grumpy when I get tired, but I don't know what pushes your buttons."

"Did you know your husband's buttons before you got married?"

"I thought I did, but things changed after we got married."

"So don't you think we'll have to learn about each other just like you did before? Will waiting make that much difference?"

Beth considered for a moment. "I guess there is only one way to find out. Let's make it September 15 then."

"Thank you, my love. I'll handle the reservations in Estes, a place along the river?"

"Oh yes, I love the sound of moving water. Try to find one with a hot tub so we can soak our old bones. Maybe an outside one so we can soak and sip wine and look at the stars?"

"Done, my love. Leave it all to me. I know just the place. Now next item—do you still want to get married by a justice of the peace or do you want to be married by your minister with our immediate families? That would be a problem with Gloria, wouldn't it?" Dale took a deep breath. "Would your son be upset if he didn't give you away?"

"I don't think so but I'll talk to Steve. My feeling is to just keep it simple, and we can have a reception later, can't we?" Beth hesitated. "Or maybe we don't need to. Most of the ones I would want were at the engagement party. Do you have people you would want to invite to a reception?"

"Not very many. Why don't we just table that until after we get married?"

Beth laughed. "You certainly do keep harping on this marriage."

"I do not harp. I'm pleading with my reluctant fiancé. I—"

"Oh, I just remembered," Beth interrupted. "A friend of mine told me that you can just marry yourselves, get a form, say your 'I dos' to each other any time within a certain period, and then just get the license recorded after you sign it. They were living together and got married in her kitchen after she got off work one day. So that gives us three options."

"It doesn't sound very romantic."

"I thought so too, but she said her man said things to her as they made their vows that he would never have been able to do with other people around. So they were very happy with it."

"Where do you get the license?"

"I can't remember but I'll call and ask her."

"I really don't care, darling, but I think the simpler the better. I'll take care of the reservations in Estes, you find out about the license. I'll call you tomorrow as usual."

"All right, love. I see the sun is about to go down. One more day gone. Soon we won't have to call each other on the phone. Won't that be nice?" She sighed. "Talk to you tomorrow. Good night."

Beth hung up the phone and sat in the darkening office. She felt relieved, the decision had been made, the plans set in motion. *I will not look back*, she thought. *I will not worry about the future. I will live in the present and enjoy every possible moment.*

Finding her owner seated, Taz jumped onto Beth's lap. Beth stroked the soft fur and stared out the window at the emerging stars.

The phone shrilled, making her jump, and Taz spilled out of her lap as she rose abruptly, reaching for the receiver.

"Hello, May. I knew that was you."

"See, I keep telling you that you have the special sense too. Beth, I am so sorry I could not be at your engagement party. But I already had my ticket and all."

"I understand. I'll tell you all about it. But first, how was your trip?"

"I loved being with my grandkids, but I decided I couldn't live in Seattle. It's lovely, but it rained the whole time I was there, and I was dying for some blue sky and sunshine. I am so glad to be home, and I was thinking why don't you come into town tomorrow morning for tea? I will make my special sticky buns, and I can catch up on all your news and tell you all about my trip."

"I couldn't pass up a chance for those. I'm glad you're back. I miss you when you're off gallivanting all over the place, so I'll be there close to nine. Will you to do the cards for me?"

"We can do that," May said. "It's been almost six months since I told them for you, so it won't be too soon. You wouldn't want to know about your marriage, would you?"

"Nah, why would I want to waste your time talking about that? I'm glad you're back safe, and I'll see you in the morning. Get some rest."

Beth hung up and yawned as she turned out the light in the office. Taz was waiting for her in the foyer, and she paused to lean down and pet her cat. "I think it's time for bed, don't you?"

"Mmmrowph."

As they made their way to the bedroom, Beth said, "Just to let you know, your highness, I'm getting married so you're going to have to learn to share me."

Taz refused comment.

# CHAPTER 20

The next morning in May's snug kitchen, Beth concentrated on making a wish as she shuffled the deck of cards. *Will my marriage be happy?* she silently asked as she watched May turn the cards over one by one.

"You're concerned about your marriage, which is obvious. All the cards are concerned with love." May put another card face up on the table and frowned. "You will get married again . . . it will not be soon." She looked up at Beth.

"But we're going to be married in two weeks. We just decided last night." Beth's finger poked at the card that had imparted such offensive news.

May slowly shook her head. "No, I do not see it happening soon. There is darkness there . . . a trip?" She frowned at the cards.

"We're going to Estes for a few days." Beth could feel a knot form in her stomach. "Is it his daughter?"

"It isn't clear."

"But we will get married?" Beth warmed her suddenly cold hands on her cup.

"Yes. But not as you expect." May gathered the cards and handed them to Beth. "Shuffle and cut them and ask your wish again. It might read clearer a second time."

Beth's hands trembled as she shuffled the cards and handed them to May. She concentrated on her wish, adding a simple prayer for a clear answer.

May carefully placed the tarot cards on the table, turning them over slowly. "It is the same. See? These cards are concerned with love. That is plain, but there is darkness and confusion and loss. I do see a trip, but it is not soon, so I don't think it is your honeymoon trip to Estes. You are with a woman."

Beth looked at May in confusion. "A woman? Who?"

"I wish I could tell you." May shook her head and swept the cards together and put them to the side of the table. "I can't tell you more at this time. Some things just don't come through clearly."

The women sat, lost in their own thoughts. The expected happy future that had been foretold now seemed elusive.

Beth stirred at last. "Well, life does as it chooses. There isn't much we can do but live through it. I know that well enough." She attempted a wobbly smile. "Thank you for feeding my sweet tooth. I'll keep you posted on what's going on. As if I need to."

"Don't worry, it will come right. I do see that clearly. You and Dale will be together and happy."

May's reassurance and the smell of the rolls that May gave her to take home failed to soothe Beth in any way.

She didn't remember the drive home, which always unsettled her. As she dumped her purse on her desk, she ran her hand over her face. It might be all right to be on autopilot at times, but if, on the way home, the Yukon had hurdled through a herd of buffalo the bloodstains on the hood would have been a total mystery to Beth.

She needed to think about something other than the conversation with May. *What clothes would she need for her honeymoon? New underwear for sure, something black and lacey, and a nice nightgown; her ratty pajamas wouldn't cut it.*

May's frowning face kept intruding, the Worry Nag hammered hard on the closet door, and sleep was filled with dark dreams.

Midafternoon the next day, Beth was at her desk paying bills as Taz watched her from the top of the adjacent filing cabinet. After she had to void two checks, she threw her pen down and ran her hands through her hair. "Who pays attention to their fortune anyway," she growled at the cat. Taz stared at her with knowing eyes. "What are you, my familiar? Knock it off." She plucked the cat off the filing cabinet and put her outside.

After watching Taz walk the perimeter of the orchard fence, Beth gave in to her restlessness and called Dale. His machine picked up. "Hello, darling. I was just wondering what you were up to since you didn't call me yesterday."

She stared at the wall and tapped her fingers on the desk and finally got up with a groan to go out the front door. Outside, the summer heat had her flower beds looking like dried-out old maids. The only flowers doing well were the marigolds she planted to keep mosquitoes away. Deadheading the plants to make them look less messy would also stimulate their regrowth when the weather cooled down.

She worked until she was unsure if she was pulling weeds or flowers. Taking her time, she carefully cleaned her tools, hung them on the pegboard, closed her garage door, and went into the house.

There was no red light on the answering machine signaling a missed call. Dale never waited this late in the day to check in and see how she was doing. She marched to the desk and snatched the receiver off its base and punched in his number.

"You have reached 970-332-2222. Leave a message."

"This is your almost bride. You said you were going to call me. Is this what I get for setting the date? Call me, I'm missing you." Beth slowly put the phone back on the base.

By midnight she was falling asleep in her chair and forced herself to go to bed. Two other calls made earlier in the evening had been cheerfully taken by the answering machine that she was beginning to hate.

Her sleep was restless. She woke in the night full of dread. She had been dreaming of Dale. She couldn't remember any details except he had been calling her name. Beth was so disturbed she turned on the light, and even though it was three in the morning, she dialed his number again. "Damn." She slammed the phone down as his answering machine picked up.

The Worry Nag beat on the closet door, and Beth's worried mind couldn't find the strength to keep her locked inside. The Nag strutted out, dressed in a worn flannel nightgown. She stood with her hands on her hips, the expression on her monkey face gleeful. "And where's your lover now? You really expected him to stick around when he got what he wanted?"

"And what was that?"

"Your heart and soul. Isn't that what they all want?" The Nag's thin lips stretched into a sour smile. "Men never change. It doesn't matter the era. Once the chase is over, they go hunting in new pastures."

"Something must have happened to him. There's a reason he didn't call."

"There's none so blind as those that will not see."

The Nag's self-satisfied expression exasperated Beth to the point she was able to find enough strength to push the image away. She wouldn't believe the Nag, she wouldn't.

She turned out the light and tried to go back to sleep, but it was a lost cause. She sat in her bed and watched the sun turn the mountains pink, feeling alone and unreasonably frightened.

Beth called Dale all the next day and never got anything but the machine. She grew more and more upset. *My God,* she thought, *this is the way I remember it when he would disappear when we were young. Surely I'm not going to have to go through it again. Please don't let it happen again.*

# CHAPTER 21

Two days later, Beth watched Larimer County police officer Clarence Pridley pop the lock on Dale's front door. Her concern about his unresponsiveness to her calls had finally convinced the police he might be in trouble and unable to get to the phone.

"Hello, the house," Officer Pridley yelled, waited for a reply, and, when there was none, walked in with Beth close on his heels. Dale was not huddled in the bathroom with a broken leg, not dead in his bed from a heart attack, just not there.

"You said his daughter lives next door?" Officer Pridley questioned as they stood in Dale's living room. "You called her about her father?"

Beth nodded. "I never got anything but her answering machine, but she probably wouldn't get back to me anyway."

"Why not?" The young officer watched Beth closely.

"She doesn't like me."

"Why not?"

"She thinks I'm stealing her father away from her. She is totally against the whole idea. So if she knows what is going on, she is probably tickled to death."

"You really think something has happened to him?"

"Yes, Officer, I really do. We were planning on getting married in two weeks, and he called me every day at least once." Beth thinned her lips as she looked at Pridley. "Something is very wrong." As Officer Pridley looked around the living room as though he expected Dale to materialize out of thin air, Beth added, "What do we do now?"

The young officer sighed and motioned Beth out the door. "Let's go see if the daughter is home, and if not, I guess you better file a missing person's report. I don't know how much good it will do, but at least it will make it official. If he doesn't show up, we will already have the paperwork done."

\* \* \*

Gloria wasn't home. Half an hour later, Beth found herself passing through the door of the new Larimer County Police Department building. Never in her wildest dreams would she have thought she would have any reason to be here. Disbelief sat on her shoulders as she waited for the detective that would take her report.

"Ms. Waterford?" Detective Ben Rojas was short and stocky. He looked tired. "You want to file a missing person's report?"

"Yes, my fiancé has been missing for four days. Something is seriously wrong."

"Why is that?" Rojas shuffled through the papers on his desk, which looked like the aftermath of a bombing run.

Beth grit her teeth. It wouldn't help Dale to get annoyed at the police. "Because"—she strove hard to keep a civil tone in her voice—"he was making plans for our honeymoon. Also, he calls me at least once a day. I haven't heard from him for three days. All my calls get shifted to the answering machines, both his landline and cell phone. And he wasn't planning on going anywhere."

"You're sure of that?" Rojas scratched at his head of dark hair. A thriving case of dandruff lightly dusted the shoulders of his navy jacket. The sleeves of the jacket were too short; his wrists hung out.

"Yes, Detective, I'm sure of that."

"Anyone else you can think of that would know where he is?" He was scribbling on a form he had finally unearthed from the rubble on his desk.

"He has a daughter that lives next door, but I haven't been able to get anything but her answering machine either. She doesn't like me, and I don't think she will call me back. She will love the idea I'm upset."

"And why is that, Ms. Waterford?"

Beth shifted in her chair and took a deep breath. "Because she doesn't like the idea of her father marrying me."

"Thinks you're after his money, eh?" Rojas had a half smile on his face.

"No, Detective, I don't think it's that, as I'm in good financial shape. No, she's very possessive of her father. She's his only child, and she doesn't get along with her mother. She isn't very rational about it."

"How do you mean?" Rojas leaned forward. "You think she would harm her father?"

"No, not really, but she has thrown several cat fits in public and refused to speak to him after he told her we plan on getting married in two weeks."

"Does she have a job?" When Beth nodded, he asked, "Where?"

"I really don't know. She's a trauma nurse, but if I was told where she works, I don't remember. That has made it impossible for me to get in touch with her."

"Uhm." He leaned back in his chair to regard Beth for a long moment. "This isn't a question I like to ask, but you don't think he got cold feet?"

Faced with the idea Beth dreaded, she replied firmly, "No, Detective, I do not." And as she said the words, she realized she really didn't believe Dale had voluntarily walked away from her again. *But if he hadn't, what had happened to him?*

"Well, there isn't much we can do at this point. If you could find out where the daughter works, it would help. Get back to us in a few days if you're sure he still isn't home."

As she walked toward her vehicle, the wind tugged at her hair and whipped it into her eyes. Irritated, she swiped at it. What a waste of time that all had been. Although she had the relief of knowing Dale wasn't dying of dehydration from a fall and the inability to get to the phone. She felt Detective Rojas figured Dale had taken off for a breather to think about the wedding despite her assurances that he hadn't. His promise to look into the matter only made her feel like he was laughing at her for being left at the altar. She hoped his dandruff was terminal.

*     *     *

It was after lunch by the time Beth returned home. She spent a miserable two hours worrying about Dale with unwanted comments from the Worry Nag until Nancy called.

"Hey, girl, how about a ride on the canal before it gets too late?"

Her friend's cheerful voice triggered the tears that had been threatening to overwhelm Beth ever since she was unable to contact Dale.

"Hang on. I'll be right over," Nancy said. She was at Beth's door in five minutes, took one look at Beth's chalk-white face and red eyes, went into the office, pulled the bottle of Jack Daniel out of the bar cabinet, and poured two stiff drinks. "Here, you need this, and I have a feeling I will too. What's going on, sugar?" She listened in growing disbelief as Beth stumbled through her fears about Dale. "You don't think he decided on a trip to Estes to check on a nice place to stay?"

Beth mopped her eyes and blew her nose. "It wouldn't take four days, would it? He was going to do that by phone. He's pretty familiar with some of the nice condos up there. He was going to call me the next day." She choked down a mouthful of the whiskey. "I know something's wrong, I just know it. You know he called me at least once every day since he proposed. I know he had a lot of things to do. The reservations, the condo . . ." She stared at the wall. "The realtor, maybe he can tell me something."

But the realtor hadn't heard from Dale either, and he had a prospective buyer.

*   *   *

"Rojas here."

"This is Beth Waterford about my fiancé's disappearance. You remember me?"

"Of course, Ms. Waterford. He showed back up again?"

"No, he didn't show back up again, but I thought to contact the realtor that is trying to sell his house."

"And?"

"He has a prospective buyer and had Dale's cell phone number and he hasn't been able to contact him either. So that would suggest to me he isn't just screening his calls." She swallowed a sob. "Please, can't you help me?"

"I'm sorry about your pain, Ms. Waterford, but we're doing what we can. We did check all the area hospitals. There's no record of your fiancé being admitted or treated. No body at the coroner's department. We also managed to cross those off as possible places for your proposed daughter-in-law to work." There was a small silence, and then he said in a gentle voice, "We're doing all we can, really."

"Thank you, Detective." Perhaps she had misjudged him.

Beth felt old and defeated as she gently hung up the phone.

\* \* \*

*I've done all I can think to do,* Beth decided on Friday of the third week. Rojas had talked to the realtor. There had still been no contact from Dale. The prospective buyer had given up and was looking at another piece of property.

The sandwich she was supposed to be eating was in shreds on her plate. *I won't do anything over the weekend. He will call Monday, and it will all have been a miserable mistake. And then I will hit him, a lot.* She gave a weak laugh that didn't even deceive Taz and decided to clean out her utility room.

The Worry Nag worked right along with her, throwing out a huge pile of boxes from her closet.

"Do you want to know what all those boxes contain?"

"Not really, but I don't see how you could have all that in your closet."

The Worry Nag chuckled. "Those are all the worries from the first time Dale pulled the disappearing act on you. I figured I would need to get rid of those to have room for all these new ones that are just starting, if you ask me."

Beth sighed as she scrubbed down the wall behind the utility sink.

"You're taking the paint right off the wall!"

"Please go away. You're giving me a headache."

When Monday morning finally dawned, she had cleaned the entire house from top to bottom. The Worry Nag worked right beside her but did keep silent most of the time.

Dale still didn't answer his phone.

"May, could you come out here? I just need to talk to someone, and I'm not fit to drive. I'm so upset," Beth pleaded. It was either talk to someone or explode from frustration and fear. Nancy and Len had gone to their condo in Steamboat and wouldn't be back for a week.

It was ten o'clock when May drove in. Beth met her on the deck and practically yanked her in the house. "Slow down, slow down," May said.

"You almost pulled my arm out of the socket." She gave Beth a hug and added, "Fix us a cup of tea and tell me all about it."

Beth made a mess out of getting tea until May took pity on her. She gently pushed Beth out of the way and took over while Beth talked disjointedly about Dale's disappearance. The two friends sat opposite each other at the dining room table. May frowned as she watched Beth wring her hands.

"I'm sure one minute something terrible has happened, and the next minute I'm furious because it's so much like the times when we were young and he just disappeared." Beth picked her cup up, but her shaking hands had the liquid slopping over the rim. She put it down with a bang that filled the saucer.

"Do you really think he's gotten cold feet?" May queried gently. "After that beautiful proposal? I felt no deceit in the man."

"He doesn't have any reason to back off this time. He had to chase me down, and I was the one backing off. I gave him every chance to disappear." Beth sighed. "The only negative we had was Gloria."

"Ah, Gloria." May leaned back in her chair and gazed at Beth. "You said you can't get in touch with her either? Did you try the hospital where she works?"

"When the police talked to the hospitals about Dale because they thought he might have been brought in because of an accident, they checked to see if Gloria was employed at one of them. But there was nothing at any of them. I never did know where she worked. If I was told, I don't remember. I don't know what to do. I cleaned my entire house over the weekend just to keep from going crazy."

"Come clean mine if we don't find your Dale soon," May said absently as she tapped her fingers on the table. "The fact that both of them are gone is the key, I think. Yes, they are together. I feel it."

"But where?" Beth twisted in her seat. "I just can't imagine him going somewhere with her and not letting me know he was going to be gone this long. They might have had a fight. Oh God, you don't think she could have killed him in one of her fits?" Beth asked desperately.

"No," May said slowly. "He is not dead." She looked at Beth, who stared back at her. "You do believe me, don't you?"

"You asked me one morning what was wrong with Far's leg, as he had told you it hurt. That was the morning after he rolled into the fence and got himself tangled up. I had to cut him out of it, and he took some hide off his leg." Beth gave a laugh that turned into a sob. "If you're telling me you know Dale is still alive, I believe you."

"If we find the daughter, we will find Dale," said May.

"But how?"

"Keep after the police and we will pray. You must not give up hope. You will find him."

# CHAPTER 22

One month after Dale disappeared, Beth caught a glimpse of herself as she passed by her bedroom mirror. Backing up, she peered closely at her image and sucked in a shocked breath. An old woman looked back at her. She had not been coloring her hair. It was a mélange of unflattering colors ranging from several shades of gray to faded reddish blonde. A comb had not been near the shaggy, grown-out haircut for at least a week. Dark circles under her eyes accentuated the lack of the usual careful darkening of her eyebrows. She ran her fingers over the sallow skin of her face and sighed. She looked as sick on the outside as she felt on the inside.

She turned away from the mirror and sank into the wicker chair next to the dresser. How to wake from this nightmare? The days had passed like water under a bridge as she struggled to find the energy to carry on her life and daily failed. Her desk was piled high with overdue bills. She was avoiding her office because the wet bar tucked into the one corner offered oblivion, and she refused to yield to liquor. Hunger pangs would catch her unaware, and she would realize she hadn't eaten. Her clothes hung on her. Sleep was unattainable; she roamed her house at night or stared unseeingly at her TV.

Everything had come to a dead end. The disappearance of Dale and Gloria Runnington was official now, but Beth knew the police were no longer spending any time on the case. Possible leads had led nowhere. The understaffed police had their hands too full to waste any more time on a mere disappearance.

Beth shifted in the chair and looked out the window. Far Horizon was grazing in the west pasture. She should be riding to keep them both in condition, and it would be a lovely day to ride. She couldn't bring herself to care.

Dealing with Dale's disappearance in many ways seemed harder to her than trying to get through her husband's death. *I had so much to do,* she thought as she levered herself out of the chair. *Dealing with the estate demanded I keep going. This time there is nothing to fill the void, to keep the pain submerged.*

She went into her bathroom, stared at the deep steeping tub. *I should take a bath and get dressed.* She considered the thought for several minutes but could not dredge up any energy. Turning away, Beth moved like a zombie down the hall.

The ten o'clock news was blaring away when Beth realized the phone was ringing. She ignored it. The answering machine would pick up any message. She heard the click, and her son's voice brought her out of her chair, had her scrambling to pick up the phone.

"Hello."

"Mom? What's the matter? You sound awful. Are you sick?"

"No, hon, just tired. How are you?"

"We're all right, just checking. I haven't heard from you for a while and wanted to catch up. I'm sorry I haven't called sooner, but we've been busy. But I imagine you haven't missed me with Dale hanging around."

"He isn't hanging around," Beth said in a very small voice.

"What?"

The disbelief in Steve's voice pierced Beth to her core. She took in a hitching breath. "I haven't heard from him for a month. He just quit calling and . . . he seems to have disappeared."

"Did you have a fight? What happened?"

"No, nothing like that. We were talking about our wedding plans, and he was going to get back to me after he made reservations in Estes. That was the last I heard from him." Beth paused, fighting against tears. "I don't know what happened to him. I went to the police after three days. He wasn't in his condo, and the realtor hasn't been able to find him."

"I can't believe he would do something like that after watching the two of you together, and that proposal. I really thought he was crazy about you."

"I did too," Beth replied in a choked voice.

"It just doesn't make sense. Did the police have any luck figuring out where he is?"

"No, I think they really feel he just changed his mind." She could feel Steve's hesitation. "And no, I don't think he did. I think something happened. Gloria is gone too."

"Ahh, the wonderful daughter. I haven't had the pleasure, but there hasn't been too much good said about her. I don't imagine she was thrilled about your engagement."

"No. She wasn't speaking to her father once he told her we were getting married, but it's strange they're both missing."

"What can I do, Mom?"

His concern for her made Beth's throat constrict. She was unable to answer.

"Mom?"

She cleared her throat. "I don't know, love. I'm just waiting. I don't know what else to do. Just hope that something breaks. I just want to know he's all right. The rest of it doesn't matter, just that he's all right." Beth tried to swallow a sob, but she was sure Steve heard it.

A long minute later, Steve murmured, "I'm so sorry, Mom. You both were so happy together. I would have never imagined this would happen. I wish I could do something."

"I know," Beth said softly. "But I have done everything I can think to do. I will keep after the police, but other than that . . ." She was drowning in a well of tears. "I'll call you later. I can't talk anymore right now, love. I'm really tired."

"I love you, Mom. Take care of yourself."

"I will, thank you." Beth gently put the receiver back on the base and let the tears pour.

\*    \*    \*

A knock on her front door the next morning startled Beth. Nancy opened the front door, yodeling her presence. She stopped in the foyer at the sight of her friend sitting in the big leather chair in the living room with Taz on her lap.

Nancy shook her head. "Weren't you in that position the last time we talked?" She walked into the living room and looked around, her hands on her hips.

"My Lord, this place is a mess," Nancy scolded. Ignoring Beth's feeble protests, she picked up plates, hauled them into the kitchen, and gathered the mail cluttering the end tables. She put it in careful stacks on the desk in the office. She took Beth by her wrists and hauled her out of the chair. "Come on, my friend, get out of those pajamas. It's a beautiful day, and your horse is calling for you. Let's get out of the house and go for a ride."

She pulled Beth down the hall to her bedroom. "Now you've got two choices," she said, ignoring the glare directed at her. "You can dress or be dressed—which is it?"

Beth hesitated and then slowly walked to her closet.

Far Horizon was already saddled, tied across the rail from Nancy's horse, and he nickered as he saw Beth come out of the house. When Beth came through the gate, the gelding tugged at his lead rope, watching his owner as she approached. Beth came slowly up to him and wrapped her arms around his neck, burying her face in his mane. The horse nuzzled Beth, grumbling softly until she raised her head, untied him from the fence, and gently put his bridle on.

Let's not talk, just ride." Nancy said, glancing at Beth as she got on her horse.

After a moment spent stroking Far Horizon's nose, Beth mounted her horse and settled onto the saddle. She swept her hand along the crest of the gelding's neck and nudged him forward. Far Horizon moved out willingly with his long swinging walk.

The riders cut across the pastures to the big irrigation canal, where Beth gradually lost herself in the motion of her horse as she listened to the creak of leather, the jingle of the bit, and the sound of hooves striking the ground.

Beth came alive to the world again. The day was warm and sunny with a slight breeze. Birds warbled their particular brand of song. She could hear meadowlarks, blackbirds, and the lonely shriek of a hunting hawk overhead. Someone had cut alfalfa. The smell was so sharp it hurt her nose. Fall was near; the trees were still green, but the leaves had the undertone that precedes their turning.

It was like waking from a dark unpleasant dream. The dismal facts were still there, just under the surface, but she fought them, concentrating on the moment. She hummed to her horse and watched his ears swivel back and forth as he listened to her.

The friends didn't say a word to each other during the ride or while they were unsaddling. After Nancy pulled the sliding door to the lean to shut, she looked at Beth closely and said, "Feel better?"

Beth heaved a huge sigh. "Yes, thanks Nancy. There's something about horses that make my troubles bearable. After Rob died, when I was really blue, I used to come out and just lean against Far Horizon to let his warmth and smell unwind my kinks. It's almost magic how he can improve my mood."

"I hear you, girlfriend. I've experienced the same thing." Nancy put her arm across Beth's shoulders as the women walked slowly toward the house. "I hoped it would help you get back on your feet. I've been so worried about you."

Beth stopped and turned to Nancy, smiling sadly at her friend. "I've been completely tuned out. It was the only way I could fight the pain. It's been almost worse than when Rob died. I just can't find the energy to do anything." Beth wearily rubbed the back of her neck.

"It's because you don't know," Nancy said. "You knew what happened to Rob. I can't imagine what it must be like to not know. But you can't give up. You still have your son and his family, your friends, your horse."

"This is exactly why I didn't want to get involved with someone again," Beth said shakily. "I get to the place where I don't think I can stand it."

"Do you have a choice? No, I mean that. You did so well after Rob died, you can start again. You didn't want to be a burden on your son the last time. Do you want to be one now? I know he's worried about you. He calls me all the time."

"Oh Lord, he does?" Beth groaned. "I didn't know that."

They walked the rest of the way to the house in silence.

"So what are you going to do?" Nancy put her hands on Beth's shoulders as they stood in the sunshine on the east deck. Far Horizon watched them from the corral. Would Beth remember he deserved a treat?

"I don't know where to start," Beth said. Her hands were fists in her pockets.

"Why don't we go into town tomorrow and get your hair and nails done? There are a lot of silver threads among your locks, and I don't think you're ready to be gray headed yet, are you?"

Beth shook her head.

"There's nothing like getting our hair done to make a woman feel better—unless it's a bit of chocolate. Maybe we should stop at the Chocolate Shop in the mall. If anyone deserved a little treat, it would be you. And of course, I'll have to join you. Watching a friend eat chocolate alone causes brain damage."

A small smile worked its way across Beth's face. "I don't know what I would do without you." Beth pushed her bangs back from her face and tilted her face toward the sun. She let out a long shaky breath.

"You'd be fine but maybe not have as much fun," Nancy said. "I've got to get home. Are you all right?

"Much better, thanks. I guess I needed a poke in the rear. Thanks for being there with the stick."

*    *    *

The phone rang at seven the next morning. Beth picked it up, almost spilling her cup of coffee in the process. "Who?" she croaked.

"My goodness, there's a frog at Beth's house. Does it want to go have breakfast with me?" Nancy's voice was so cheerful she might have been singing.

"The frog says no." Beth took a swallow of coffee. "I'm not dressed."

"Figured. Well get yourself clothed because I will be banging on your door in an hour. You need a monster breakfast because we're going to spend all day getting you whipped back into shape."

Beth groaned.

"I take that as a yes. See you in an hour."

Seated in a red leather booth at the IHOP, Beth felt much better as she swiped a piece of toast across her plate, getting the last of the egg yolk. "That was good."

Nancy shoved her empty plate to the end of the table. "I'm sure you haven't been eating right."

"Who ate?" Beth poured herself another cup of coffee. "Or if I had an eating fit, it wasn't something that was good for me. Ice cream or potato chips and dip. If I'm hurting, I can eat anything I want, can't I? I'm entitled because I'm in pain?"

"I'm sure I would feel the same way, but we aren't going to let this finish you off. We have an appointment with Michael in half an hour to do something adventurous to your hair after you have a facial and manicure."

Beth peered sideways at her friend. "Adventurous? That sounds downright dangerous. You know my hair will only work one way. Short and simple."

"And it looks good on you too, but let's modernize it a bit . . . spike it maybe?" Nancy gave her friend an innocent smile.

"Oh Lord, help me," Beth groaned.

Her hair was spiked after much discussion and the hairdresser's promise that he would wash it out if she didn't like it and just blow it dry like she normally wore it. Beth had to admit it looked good.

"I won't ever be able to do this to myself," she complained to Nancy as they drove toward the mall.

"Sure, when you get up in the morning, don't brush it, just gel it. Most of these modern hairdos look like you just got out of bed. This do looks really good on you, and you can use it when you want to dress up or just want a change.

Beth snorted but had to grin. "Okay, you win. I do feel better because I look better. You are a good friend. Thanks." She sighed and settled into her seat. "Where are you headed now?"

"Silly woman, we must have chocolate. To the Rocky Mountain Candy place of course." Nancy licked her lips and made chewing noises until she had Beth hooting with laughter.

"You're going to be all right, Beth. You're too strong to opt out of life. Right?"

Beth looked at her friend, small and energetic and caring. "How can I not? You'll be dragging me to the hairdresser to dye my hair purple or something if I don't, knowing you."

"Damn betcha, girl. I'm a force to be feared. And you know you can call on me any time, right?" Nancy took one hand off the steering wheel and reached toward Beth.

"Right," Beth said softly as she leaned over and took her friend's hand and squeezed it with gratitude. "Now how about a little hurry toward the mall. I am beginning to feel like chocolate, a lot of chocolate."

# CHAPTER 23

By mid-October, Beth was sleeping most nights, which made her feel she was starting to function somewhat normally again. The Worry Nag had less excuse to come out of the closet.

One afternoon, Beth was in Fort Collins running errands and, on impulse, decided to drive by Dale's place again. The For Sale sign was still up; the condo had been taken over by the bank. She was almost past Gloria's condo before it registered. A realty sign was in front of it too. She hit the brakes.

Beth backed the Yukon up and stared at the sign. It was a different realtor than the one Dale had used. She dialed the realtor's number on her cell phone, asked if there was any possibility someone could come out now to show her the place since she was sitting in front of it. She was in luck; an agent was available and could be there in twenty minutes.

"I'm Judith Miracle," the real estate agent said. The woman was close to Beth's age, with a kind face and a motherly manner. She unlocked the front door of Gloria's condo, keeping up a chatter Beth hardly listened to as she looked around. This condo was identical to Dale's but stark, with very little furniture, no pictures on the wall. It had the feeling of a motel room, seldom occupied. It smelled dusty.

"Why is the owner selling?" Beth asked as they walked into the kitchen.

"She said she was changing jobs and leaving town. She has it priced very low so it's a very good deal. She wants to move it as quickly as possible," Judith Miracle said.

Beth continued to pretend to be interested in the condo as they went through the rooms. She was looking for anything that might help her understand what had happened, but there was nothing personal here.

"It looks like she has already moved out."

"Yes, she's not living in it."

"Do you know where she is?"

The agent looked warily at Beth. "No, she came into the office and said she would be in contact with us, as she is traveling a lot and has no permanent address at this point."

"A cell phone number, did she give you a cell phone number? Please, I must get in touch with her."

"She didn't, but even if she did, I wouldn't give it to you. Are you interested in this condo or what's the deal?" Judith asked.

Beth knew she wasn't going to get anywhere further with this kind of questioning. She walked into the living room and sat down on the couch, looking up at the agent.

"You noticed the condo next door was for sale too?" When the agent nodded, Beth continued. "It's a long story, but I need to be honest with you because I need your help. Please sit down and I'll tell you what's going on." After a brief hesitation, Judith sat beside her.

Beth told her why she was so desperate to get in touch with Gloria.

"I can't believe it. That is the kind of story you read in books. But I don't know you. Maybe you're making it up," Judith Miracle said after listening raptly to Beth's story.

"It's all true. You can ask the police if you don't believe me, but this condo sale is the only lead I have to go on, the only contact I have with Dale's disappearance. Will you help me?

"How?" Judith asked.

"How would you get in touch with Gloria if you get a buyer?" Beth asked.

"She calls in most Mondays to see if there is any action on the place."

"Would you tell her you have a buyer? She would have to come and sign papers, wouldn't she?" Beth asked eagerly.

"Yes, but I can't do that. It would be fraud, I think. I could lose my license." Judith chewed at her lower lip. "But what I could do would be to notify you about the closing date if we do get a buyer. You could confront her then."

"Oh Lord, it could take months to sell this place." Beth rested her elbows on her knees, bent forward, and scrubbed at the back of her neck.

"These usually sell within a few weeks when the market's good, and it is. We've had the listing for three weeks, so it might not be long at all." Judith rose to her feet. "I wish I could do something else to help."

Sighing, Beth got to her feet. "This is as close as I've come to being able to do anything at all, so I'll just have to be patient." She smiled crookedly at Judith. "That's not one of my strong points. Thanks. You don't know how much this means to me."

"I might, my dear. You see, I lost my fiancé in Vietnam," Judith said. "He was missing in action. We never have known what happened to him. So I do understand how you feel."

Judith put her arms around Beth, held her close for a moment, released her, and then said, "Lock the door when you leave. Call the office and leave your number. I'll keep you posted on any progress we make on the condo. Let's hope for a hot prospect to show up ASAP." She smiled at Beth as she walked out the front door.

For the first time in months, Beth felt a touch of hope but also a touch of fear. Fear of what she might find out. "Knowing is better than not knowing, isn't it?" Her question hung in Gloria's empty living room as Beth went out and closed and locked the door.

\*     \*     \*

Beth called Nancy to bring her up-to-date.

"Do you want me to go with you? Between the two of us, I bet we could beat the truth out of her," Nancy growled.

"We might kill her before we find out where Dale is, better not risk it. You're a true friend, always ready to create mayhem on my account. Your husband wouldn't appreciate having to bail us out of jail."

May was less confrontational when Beth called her with her news. "This is the first step. You will be with him. Believe it, my friend."

"How do you know, May? You keep saying that, but how can you know?"

"Because I do not see him on the other side. He would be there if he was dead."

"Oh."

"Some things come through to me without talking to those that have gone before, but usually they are there behind the veil, and they tell me what they want their loved ones to know."

"The veil?"

"Think of a gauzy scarf, fine enough that I can identify features but not as clear as it would be if they were standing in front of me without the curtain."

"I've always believed in life after death, but it's such a comfort to know," Beth said. "It seems so unfair we all can't do what you do. I would have given anything to have seen and talked to Rob after he died. There were times I felt that he was with me as I sat crying, but there was no way I could be sure."

"Be glad that you don't have the sight." May was silent for a few seconds. "It's exhausting to deal with, all those people clamoring to break through to me. At times I just have to tell them to go away. I feel God protects most of us by not allowing communication between the living and the dead. If we could continue a relationship when a loved one died, would we continue a normal life in the here and now? He has a perfect plan, and it doesn't include our living in two worlds."

"It's strange. All these years I've known you, you have this ability, but we haven't really talked much about it unless I ask for a reading. Why is that?"

"Ah, love, you have cared about me as a friend, not just as a psychic, which has been a blessing to me."

"I guess that's true. We were so busy raising our kids and living life. It was just part of who you were. I guess I never really thought much about it." Beth laughed. "I had freckles and you were psychic."

"I would much rather have freckles. I will pray the realtor gets back to you soon."

# Chapter 24

"Beth, this is Judith Miracle. Gloria Runnington is coming this morning at eleven to close the sale on her condo."

It had been two weeks after Beth had first talked to the real estate agent. It seemed more like two months to Beth's tortured mind.

"Oh, thank God," Beth said. "I will be in as soon as I can. How do we handle this?"

"Do you have a cell phone? The number you gave me was your landline." Judith asked. When Beth answered in the affirmative, she continued, "There's a coffee shop right across the street. Wait there. Once she goes into the conference room, I'll call you."

Beth hesitated. "What if she decides to pick up some coffee? That would just be my luck."

"Oh, I hadn't thought of that, "Judith said. "Mmmm, how soon can you get to the office?"

"I can be there in forty-five minutes, thirty if the lights aren't against me," Beth said.

"That would give us about an hour, which should be enough time even if she comes early. There is a back entrance to the office. Park in the alley and come in that way. I'll be watching for you, and I'll put you in the storage room until she goes in to sign the papers." Judith hesitated. "I hope this will help somehow. Maybe you should contact the police?"

"I don't think I can depend on the police. They think it's a case of cold feet, although since he has completely disappeared and nobody has heard from him all this time, I don't see how they can think that." Beth sighed. "But I guess it happens. The police might foul up the timing, so let's try it this way and see what happens. Thank you so much, Judith."

Beth made very good time going into town and was hidden in the storage room with half an hour to spare. *I should have brought a book*, she thought. *Yeah, like I'd be able to read.* It seemed like hours until Judith slipped into the storage room. "They've just signed the final papers. Come with me, and I'll try to delay her while the others leave."

Beth followed her into the reception room and waited while Judith disappeared into a room at the end of the hall.

Beth watched as a couple, and then another man, came out of the conference room; and after a moment, Gloria came out with Judith close behind. Gloria stopped dead in her tracks just outside the conference room door when she spotted Beth waiting for her. Judith edged around both women unnoticed.

"You," Gloria spat.

"Yes, me," Beth said, glaring at Dale's daughter. She stepped toward Gloria, and Gloria backed up through the conference room door. Beth crowded her into the room and shut the door. "We have something to discuss. Where's your father? Is he all right? What on earth is going on? I have been crazy . . ."

Gloria set her jaw, thrust her chin toward Beth, and sneered, "It's none of your damn business. Can't you get it through your head that he isn't interested in you anymore?"

"I don't believe it. Your father was the one pushing me to marry. He loves me. He wouldn't just go off without a word."

"Why not?" Gloria asked with a sour smile. "He did it before didn't he?"

Beth flinched and then took a deep breath. "I don't believe it, not this time. Why don't we go to the police, and you tell them what's happened to him? They're looking for him too. It's suspicious he would just disappear like that. Yes, when he was young and unsure of himself. But not now. I don't believe it and I don't think they will either. You tell me what's going on or I'm calling them." Beth had her back against the door, and the look in her eye dared Gloria to call her bluff.

Gloria took a step toward Beth, thought better of it, and then gave a harsh laugh. "Well, you asked for it." She sat down, lit a cigarette, looked at it for a long moment, and then looked up at Beth. "He's dead."

Beth stared at her, unable to speak. "How?" she finally managed.

"We had a car accident."

"You're lying. We checked the hospitals," Beth said. She had to lean against the conference door to keep from falling.

"We were in Sterling when it happened. Dad had some stuff in storage there he wanted to go through." She took a long drag on her cigarette. "I went with him because a few of the things were mine. It was an impulse. We were supposed to be back that afternoon, so he didn't call you. A drunk came across the centerline and hit us head-on. Dad died in the emergency room. I was in the hospital for a few days because it banged me up pretty good too."

She flicked the cigarette ash on the floor and looked up at Beth, who still gaped at her in shock. "I had him cremated, and I spread his ashes at the reservoir north of Sterling. If it wasn't for you, we wouldn't have been there, and he would still be alive. End of story." Gloria ground out her half-smoked cigarette, stood up, and walked toward Beth. "Now get out of my way," she hissed. Her voice was flat, her eyes cold stones.

A wave of grief paralyzed Beth. She was incapable of resisting as Gloria shoved her roughly away from the door and stalked out. Beth heard Gloria's voice raised in anger as she fought to keep from fainting.

Judith came back into to the room, took one look at Beth's chalk-white face, gently led her to a chair, backed her into it, and sat her down like she was a small child. Beth bent over her knees and rocked her body. Judith leaned down and could barely hear Beth whisper over and over, "Dead, dead . . ."

Her grief shut Beth down; she was not aware of her surroundings or of Judith putting a glass of water in her hand.

Folding Beth's hands around the glass, Judith said, "You've had a terrible shock. Sit here as long as you need to recover." She sat down next to Beth.

The two women sat in silence.

Beth was so numb she wasn't able to cry.

Finally, Beth sat up, gave a huge sigh, and got to her feet. "Thank you for your help, Judith," she said dully. At least now I know. He didn't run away this time."

She was still in shock and kept dropping her car keys as she walked unsteadily through the real estate office.

Judith followed Beth out to her car. "Are you sure you're all right? Maybe I should drive you home."

"I'm all right," Beth said. She just wanted to be alone, to go home. "Thank you for your help. At least I know. That will help. Eventually."

Judith placed her hand on Beth's shoulder, hiding her pity, and said, "Please take care of yourself. I am so very sorry."

Beth got in her vehicle, got it in gear, and drove slowly down the alley.

She managed to get out of Fort Collins, but halfway home, she had such a crying fit she had to pull over to the side of the road until it passed. *I wish a garbage truck would come along and total the Yukon and me with it,* she thought as she stared unseeingly at the canal that ran along the highway. *I don't want to go on without Dale. I can't handle losing him twice. I just can't.*

It took a half hour before she could continue home. When she parked in the garage, she just sat in the Yukon, unable to find the energy to go into the house. Again, her life was shattered. *I'm not strong enough this time,* she thought as she struggled out of the vehicle. She went up the steps to the kitchen door and fumbled with the doorknob. Another crying fit hit her, and she leaned her head against the door and sobbed until she was hiccupping. She tried again to get into the house but kept turning the knob the wrong way. She finally got the door open and staggered into the kitchen.

She realized the phone was ringing. She waited until the machine picked up, but when she heard Nancy's voice, she picked up.

"I saw you coming up the lane. Did you see Gloria?"

"He's dead, he's dead, he's dead," Beth choked into the receiver.

There was a prolonged silence. "Oh, I'm so sorry my friend, so sorry. How did it happen?"

"They were in an accident in Sterling . . . Dale didn't survive. Gloria delighted in telling me that. She is the most unfeeling person . . . would it have been too much for her to call me?" Beth choked off another sob. "She said I killed Dale . . . if I hadn't gotten involved with him, they would have never been in Sterling. It's my fault."

"That's pure nonsense. It was his time. I know you believe that. What an awful person she is to let you wonder all these months." The two women were silent for a few moments. "What can I do for you, Beth? Do you want me to come over?"

"Thank you, but there's nothing anyone can do for me right now. I'm exhausted. I'm going to take a sleeping pill and go to bed. I know it won't solve anything, but at least I will be a little stronger when I wake

up. I promise to call you so you'll know I'm alive, so you won't worry."
Beth's voice sounded as dead as she felt.

She fell into a drugged sleep, but it was all there when she woke up
as she knew it would be. She let herself cry. She stumbled over a pair
of shoes when she went into her closet to get a pair of jeans and, in a
rage, threw all her shoes out into the middle of her bedroom floor. *If
Gloria was here, I would tear her into confetti, one bloody strip at a time,*
Beth thought furiously and kicked a pillow until feathers flew all over
her bedroom.

When the worst of her anger at Gloria was spent, she went outside
to do her chores and found that they had already been done. Nancy and
Len had also left soup in a pan on the stove for her dinner. *I'm blessed
with my friends,* she thought, although the work would have been better
for her.

She prowled the house until it got dark. A bath and pajamas didn't
help her sleep, and she spent the night twisting in torment in her big
lonely bed.

\*   \*   \*

When the phone rang the next morning, she let the answering
machine pick up her messages and didn't listen to any of them.

Midmorning the next day, her front door opened, and May walked
into the house. "What happened? You didn't call and you didn't answer
my messages." Beth and Taz were huddled in the big leather chair. May
knelt and Taz rubbed her head against her shoulder in greeting and then
dropped to the floor and left.

Beth stared at May with dull eyes. "Dale's dead. Gloria came to sign
the papers on her condo, and I managed to confront her. She told me
he'd been killed. They were in a car accident." Her mouth twisted in
pain.

May shook her head in denial. "He's still alive. I don't know why he
hasn't let you know where he is, but he is not dead. He is not behind
the veil, I swear to you." She stroked Beth's hand then hauled herself to
her feet. "We need tea and talk to figure out what to do. Get out of that
chair and tell me what happened. Come, love," she coaxed as Beth just
stared at her. "Trust me, Gloria is lying." May pulled Beth to her feet.
"Go get out of your pajamas."

Like an obedient child, Beth slowly went down the hall to her bedroom and pulled on a set of sweats. The house was chilly.

May knew Beth's kitchen almost as well as her own. She took a teapot decorated with strawberries out of the cupboard, added loose tea, and put water on to boil. Beth watched, mute, as her friend bustled around the kitchen. May had slipped her shoes off. She went barefoot unless she was outdoors.

When the kettle boiled, May added hot water to the pot and carried it into the dining room. "I turned the furnace up a bit. It's too cool in here. Sit down, dear, while the tea brews and tell me what that woman told you."

Beth looked out the window at the early November afternoon. Thin, high clouds dimmed the sun, and a breeze was coming up. Indian summer was gone; the bitter days of winter were waiting to be born.

May listened intently as Beth told her about the meeting with Gloria, her voice breaking as she fought to deal with all the grief and anger that was tearing her apart.

"If Dale's not dead, why would she lie about it? Surely she can't hate me that much?" Beth took a shallow sip of the tea and put the cup back in its saucer.

"I think her fear of losing her father might have pushed her over the line. She can't be a very stable person to act the way she has about the whole relationship. It is very obvious she is self-centered, or she would be happy her father has a second chance for happiness. Are you still dreaming about Dale calling you?"

Beth shook her head. "No, but I haven't been sleeping much."

May leaned forward and said slowly and distinctly, "You must believe me. Dale is not dead. I see him in a hospital bed, and he is alive. Look at me, Beth. Believe me." She sat back in her chair.

Beth looked at May steadily for several minutes and then took a huge breath and let it out. "I believe you," she said slowly. "I guess if he was really dead, I wouldn't be dreaming about him. No, that isn't true, I did dream about Rob right after he was killed when he let me know he was all right, and then I had those dreams about the Colorado River trip." She pushed her chair back and went into the living room, where she paced around the large footstool that matched the big Indian-patterned chair.

May followed and stood in the doorway, watching.

After several circuits, Beth flopped down on the stool and put her head in her hands. "I just feel so helpless. I don't know what to do. Should I go to the police again?" She grimaced. "They'll accept Gloria's word, won't they? After all, she's Dale's daughter and a registered nurse. Why would she lie?" She gave a sharp bark of laughter as she looked up at May. "Tell me what to do."

"I think you need to check with the Sterling hospital first to see if they were admitted to the emergency room. It may be difficult to get information because of this stupid privacy law since you aren't a relative, but we should be able to find out if they did have an accident. And you are his fiancé. That would be a start." May sat down on the couch.

The friends were quiet, both thinking hard. After a few minutes Beth got up and started pacing again. "I guess I better go to Sterling and see what I can find out. I'll go tomorrow. At least it will give me something to do." Leaning over the footstool, she rubbed her hand over it. "Although from the looks of this, I need to work on the cat hair Taz so generously distributes on the furniture and everything else."

"I would go with you, but I have some old friends coming in tomorrow for a few days. Will you be all right by yourself?"

Absently rubbing her hand over the footstool, Beth looked up at her friend. She straightened up with a groan. "I'll take Nancy with me if she can get away. If she can't, I'll have a lot of memories to keep me company. Rob and I met when we were going to junior college there, you know."

"I remember. He will be watching over you. He's worried about you."

"And mad at me, you said."

"He's past that now. He sees your pain. He loves you and wants you to be happy."

"Everyone wants me to be happy but Gloria."

"Should you tell your son you will be gone?"

"No, he has enough to worry about. The only thing he really knows is Dale isn't coming around anymore, and I don't want him to know I'm trying to be a detective. He would freak out. If he calls you looking for me, tell him I have been getting out a little and have probably gone to a movie or something, will you? I don't want to make him crazy too."

# CHAPTER 25

"It's about time you called me. I've been chewing on the corral posts worrying about you. I saw May's car over there so I left you alone yesterday. Do you need me to come over?"

"I'm sorry, Nancy. I've had a lot to think about. May says Dale isn't dead, that Gloria is lying, and you know how right on she usually is. The only lead we have is the Sterling hospital, so I'm going to go see what I can dig up about the accident."

"Gloria," Nancy spat, "we need to put a contract on her, make her disappear. What a piece of work she is . . . is May going with you?"

"No, she has company coming."

"When are you going?"

"Tomorrow."

"Oh darn, we have reservations for that trip to Santa Fe, but we'll be back in three days. Wait until I can go with you, Beth," Nancy pleaded.

"Please don't worry about it, Nancy," Beth soothed. "I appreciate you wanting to help, but I need to do something. I'll go nuts pacing around here for three days."

It took Beth fifteen minutes to calm Nancy down and get off the phone. The urge to get in her vehicle and drive away consumed her, but she needed to make arrangements for her animals. Far Horizon would be fine; the automatic water tank would take care of his only real need. He wasn't a horse that would overeat, so she didn't worry about giving him free access to the pasture. She would leave Taz in the shed with plenty of food and water so she could terrorize the mouse population.

A few articles of clothing were flung into a bag; she took a shower and, knowing she wouldn't sleep, took a sleeping pill. She would need her wits about her tomorrow, and staring at the ceiling all night would not keep her awake on the monotonous drive across the drylands.

\* \* \*

*I haven't been back to Sterling since I married Rob in '61,* Beth thought as she drove east of Ault on Highway 14 early the next morning. Memories of their courtship drifted through her mind as she sped through the bright fall day. The wind was blowing, and at times it rocked the Yukon. *Rob rocked my world,* she thought as she remembered how they met at the junior college in Sterling during their second year.

"I noticed you last fall," Rob told her after their first date. "But I had to study hard to get my grades up so I could go back to CSU. I didn't dare get involved at that time. And I had a feeling if you and I got together, we would definitely get involved."

"Partied a little too hard when you were at CSU, did you?" Beth had given him a mischievous grin.

"Oh yeah, big time. The farm was all work and no play, although my dad allowed me to do sports. When I got away on my own, I tried to make up for the fun I thought I had missed. I totally flunked the first semester. That was a wake-up call. I realized I was wasting my dad's money, so I went into the marines and spent four years there. I'm starting the rest of my life now, and I want you in it."

"Oh, you do, do you? Sure of yourself, aren't you? What makes you think I want you in my life?"

"I'll wear on you. You'll see."

Beth smiled, wrapped in her memories, hardly aware of the steering wheel her hands gripped so tight.

*Remember how it was, my love? How we were like a pair of old shoes from the start?* Beth laughed to herself. *Oh, how insulted you were when I told you that until you realized what I meant. We were comfortable together. There was no pinching, it wasn't necessary to break in our relationship. We could almost read each other's thoughts. Being broke didn't bother us—we did simple things: an afternoon drive, picnics by the river, an occasional movie. Remember the heavy snowstorm that hit just as you took me home? I talked you into walking for a while. I can still see those huge snowflakes drifting slowly down past the street lights. There was no sound, the snow muffled everything. We felt insulated from the world. How gentle you were as you brushed the snow off my face.*

*We wanted to spend every minute together, but we both had jobs. You were working in a filling station. What was I? Oh yes, a bookkeeper for the office supply store until they couldn't put me on full time after we graduated. I went to work for the photography studio, and you went back to your father's farm to work for the summer before you went back to CSU.*

*That summer was hard, wasn't it? Being apart all week and sometimes you couldn't get back for the weekend. You were good about writing, but I could hardly read your letters. You must have flunked penmanship. You wrote me that you had been so sleepy one night driving the ninety miles back to the farm you stripped down to your shorts and ran up and down the road to get your circulation going so you could wake up. That would have been a sight to startle any passing motorist but not a worry on that highway in the dead of night.*

*Everything was wonderful until I broke my ankle,* Beth thought.

The Yukon picked up speed as it went down the only hill on the entire trip to Sterling.

*My sister insisted on me running for rodeo queen because she wanted to, and that borrowed horse buggered me up.*

*I should never have walked up all those stairs. Whoever told me "if you could walk, it wasn't broken" didn't know what they were talking about. I had never had a broken bone, come to think of it, until that point, and I sure did a bang-up job on that ankle.*

*It's still hard to believe you talked your mother into letting you bring me to the farm for a couple of weeks. The doctors wanted to see if the bones would knit or if surgery was needed. I still remember my reaction.*

*"You can't possibly expect your mother to take care of me. She hasn't even met me yet, and you're going to take someone who is helpless because she can't walk to add to your mother's chores? I'm sure she will love that!"*

*"You can't put weight on that foot until they put a walking heel on your cast, and everyone in your family works through the day. How are you going to manage?"*

*"I'll be all right."*

*You just ignored me, told my mother what you were going to do, and hauled me to the car and dumped me in. I realized you meant to take care of me, however inconvenient it might be. I had felt it before this, but that settled the question for me. I never looked back.*

*Remember how you massaged that ankle when it came out of the cast just two weeks before our wedding, my love? I couldn't bend it and was so upset. You just said it was no problem, we would have it ready so I could dance down the aisle . . . and I did.*

Beth realized that even though she was smiling, tears were leaking from the corners of her eyes. How she missed her husband. She always would. Even with Dale in her life, she would forever have her first marriage in her thoughts.

\*    \*    \*

As she wiped the tears off her cheeks, she realized she was just outside of Sterling. Her past was full of love and laughter, but it also brought pain. How strange life could be. Love came to her in this town early in her life. And she was back full circle. Would she find loss this time instead of love?

Glancing at the dashboard display, Beth saw it was ten o'clock. She drove slowly down Main Street. Very little looked familiar except the town square and the Presbyterian Church where she had been married. She went through the campus of the junior college where she and Rob had met, but it was unrecognizable. Nothing remained of the old buildings; it was a totally new landscape.

Her senior class of '59 felt special when they were the first students to graduate from the new high school. Now it looked out of date as she drove by, like a harvest-green and avocado-gold kitchen.

Her mother's house was only recognizable by the address over the garage door. It felt like Beth had never been here before, even though the memories were as sharp as new photographs.

*Quit stalling,* she snarled at herself, *you need to go to the hospital. Better try the old site first.* It wasn't far from her mother's home.

She found the hospital in the same location, but growth buried the original building. Beth parked the Yukon and sat in the lot, remembering herself as a seventeen-year-old girl working here as a nurse's aide. *How I loved the job—dealing with the patients, helping them feel better. Those were the days each patient got a back rub before they slept. I had the reputation of giving the best one. Oh, the one I gave to the senior class jock who thought he was such a lady-killer. The suggestive remarks he made while I gave him the massage turned sour when I told him I would take his temperature rectally if he didn't knock it off.* Beth snickered, remembering the look on his face.

*I sure got over any body shyness: shaving men for surgery, giving enemas, and chasing Mr. Willmoth down the hall during visiting hours because he didn't have any clothes on. He was going home. He almost got to the fire escape before I caught him and wrapped a blanket around his stringy body and tried to deal with his poor deluded mind. No wild parties for me. Instead I dealt with blood spurting from a cut artery, bathing a screaming baby in ice water to bring its temperature down while the doctor plunged needles into both fat little thighs to give the baby a lifesaving IV to fight the dehydration a high fever was creating. The look on the mother's face as they worked frantically on the child, cringing at what they were doing but knowing it had to be done. The child's exhausted screaming . . .*

Beth got out of the Yukon, locked it, and went into the building.

Recently updated, the hospital lobby was pleasant with an aquarium bubbling away. The woman at the reception desk gave Beth directions to the billing department, where she stood outside the door, hesitating. Would she be able to keep it together if she managed to find out about the accident and was told Dale had died? Her hand was shaking as she opened the door and went in.

"Can I help you?" A petite, slightly chubby woman with beautiful silver hair and a tag that said she was Marilyn smiled at Beth from behind the counter. Computer operators huddled at their screens throughout the rest of the room.

*Answer her, idiot!* Swallowing, Beth put her purse on the counter and leaned forward. "I need a copy of the bills for Gloria and Dale Runnington. They were treated here August 20."

"And you are? I can't release records to anyone but family or insurance companies."

"I'm Dale's fiancé, Beth Waterford. He needs copies for a problem with the insurance company. I was coming to Sterling, so I told him I would pick them up. He still isn't doing very well, and Gloria works." She forced a smile.

"That's a little odd. Usually we deal with the insurance companies." Marilyn frowned at Beth.

"But a patient has a right to have a copy of his bill, doesn't he?"

"Oh yes, and I would be glad to turn them over to Dale or Gloria, but I don't know . . ."

"Please, they're having a terrible time with the bills and insurance and all. You know how it is—pay your premiums, then try to get the company to pay your bills? It's criminal."

"I know, I had surgery here six months ago, and my insurance hasn't paid a dime on my bill yet." Marilyn thought a moment. "Well, I don't see how it would hurt. Let me see some ID though, please."

"Of course." Beth pulled out her driver's license and blew out a sigh of relief. So much for the privacy laws.

The lobby offered comfortable purple chairs, and Beth settled in one to look through the bills. She discovered that Dale did have surgery. Gloria's bill was much less extensive and ended almost a week earlier than Dale's. But had he died of his injuries like Gloria insisted?

Folding all the papers, she stuffed them into her purse and went back to the admissions desk to ask directions for the emergency room.

*I wouldn't be able to do this in Fort Collins*, she thought as she walked into the ER. *I would have to be escorted by someone at the desk and have to be family. Thank heavens for small towns.*

There was no one in sight. Only one of the beds was occupied. She could see feet under the covers; the rest of the body was hidden by a curtain. As she hesitated, a male nurse that had been behind the curtain appeared, patting the covered feet as he came around the end of the bed.

"You'll be all right, Mrs. Bender. Just rest and let the pain meds do their job." He came toward Beth with a pleasant smile. "Can I help you?"

"How can I find out about a patient that was treated here? I know he was in a car accident and then had surgery. I can tell from the bills that he was in the emergency room. Were you working on August 20?"

"Sorry, I wasn't, and it is going to be hard for you to speak anyone that was. ER personnel are contracted in, and none of the August people are still here." He looked at Beth closely. "Why do you want to know?"

"My fiancé has disappeared. The only lead I have is this hospital. I need to know if he left here alive . . . or dead." She took a quivering breath.

"Come, sit over here." The nurse took Beth by the arm and led her to a stool. "You're shaking."

She crumpled onto the stool and looked at his name tag. "Michael, please help me. Who could I talk to that might remember Dale?"

He frowned at her. "I would be glad to help, but I don't . . ." He thought a moment and then put his hand on her shoulder. "You said he had surgery?"

Beth nodded.

"Mmm. There is one person I can think of that's almost always here. Rachel Warren. She's the head of the recovery room. She's a widow and this hospital is her life. If anyone might remember something, it would be her."

*   *   *

"You were right, May, thank God." Beth sat in her car, sheltered from the wind that was whirling stray pieces of trash away from the dumpster area of the hospital parking lot. She shifted her cell phone to her left ear as she fumbled her keys into the ignition. "They were here for over a week, so she was telling the truth about the accident. According to the bills, it looks like Dale did have surgery. I told them I was Dale's fiancé, which is the truth, and I needed a copy of the bill for his insurance, which was a lie. The address Gloria gave was a post office box in Fort Collins so that won't help. Hopefully he was still alive at the point his billing stopped. The ER people are hired from out of town and only stay for their contract. No one is still here from the August staff."

"I'm sure you feel better now you know Gloria was lying about Dale dying in the wreck."

"Yes, but I still don't know if he was alive when he left the hospital."

"What about records for the morgue?"

"That would be just too easy, wouldn't it?" Beth choked off a bitter laugh. "They were destroyed in a fire."

"So now what?"

Beth could hear the sounds of water running in the background. May was probably making dinner. "I'm going to talk to a nurse that's in charge of the recovery room. Chances are she was working during those dates. My luck, she's off today, but she'll be on duty tomorrow morning."

"You sound worn out, sweetheart. Try to get some sleep," May said.

"I promise. I'm going to get a motel room as soon as we hang up. Get a large pizza brought in, eat the whole thing, and sleep like a log."

They both knew it would be a difficult night. Beth expected the Worry Nag to barge in, but she had been unusually silent. Beth was grateful she hadn't had her to argue with. She just didn't have the energy.

*   *   *

*I hope this isn't another dead end,* Beth thought wearily the next morning as she pushed her way back through the hospital doors and made her way to the recovery room. *I pray the nurse wasn't on vacation during the time Dale and Gloria stayed in the hospital.*

"Oh yes, I remember them," Rachel Warren said. She was a good-sized woman with a peaceful face, one that would soothe and inspire confidence in her patients, Beth was sure. "The man had two broken legs, some fractures to his pelvis, and a broken arm. He had to have pins in the right femur, but the surgery turned out well, and he should be able to get around in about six months. The daughter was banged up some, but her injuries were mostly bruising. I talked to her when she was visiting her father. They were lucky. The wreck totaled their car from what the daughter told me."

"He left after a week?" Beth was so tense her neck ached.

"About that. Like I said, he did well after the surgery, and since she was a registered nurse, we let him go home to her care. You know these insurance companies don't like a long hospital stay any more. All he really needed was bed rest and good nursing, and she could do that for him, as she was fine after three or four days."

Relief flooded through Beth. Dale had left the hospital alive.

"Let's see"—Rachel pursed her lips, concentrating—"he was on a lot of pain killers and wasn't sure what was going on around him at times, but that was probably just as well. He was really bruised. He may have had some broken ribs too. I can't really remember."

"Do you know where they went after they left the hospital?" Beth asked.

"Why home, I imagine. She said she had a hospital bed and everything set up." Rachel looked at Beth oddly.

*Yeah right,* Beth thought as she thanked Rachel for her time. She was no closer to finding Dale than she had been when she drove into town. Her feet, head, and heart all hurt by the time she went back to the motel to ask for another night's stay. She was too exhausted and upset to try to drive back home.

But Dale was alive.

Beth sat on the bed in her dreary motel room late that afternoon. "Hi, May. It's me. You were right as always. I shouldn't have had a doubt when you told me Dale was still alive, or at least he was when he left the hospital. He was busted up, but his injuries were not fatal. He left the hospital with two broken legs, a cracked pelvis, and his loving daughter. So he isn't mobile. She has stashed him away somewhere, like the Steven King novel *Misery*. Hopefully she won't start using an axe."

She shifted position on the lumpy bed. "How do I find them? Knock on every door in Sterling? She may not even have stayed here, but that makes the most sense, particularly since she has disappeared from Fort Collins. The only other bright idea I can come up with is to check with the utility companies to see if there is any record of Gloria having a phone. Probably a fat chance as everyone uses cell phones now. Maybe water and sewer will give me a break if she is renting a house. I'll call around after I rest for a little bit."

The city of Sterling had no record of Gloria. If she was living there, she was using a different name. The search had consumed the rest of the day with no results.

"I guess that's about it. About the only other thing I can think of is to stake out the one grocery store and hope she gets hungry," Beth reported to May that evening as she picked at the fried chicken dinner she had taken back to the motel room. Her eyes were on the muted television, but she didn't see it. "I guess I might as well come home."

"I wish there was something I could do for you, Beth. I can imagine how helpless you feel. I still see Dale in that hospital bed, but I can't see anything that would tell me where he is. You know how cryptic seeing can be."

"Oh yeah, I remember the time I was talking to you about my mother last December and happened to mention her name. You almost fell off your chair. You told me a woman whose name started with a *V* had been driving you nuts trying to come through, and you were ignoring her because you didn't know anyone who had a name starting with *V* or anyone who had people that had a name with that letter. Vonda isn't a name you hear much."

"She certainly was frustrated with me, waving that huge cake with all the burning candles on it around and around. I did finally get that she wanted me to wish someone a happy day. It's a wonder the candles didn't set her hair on fire."

"It was either Steve's birthday or my wedding anniversary. Both of those happened in December." Beth sighed. "Rob and I would have been married forty-five years."

"From the size of that cake, she was probably trying to send wishes for both events." May chortled. "The icing almost melted."

The image made Beth snicker. "Thanks, I needed a laugh. Unless I get another bright idea, I will be home tomorrow." She started to hang up the phone and then asked, "I keep forgetting. Did your company get there all right?"

"Lord, yes," May groaned. "And they left just in time to keep me from kicking them out. They are the kind of people that expect to be waited on. Never think of helping with the dishes, left the bathrooms and bedrooms looking like pigs had rooted there. Too bad they're relatives, but I've figured it all out. I will just make sure I visit them at their homes from here on."

"Good idea, seems like there is one bunch like that in every family I know. Love you, thanks for the support. I'll call you and let you know I got home all right."

Exhaustion settled on Beth's shoulders, making her efforts to get ready for bed feel like she was moving underwater. Surely she would sleep tonight.

With the covers of the bed pulled up to her chin, she dredged up the image of the worry closet and knocked on the door.

"Who is it?"

"Well, who would it be? You come out of there. You owe me an apology."

The Worry Nag sheepishly sidled out of the closet. "I don't know why I should apologize. I was just voicing what you were feeling. It's my job, you know. It would be nice to get a little appreciation for a change." She glared Beth.

"I didn't appreciate you bashing Dale just because a lot of men are creeps. You didn't help my frame of mind one bit. Now I still want an apology, and I don't think I will need you anymore. Go back to your knitting or whatever it is you do when I'm not worrying."

With a toss of her straggly gray locks, the Nag sniffed and went back into her closet. She slammed the door. Hard.

Even though Beth realized she hadn't been on the receiving end of the apology she wanted, she decided to let it go. She was just too tired to argue.

She woke with a start early the next morning in a cold sweat. In her dream, Dale cowered in a hospital bed. Gloria stood over him with an axe. He was looking at her with an expression of total disbelief as she slowly raised the weapon above her head.

Unable to get back to sleep with that image stuck in her mind, Beth showered, packed, and left Sterling as the sun tentatively peeked above the horizon.

# CHAPTER 26

"I know that you're sick of seeing me in here, Detective, but I need to tell you what has happened on Dale's case."

"Oh, something has happened? You know why he disappeared?" Rojas put down the pencil he was playing with to give Beth his full attention.

"Yes, I know. I found out his daughter was selling her condo. I confronted her at the realtor's office. She told me they had been in a car accident in Sterling, and Dale had died. She had him cremated and scattered his ashes."

"I'm sorry to hear that, Ms. Waterford. At least you know what happened."

"No, I don't, Detective Rojas. That's just the point. I have a friend that is a true physic." Beth hurried on as Rojas opened his mouth. "The police use her from time to time. You can check it out. May assures me that Gloria is lying, and Dale is still alive."

"Ms. Waterford . . ."

Beth put her hand up to forestall him. "I know, but I still dream about him calling me, and I have known May too long to doubt what she tells me. He is still alive somewhere and Gloria is with him. She told me they had a car accident close to Sterling, so I went there to check it out. Here are copies from the billing department of the hospital showing the dates and treatment. I also checked with the utility companies in Sterling, Brush, and Fort Morgan without any luck, so she has to be using another name."

Rojas took the papers Beth held toward him and slowly thumbed through them. "You have been busy. Let me get this straight. They both were in an accident in Sterling, and he lived through it although she said he died?"

"Yes, I talked to a nurse who remembered them. She said Dale was released to his daughter's care, and she took him home from the hospital. Of course she didn't. She's hiding him from me somewhere, but I haven't been able to figure out where."

"You should have called us. We would have . . ."

"What, Detective? Grilled her to get her to tell you where he is? That is if you could find her. I think she would leave him to die rather than give him up to me. She isn't quite sane. I've come to believe that. You didn't see the look on her face when she saw how I reacted when she told me her father was dead. She was gloating." Beth took a deep breath. "From what the floor nurse told me, he would not be able to take care of himself for a while yet. Gloria is a nurse, if you remember."

"Yes, I remember," Rojas said slowly. "Well, we will check the banks and see if we can find any receipts from credit card usage. That might give us an idea where she's keeping him." He stood up and extended his hand to Beth. "I promise I will give this my immediate attention."

As Beth started to turn away, Rojas cleared his throat. "Ms. Waterford?"

"Yes?" Beth looked back at him.

"Your fiancé is one lucky guy." He smiled at her. "I will get right back to you on the bank and credit card info we dig up."

Beth nodded and left. At last they were starting to take her seriously. Maybe she would take him a bottle of the special shampoo a friend of hers swore worked wonders on dandruff.

*   *   *

"How relieved you must be to know Dale is still alive. Oh, I'm so happy for you," Nancy said when Beth told her about her trip and the visit to the police over the phone a day later.

"My life was given back to me when I saw those bills at the hospital. And the police have decided I'm not a jilted lover."

"They were idiots to think that," Nancy huffed.

"Well, a lot of that does go on, so I suppose they have good reason, but it's nice to not have them look at me like I'm a discarded toy . . . can you hang on a second?"

Beth put the phone down, pried Taz off her lap, carried her to the front door, and deposited her on the deck, ignoring the hurt look the cat shot at her.

"Sorry," she said, "Taz was rubbing her chin on the phone and on my neck, making it hard to think. She is so glad to have me back home. Where was I? Oh, Rojas. He said Gloria closed out her bank account, and there is no activity on her credit cards. She's paying cash and lying low. She had about a hundred thousand in the closed account, so she may be out of the country."

"She can't move him very easily yet with those injuries, can she?"

"I wouldn't think so," Beth said.

"So she is probably not far from Sterling," Nancy assured Beth. "How long has it been since he disappeared?"

"It was late August, so it would be going on three months. Lord, it seems much longer than that," Beth groaned. "I don't know how I will ever find him."

"Don't you think when he is well he'll be able to get away from her? I don't know how she thinks she will be able to keep him prisoner then. But she can't be too rational, or she wouldn't be doing this."

Beth sighed. "I'm beginning to think that a lot of her bolts and nuts aren't screwed on right. She will be in a lot of trouble if she's doing what we think she is. If I had only known she was lying when I saw her in the realtor's office, we could have gotten this all into the open then. But she played it so real I believed it. I'm sure it made her day."

There was a brief silence on both sides of the phone line.

Beth rubbed her temples, another headache was coming on. "Thank you, Nancy, for listening to me rant and rave about this. I'm sure you're sick of my problems, but if I hadn't had you and May to talk to, I think I would have gone mad."

"You would do the same for us, Beth. We care about Dale too, and you're welcome," Nancy said softly. "Hang in there, pal."

"I will. I don't have much choice. At least we know a few more pieces of the puzzle now."

As Beth got up from her chair after she finished her call, she glanced out the window and saw Taz sitting on the deck, glaring at the house.

"Oh boy, I'm in the dog house now," Beth muttered and went to let her cat in.

---

*     *     *

The next day, Beth was in the grocery store when a sneeze caught her by surprise. By the time she got home, she was freezing and her nose was running. "Oh damn, I think I'm catching a cold," she complained to Taz as she carried groceries into the house. Another sneeze exploded, loud enough to make the cat jump.

"Oh great, just what I need." Beth sighed. She had been under too much stress; no wonder she didn't feel well.

After she put the groceries away, she took a large dose of Vitamin C, some zinc, and then fixed herself a very large toddy composed of tea with a generous slug of Jack Daniels, lemon, honey, and a stick of cinnamon. While that was mingling, she filled her tub with hot water and crawled in, shuddering from the chills that were chasing through her body.

*Ah, bliss. A hot bath is one of the best inventions since fire,* she thought as she slid down the back of her steeping tub until the water lapped under her chin. She drank the hot toddy as fast as she could, soaked until she felt the temperature of the water drop, let water out, and put in more hot. She kept that up until she started sweating, got out, and wrapped her heavy terry cloth robe around her. Hurrying into the bedroom, she crawled into bed with every cover pulled up to her ears. Sighing, she relaxed; her body finally warmed. Within fifteen minutes, she was deeply asleep.

She slept until early morning, but when she woke, she had a raging cold. *Oh boy, this is going to be a doozy,* Beth thought as she staggered down the hall to the kitchen to make coffee. It was the last week in November. There had already been one early snowstorm, and the weather was chilly. She was lucky; there was no snow left on the pasture now. She needn't go out in the chill. Far Horizon could manage on his own for a few days, although he wouldn't be happy about it.

The phone rang. Beth hurried into the office, trying not to spill the coffee she had just poured.

"Mom? I wanted to check to see what you were doing for Thanksgiving."

"Thanksgiving," Beth croaked. "Oh Lord, I had completely forgotten about it."

"Wow, you sound great, like a rusty pipe. You're sick."

"Afraid so, a cold slammed me in the grocery store. I came home and did the old treatment . . ."

"Hot tub and toddy?"

"Yep, it helped me sleep through the night, but it's still here this morning. What's up?"

"We were wondering if you wanted to come for Thanksgiving. Have you ever had deep-fried turkey?"

"No. But I've never tasted anything deep fried that wasn't good. Are you going to try to add that to your recipes?"

"Uh-huh, come join us. We'll ingest enough cholesterol to plug your arteries solid."

"Let me see how this cold goes. If I get to feeling better, I'll come up, but Thanksgiving is only a week away, isn't it?"

"Three days. Sorry for the short notice, but you know how we plan. It's mostly last minute."

"It only drives me a little crazy. Mmm, let's do it this way. I don't think this is going to give up in three days, and I don't want to pass it on. If I'm coming, I'll let you know at the last minute. Ha ha." Beth's laugh sounded like it came from a fog horn, and she could feel the cold beginning to move into her lungs. She sneezed so hard her eyes watered.

"Wow, you do have a good one. You'd better go to the doctor. What about the horse?"

"I'll go if I'm not better tomorrow. I'll stay in bed today and gobble vitamin C and be a good girl. Far Horizon will be fine. The grass is clear of snow."

"Please take care of yourself, Mom. I know things have been rough, so be careful."

*You have no idea*, Beth thought. "I will, don't worry and have a happy Thanksgiving. Let me know how the turkey turns out, and if a miracle happens, I'll be up, but don't count on it."

\*     \*     \*

Her cold lingered for the full ten days. Beth did have to go to the doctor, and she did baby herself. She reread some of her favorite books. She loved the Diana Gabaldon romance series about time travel in ancient Scotland. They were extremely well done. Steamy sex and bloody battles held her attention while her body rested comfortably in bed. She even learned what haggis was. Ugh, glad her oats came in a box instead of being boiled in a sheep's bladder. She cried buckets of tears at the tender love scenes. The rest and purging tears helped her to heal a little from the stress of Dale's disappearance.

\*　　\*　　\*

By the time she was back on her feet, the calendar said December. It came in cold and started marching toward Christmas much too fast. The stores were packed, traffic was horrendous, and Santa Claus was grouchy. It certainly was the season.

The only sign of Beth's cold was a lingering intermittent cough. *Too bad that cold isn't hitting me now*, she thought crossly. *I would have a good excuse for ignoring the whole thing.*

She stared at her neighbor's Christmas lights. Nancy and Len had gone a little mad this year. Their house looked like it was on fire. Her place was the only one on the road that didn't have at least a few decorations.

*I hate Christmas*, she thought sourly. *The whole idea has become an excuse for a shopping frenzy. There are people getting trampled in the stores just to buy things on sale. Has everyone forgotten the Christ Child? That his birthday is what the holiday is supposed to be about?*

She pulled the shades down on the windows to close out the cold and the sight of the cheerful lights too, if she was completely honest.

There was a list on the desk of people she usually sent Christmas cards to, but she put it away in her address file. *What do I tell them this year? The one three years ago told them I lost my husband. I'm not going to tell them I lost my fiancé. I'm not ready to give up yet.*

Gifts this year will just be a check, she decided. That always fits, is the right color, and in the right taste.

*Didn't I used to love Christmas?* It used to be a joyful month—big family dinners, everyone together. *I thought it was going to be that way this year because I would have been Dale's wife.* Beth crossed her arms on the desk, rested her aching head on them, and drifted into Christmases past.

*We got married on December 17, 1961, which was inconvenient to everyone but us. But that was the Christmas break for CSU, and we didn't want to wait until summer.*

*I remember my first Christmas as a bride. We had only been married three weeks. Rob found a huge perfectly shaped tumbleweed. I spray painted it and hung it with popcorn and tinsel. It looked very festive, and we were smug we spent so little making it.*

*On Christmas Day, I got a huge box from Rob wrapped in newspaper. When I opened it, I found another wrapped box, inside that another slightly smaller box. The packages reminded me of the nesting Russian wooden doll sets popular when I was a child.*

*When I got to the smallest box, it contained several objects wrapped in toilet tissue. The first tissue-wrapped object I unwrapped was a used spark plug. There was a small empty box of safety matches, a battery I assumed was used, a small comb with only a few teeth, and a used toothbrush. A Band-Aid box contained a necklace, proudly boasting a small pearl. I laughed my head off and wished I had thought to do something clever. I don't have a clue what I got my new husband. A necktie? I know I didn't put near the effort into my gift.*

*Our son was born on December 8 in 1963. I remember doing what little Christmas shopping I had to do while my mother watched my new son. My cousin sent me a little Christmas suit, complete with stocking hat for the baby. Steve didn't like the hat. He was the best Christmas gift we ever received.*

*After Steve was born, we asked everyone in the family to come to our house for Christmas dinner, as we had the only child on both sides of the family. I always thought it was important to spend Christmas at home. I suspect it was because I seldom got to when I was a child. We usually spent it with my mother's mother.*

Beth raised her head and looked at the clock. She might as well go to bed. The house was chilly. Pajamas and her robe would be more comfortable. Beth left her office, made the rounds of the house, collected Taz, and went to her bedroom to get ready for bed. She continued to relive the Christmases at her house as she climbed into bed and pulled the covers up to her chin. Taz settled in next to her hip.

*I remember the first year I made the turkey,* she thought, her eyes closed. *My mother-in-law called about eight in the morning to see how the turkey was going and found out I had just put it in. She couldn't believe it was done when I took it out, but I had tried a shortcut, cooking it at four hundred degrees, tented in foil, until the last hour. I never stopped to think what would happen if the turkey came out raw. I just did it and had faith it would come out fine. My mother-in-law had always been up at dawn putting her bird in the oven. I felt smug that I had enjoyed lingering in bed.*

*The Christmas Steve was five, he set his waste paper basket on fire, got scared, stuffed it into his closet, and shut the door. I forgot who saw him coming out of his room with that look kids get when they have done something wrong. Whoever it was checked his room and found the metal can hot enough to burn a ring on the wooden floor. The whole house could have gone up.*

*It was never about the gifts for me,* Beth thought. *I am one of the few women I know that doesn't enjoy shopping. I always had a terrible time coming up with a gift idea for Rob. The few times I did, he would come home with it before I had a chance to buy it. At least it would have been something he liked if I had not been preempted. The only gift I remember giving him was a beautiful belt buckle. He gave me a funny look when he opened it, and I remember thinking I would kill him if he had bought one himself. When I opened my gift from him, I had a woman's buckle from the very same artist. We were both speechless.*

*I wonder what kind of Christmas Dale and I would have had if . . .* She stamped on the thought mercilessly. *Don't go there. You will never get any rest tonight.*

She rolled over onto her right side, tucking the comforter close to her neck. Tomorrow she would get the checks mailed. If it was a nice day, maybe she would brave the traffic and crowds to see if she could find anything for her granddaughters. *Maybe there will be a storm, and I will be drifted in,* she thought drowsily.

But the next day was beautiful, bright, and sunny. Although it was chilly, it was bearable because the wind was down.

Beth reluctantly pulled herself together and went to Fort Collins. She did find a couple of glitzy purses she thought her granddaughters might like. The oldest one was usually hauling a purse around, and the younger one liked to imitate her big sister. Finding the purses took two hours, more than enough for Beth. She treated herself to an espresso and a chocolate croissant for getting out and trying before she went home.

# CHAPTER 27

"Mom, I checked the forecast, and the roads are going to be good," Beth's son reported. "The storm they were predicting is going to poop out in Utah, so you will be able to come to Rawlins without any trouble this year. The girls were really bummed to think that you might not make it again."

"Thank you, love. It looks fine from my end too, so I will be up in a day or so as soon as I get a few last-minute things taken care of. I have someone to check on Far Horizon. That was turning out to be a problem, but I've got it handled. I'll call and let you know for sure when I'm leaving so you won't worry."

"Watch out for the idiots on the way up." Steve laughed.

"I will. I love you, son." Beth tried to smother the little hitch in her voice. Steve sounded so much like his father.

After Steve's call, Beth made a bran mash for her horse, letting the dried bran flakes plump up from the boiling water she poured into the bucket. After it cooled a little, she added cut up apples and carrots, a little molasses, mixed it thoroughly, and carried the still warm mash out to the shed.

Far Horizon trotted into the loafing area when she called him and shoved his nose eagerly into the bucket, gobbling the succulent treat. Beth stroked him gently on the neck. He paused, raised his head, and shoved a bran-covered nose at her. She looked at the smear he left on her barn coat and mumbled, "I love you too, you old sweetheart."

She stood in the lean-to, comforted by the warmth of her horse watching the night steal the day, bringing the stars out as though bestowing a gift. She thought about the star that drew the Magi to

Bethlehem so many years ago and bowed her head. "I will trust in the Lord my God in this season of his son's birth and will not fear," she prayed, tears in her eyes. She would not spoil the season for her son and his family.

*   *   *

The day before she left to go to Wyoming, Beth decided to have a good breakfast at the Silver Grill in Old Town, Fort Collins before she ran her last-minute errands. The grill was full of happy chatting people. Waiting for her order, Beth realized she still had trouble eating alone in public. The Eggs Benedict was delicious as usual, and its energy helped her get through her shopping in good shape.

That afternoon she packed the Yukon with items she had picked up in town: olive and garlic bread, blueberry bagels, and the smoked turkey she had ordered for Christmas dinner. Her daughter-in-law had the same idea about holidays—less cooking, more time for visiting.

Her mind was busy with last-minute chores. She would pull the blinds, lower the thermostats, and make sure the trash was out in the morning when she went to give Far Horizon a last bucket of pellets.

A trip to the garage made sure she had a warm hat, boots, extra windshield-wiper fluid, a snow brush, and a shovel in her vehicle. Winter in Wyoming was to be taken seriously.

Beth thought about all the ground blizzards she had driven through when she lived in Wyoming and shook her head. Without reliable weather reporting, the storms would hit without warning. She remembered creeping along, not being able to see except from one delineator post to the next, hanging her head out the window to pop the ice off the windshield wiper blades. There hadn't been as much traffic then—that was the key.

Now if you slowed down for the conditions, you were likely to be hit by someone traveling way too fast just because they had an SUV and thought that they were bulletproof because of it. "Morons," Beth growled as she slammed the Yukon door and went into the house.

*What to wear*, she pondered as she threw her suitcase on the bed. Taz immediately climbed in and sat in the middle, giving Beth an accusing stare. "You know I'm leaving, and you know I'll be home again, so don't try that guilt trip on me." Beth gently placed the cat on the floor and walked into her closet. Taz was back in the middle of the suitcase when she returned with a set of sweats. "All right, oh faithful companion, you deserve some attention. How about a treat and a warm lap for your pleasure, a glass of wine and a warm fire for mine. I can finish packing in the morning."

\*     \*     \*

"All right, all right, I'm coming," Beth groaned hours later as she hurried down the hall, trying to get her robe pulled closed. It was the middle of the night, dark and cold, and someone was ringing her doorbell repeatedly. She started to open the door, thought better of it, and turned on the porch light. She peered through the window beside the front door and saw Dale's daughter. Beth's eyes widened in disbelief, and her hand froze on the doorknob. Gloria saw her and started pounding on the window.

"Don't break it, for God's sake. Are you crazy?" Beth yelled as she yanked the door open. Gloria's arms dropped to her sides, and the two women stared at each other in silence while Taz slipped unnoticed out into the dark.

"Well?" Beth finally said as Gloria just stood there, her mouth working. "What do you want?" The impulse to slam the door in Gloria's face was so strong she almost succumbed, but her common sense stepped in. It wouldn't help Dale. Beth stepped back into the foyer and, with a sigh, motioned for Gloria to come inside.

Gloria took a few steps into the foyer. Her eyes shifted back and forth, looking everywhere but at Beth.

*Guilty, fevered eyes,* Beth thought as she stared at Dale's daughter. Her dislike for the woman was overwhelming.

"Why are you here, Gloria? And don't you dare lie to me anymore. I've been to Sterling, and I know your father survived the accident. So either tell me the truth or get out."

Beth turned her back on Dale's daughter and walked into her living room with Gloria right on her heels. She started to sit down, but Gloria grabbed her arm and swung her around.

Beth jerked her arm away. "You don't want to touch me," she said in a low dangerous voice. "You really don't want to do anything to set me off. Right now I would as soon kill you as look at you."

Gloria backed off. Her hair was dirty and uncombed, and as Beth stared at her, she started wringing her hands, her mouth working.

"Well?" Beth snapped.

"I'm sorry," Gloria gulped. "I need you to come with me, right now. You have to come to Sterling tonight. My dad needs you." Her voice sounded rusty, like an old hinge.

Beth gave a sharp bark of laughter. "That has never meant anything to you in the past. Why are you thinking about what he needs now?"

"He's trying to die, I think. You have to come with me, please." Gloria grabbed Beth's arm, started to try to tug her toward the front door.

"I told you not to touch me, and if you think I'm going anywhere with you, you're very mistaken. I wouldn't put it past you to shoot me and dump me in a ditch. I think you're crazy." Beth tried to jerk her arm free, but Gloria had it in a death grip.

"Oh please, let's go. If you care anything about my dad, you have to come now." Gloria started to sob.

Beth yanked her arm free. Rage was building; she had a mad desire to punch Gloria in her lying mouth, but she shoved it back hard. *Not now, it wouldn't help Dale now.* She clutched at her robe. "Your dad is still in Sterling?"

Gloria nodded.

"I should call the police. Tell me one reason why I shouldn't"

Gloria looked Beth straight in the face. "It won't help things much if I land in jail, will it? Can't you just help me with Dad before things get any worse? Please, I'm begging you. If you care anything about my dad—"

"I'm not promising you I won't still go to the police," Beth interrupted. "It depends on what you've done, do you understand me?" Her eyes snapped angrily at Gloria, and her face was flushed with temper barely controlled.

Gloria nodded meekly.

"I have to get dressed. I'm driving. You can pick your car up later. Don't argue with me," Beth shouted as she charged down the hall to her bedroom.

When she returned ten minutes later, Gloria was still standing in the same spot. She looked exhausted and old. Beth stamped on a faint stir of pity. "You need to move your car. You're blocking mine. Drive yours down toward the shed while I back out of the garage."

Gloria opened her mouth to protest but closed it when Beth put up a finger and shook her head. She let Beth shove her out the front door, which Beth locked, and then hurried to get her Yukon out of the garage and find Taz when she realized she was not in the house. She was not going to lose her cat to one of the coyotes that roamed through her place at night.

Beth drove through Ault and headed east into the empty prairie. The two women sat in uneasy silence while Beth started at the road with her jaw clenched so tight her teeth began to ache.

When the Yukon reached the desired speed, she engaged the cruise control and gritted, "You have ninety miles to make me understand this unholy mess, and it had better be the truth, or I will throw you out and call the cops to come and get you. You can start with what happened after you took Dale out of the hospital." Beth glanced over at Gloria and then turned her attention back to the road and switched the headlights on high.

Gloria took a deep shaky breath and then starting talking in a low voice.

"I can't hear you," Beth said roughly. "Speak up."

"I took Dad out of the hospital and to a house I rented under another name. I had all the equipment I needed, plenty of pain pills. He would get better care with me taking care of him. After all, I am a nurse. She glanced over at Beth but got no reaction except a tightening of Beth's lips. "He was in a lot of pain, so he was pretty doped up for the first three weeks, and everything went along pretty well. He kept calling for you."

"I know. I could hear him in my dreams."

Gloria sucked in a breath. "Really?"

"Really." Beth snapped. "Go on."

"After he began to need less pain medication, he wanted to know where you were. I told him you had been to see him while he was so doped up, he just didn't remember it. That stalled him, but he kept asking when you would be back. I said that you had to go to your son's because your oldest granddaughter was really ill. That satisfied him for a while."

"Didn't he think it was strange I didn't call?"

"We didn't have a phone. I kept telling him I had one ordered, but they were so busy it was going to take some time. That my cell phone was broken. I don't remember all the excuses I used."

"Lies, you mean." Beth sighed. "Keep going."

"Then I told him you died."

"What!" The steering wheel jerked hard, and the Yukon veered sharply to the right as Beth jammed on the brakes and brought the vehicle to a rocking stop. "You what!"

"I told him you fell off your horse and broke your neck, and I just hadn't been able to tell him because I knew how much it would upset him."

"There's going to be a special place in hell for you for this. My God, did you want to kill him?" Beth yelled as she turned sideways and slapped Gloria so hard Gloria's head cracked against the side window.

Gloria started sobbing.

"Stop that, I can't understand a word you're saying."

"I'm afraid I may have let it go too long. He's just given up. Giving him sedatives all the time to keep him quiet has made him weak, and now he won't eat. I don't know what to do. When I told him this morning I was lying, he wouldn't believe me."

"So rather than kill him you'll let us be together?" Beth asked bitterly. She hung onto the steering wheel with all her might, fighting the urge to hit Gloria again. "You're out of your mind, woman. How could you do this to your own father? My God." Beth's hands went into painful spasms. She pried them off the wheel and rubbed them hard, staring into the dark. She realized she was swearing under her breath.

She turned her face slightly toward Gloria as she shifted the Yukon into drive. "If he dies, you have murdered your father." She pulled back onto the road, gravel squirting out from under the tires. *And I'll see you pay for it*, she promised silently.

*　　*　　*

Gloria sobbed steadily while the Yukon hurtled through the night. A light snow began falling—big fat flakes that promised moisture. Normally they delighted Beth, but now they hardly registered, except she hoped the snow would stop before it made the road hazardous.

Dale would die, Gloria had waited too long. No, May said it would be all right. "Please God," Beth prayed over and over under her breath, a mental rosary. She was as tense as she had been before she jumped out of an airplane at thirteen thousand feet to skydive. The picture of Dale lying helpless in a hospital bed tortured her.

Gloria blew her nose. "It wasn't particularly you. I just didn't want to lose Dad. He's all I have ever had, the only person who has ever loved me. My mother never liked me, I never had any friends. I've always been alone except for Dad. I didn't want to lose him. I can't lose him . . ."

"Gloria, I want to say something. Are you listening?"

Out of the corner of her eye, Beth saw Gloria give a slight nod. She looked straight ahead, groping for the right words. "I never had any intention of taking your father away from you. I believe when people marry, they inherit each other's family. I hoped you and I could at least be friends. You certainly have made that possibility very remote, but if your father doesn't die, we might someday still have a chance. Maybe because of something my husband said to me after our first granddaughter was born, I can partially understand your thinking."

"What was that?"

"We were in bed one night and he asked me if I loved my granddaughter more than I did him. It floored me—this from a man that was running two banking systems at the time, very successful, very confident, and yet he was afraid that my joy in my new granddaughter had diminished what I felt for him."

"What did you tell him?"

"What I'm telling you now if you'll just listen. There are all kinds of love: love of self, love of family, spouse, children, your grandchildren, your in-laws, your outlaws, your friends. Love expands to fill all the needs if you know how to love."

"I love my dad."

"I'm not sure you do. I think you need him, but *need* and *love* are different things. I don't think you ever learned to love."

"That's ridiculous."

"Is it? If you really loved your dad, you'd want him to be happy. My son was thrilled that Dale came into my life. I certainly didn't get the impression you felt the same when your father had a second chance to love. You delighted in making him miserable." Beth glanced at Gloria when she didn't get a reply. "Real love puts the other person first. I think you have a heart the size of an acorn, but maybe you can learn to water it and make it grow."

There was no response, just silence. Beth loosened the death grip she had on the wheel and rolled her shoulders, trying to relax her neck. Could she manage to find a kernel of pity for the woman who had made life a living hell and brought her own father to death's door? Right now it didn't seem very probable.

Gloria gave a snuffle off and on, but Beth wasn't sure if she was still crying quietly or had gone to sleep.

*Would they never get to Sterling?* She felt a vibration and looked at the speedometer. It quivered at the hundred-mile marker. She backed off on the accelerator and tried to keep the speed down, but the vibration kept creeping back as the road stretched on and on. The snow had stopped, which was a relief. She had hit black ice once on the one hill this route contained and had spun completely out of control, barely managing to keep the car on the road.

"Please drive carefully. I'm too young to die." The Worry Nag had on a big parka and bunny slippers. She looked like the comic character Maxine, minus the cigarette and dog.

"I'm the one supposed to be worrying," Beth muttered. "How come you are?"

"You aren't right now, probably because you are able to do something about your problem? So I am. I do care about you, you know."

"Could have fooled me. I thought you lived to drive me crazy. You haven't been around much lately though, come to think of it."

"You were doing better. I didn't have the heart to nag you. I hope your Dale is alive and all comes right. If it does, you have seen the last of me." The Nag shook her head. "I don't know what I'll do if I have to retire again."

"Don't worry about it. I have grandchildren. I'm sure you'll be needed down the line."

"Well then, I'll be waiting. Good luck." The Worry Nag turned and walked back through the closet door, the bunny ears on the slippers flapping. She turned with her hand on the knob, gave a little wave, and then slowly closed the door.

# Chapter 28

Finally, a sign promised Sterling in ten miles. As they sped past, Beth glanced over at Gloria. She was asleep, her head bobbing. The sun was thinking about rising, sending shy tentacles of rosy light above the eastern horizon. Beth reached over and gave Gloria a not very gentle nudge.

"Uhnnn."

"Wake up before you snap your neck. We're almost there. I need directions."

Gloria scrubbed at her face and stretched, yawning. "Take a left at the first stoplight. Dad may still be asleep. I gave him a heavy dose of sedative so he wouldn't do anything while I was gone."

Beth choked back a rebuttal. Get there first before she tackled Gloria's behavior, she told herself. See what they found when they got to Dale.

They turned left onto a winding dirt road and travelled ten miles north until it ended abruptly in front of a dilapidated clapboard house. The dawn light revealed a badly repaired set of corrals and a barn with a broken back crouching under scraggly trees a short way from the house. A chicken coop without a roof had provided shelter for long-gone laying hens. A machine shed held the rusty hulks that had harvested crops in the distant past. All the outbuildings looked like a slight wind would tumble everything into a pile of kindling.

A cracked and uneven sidewalk led across a patchy lawn to two crumbling cement steps at the front door of the house.

"It isn't much, but we just needed a couple of rooms and a kitchen," Gloria said as she fumbled with the lock on the front door.

Beth took a long look at the surrounding ruins. "What if this place had caught on fire while you were gone? Did you ever think of that?"

Gloria ducked her head, and without answering, she shoved the door open and switched on a dim ceiling light. "Dad's in the back bedroom. I'll check his vitals then leave you alone with him." She disappeared down a dimly lit hallway.

Beth hesitated, looking around. She stepped to the opposite side of what she supposed had been the living room and found the kitchen. Outdated appliances wore their shabbiness resignedly. Part of the countertop looked like someone had hacked it with an ax. The faded linoleum kitchen floor sagged in front of the back door. *What a dump*, Beth thought, although it did look like it was as clean as old could be. She turned and walked slowly down the hall, praying, "Please God, please God." She took a deep breath as she looked into the first room on her right.

Gloria bent over the figure in a hospital bed. A framework at its foot elevated both legs, which were wrapped in casts. He might as well try to carry two anvils around. Gloria took Dale's pulse and peeled back an eyelid. She straightened and carefully, not looking at Beth, said, "Dad should be coming to any time. I gave him just as enough sedative needed to give me time to get you and get back. But it was quite a bit. I'll go fix something, and maybe you can get him to eat when he wakes up." She sidled past Beth and went down the hall.

Beth walked over to the bed and looked down. "Oh, Dale . . ." Her hands fisted, fingernails cutting into her palms as she saw the change in the vibrant man she last saw four months ago. She doubted he would have changed this much in four normal years.

Even relaxed in sleep, the new lines in Dale's face shocked her. At least twenty pounds lighter, he was so pale he looked like he had crawled out from under a mushroom. There was a dirty yellow stain on his temple. A fading bruise? Gloria had kept him clean; his hair was shaggy, but she had shaved him recently. His lips were chapped.

Beth pulled the scuffed chrome chair close to the bed. Her hand wandered all over his face as though she was using braille to see him. She leaned close enough to breathe his breath and dropped her left hand onto his chest. Its rise and fall was comforting. She wasn't too late.

"I'm here, darling," she said softly as she found his hand under the covers. She stroked it gently. "Oh, I have had such a time finding you.

I thought for a while you had run away again. Forgive me for doubting you." Tears slid down her face as she whispered into his unhearing ear. "I'm not dead, my love. I'm right here. I'll always be right here." Dale shifted slightly, and his eyelids fluttered as she talked, but the sedatives still held him captive.

Beth yawned as she watched him, a whole night without sleep demanding payment. Within minutes, her breathing began to match Dale's. Her head drooped and jerked as she tried to keep her eyes open. She sighed and rested her head on the bed, close to Dale's face. She was so tired. She whispered love to him as she slowly drifted to sleep.

Gloria came into the room, stood for a moment with her arms folded across her chest, and then gave a slight nod and left.

Beth began to dream. She wandered through strange halls, looking, looking for she knew not what. She found herself in a large dim room. A ballroom, she realized, where many couples were dancing to an excellent band. She felt heavy fabric brush her ankles and glanced down to see she wore her favorite long dress, the red sequined one whose heavy skirt swung as she moved.

She watched the dancers, admiring the women's lovely gowns. The men were in tuxedos, and in her opinion, even a homely man looked like a king wearing a tux. She knew some of the dancers. They had been friends and Rob's co-workers. They smiled and waved as they swung by. Gradually, she realized they were all exiting to her right, leaving her alone in the huge dimly lit room. She was so tired of being alone. It would be better to leave, but she could not find the exit. She began to be frightened. When she heard footsteps behind her, she whirled, the hem of her dress brushing her ankles.

It was her husband, coming toward her with outstretched arms. "Will you dance, my love?" Beth nodded and Rob gathered her into his arms. The invisible band began to play "Stardust," one of the big band hits from the forties, as they moved into the dance. She felt as though they were skating on a mirror and smiled with pleasure. Dancing was almost as good as making love, and they had become skilled at it over the years. Rob twirled her away, and as she came back, he gave her a grave nod, his eyes intent on her face. She could smell the aftershave he always wore. She snuggled against him, closed her eyes, and let herself drift with the music. The warmth of his body against hers felt familiar, safe.

She could feel the play of his muscles under her hands as he changed speed and direction in the dance. She moved without effort or thought, suspended in the moment, content. The song played over and over, and Beth hoped it would last forever. She had been so tired, so alone.

Rob stopped. Beth opened her eyes, wanting to protest. Dale stood there, his hand on Rob's shoulder. Beth and Rob turned toward him as Dale said, "Do you mind if I cut in?"

"No, I think it's time." Rob gave Dale a wistful smile as he released Beth. He kissed her forehead tenderly, took her right hand, and placed it in Dale's. "I leave her in your care."

He took a few steps back, his eyes sought Beth's, and he sent her a small smile. "Be happy, my love. Good-bye."

Dale nodded solemnly at Rob and then carefully took Beth into his arms. She gave a small incoherent sound and strained toward Rob as Dale began to move her away. Her left arm reached toward her husband, tears gathering in her eyes as her feet automatically followed Dale's lead.

Her husband turned and walked toward the dense darkness at the far end of the room.

Beth's arm fell limply to her side as Dale pulled her closer, murmuring in her ear to sooth her distress.

Rob's figure grew distant as Beth and Dale danced on through the dimness, a sparkling spinning ball the only source of light. He stopped, turned, blew her a kiss, and disappeared into the void.

Sadness engulfed Beth in a shuddering wave as she peered into the dimness, her eyes straining to see him, although she knew in her heart he was gone for good.

"It's all right, love, it will be all right." Dale's voice was low and full of understanding for her loss. Beth nodded, blinking back her tears. Her grief slowly ebbed as they danced. The warmth of Dale's body relaxed her, and acceptance finally came. She took a long shuddering breath . . .

"Beth?"

She jerked awake.

Dale stared at her in shock, his hands clutching the bed clothes. "Am I dead? Gloria told me you died, but you're here. Are you real or am I dreaming again?" Dale's face contorted as he frantically fought to pull himself upright.

Beth scrambled to her feet and leaned over the bed, pushing pillows behind Dale's back. She hugged his neck, kissed his cheek. "Oh my love, oh my love, I thought I'd lost you," she whispered brokenly. "I've hunted for you for so long. I'm here. I'm not dead. You're not dreaming." She pulled back to look at his face.

Bewilderment from the drugs and emotion made Dale speechless. He reached weakly toward Beth with trembling hands. She took them and put his hands on either side of her face. His hands quivered against her cheeks as she looked deep into Dale's eyes.

"I'm here, darling, and we'll never be parted again."

His eyes filled with tears as he tried an uncertain smile.

"It will be all right. Don't worry, my love, it will be all right."

And it would. Beth smiled at her first love. There was no hesitation in her heart now.

The first time hadn't been right for them. The rest of her life might be a waltz instead of a fandango, but they would still be able to dance. And it would be worth the wait.

# EPILOGUE

"Well, we lucked out on the weather," Steve said. "I was sure we would end up with a hailstorm, a microburst blowing the tent down or something. Then what would we have done?"

"I had the shed cleaned out," Beth said. "We would've had the wedding there, maybe not so nice, but it would've been dry. Hail on the metal roof would have drowned out the band, such as it is." Beth flinched as the band hit another sour note.

Her son skillfully maneuvered her around the small portable dance floor.

"I haven't danced with you for, oh my, I can't remember when," Beth said. She looked over Steve's shoulder. "It has turned out nice, hasn't it?"

Steve nodded as he avoided a collision with a couple dancing to their own slow beat, oblivious to the pace of the rest of the dancers.

The wedding crowd, dressed in their best, milled under a large white tent set among the fruit trees in Beth's orchard. The canvas sides were rolled up to admit cooling evening breezes. The date had been auspicious, perfect July weather with a full moon appearing in the east, to the delight of the wedding guests.

"When she insisted on having the wedding here, I thought it was too much for you, Mom, but you insisted."

"It's been my pleasure. Anything for my girls. That's been my one wish these last years—to live long enough to see my granddaughters married, and here we are." She smiled faintly as she watched the bride, who wore a dreamy smile on her lips, dancing with both her arms around the groom, her head on his chest. The groom's chin rested on her hair.

"Remember our conversation years ago when we were sure Jacklyn would get married early because she had her first boyfriend in kindergarten? When she was serious with that boy in high school, I could see the wedding. The bride with long straggly black dyed hair, black lipstick, fingernails also painted black. What was that look that she was so into at that age?"

"Goth, I think." Steve's lips twitched. "She would have worn a black wedding dress and had a black wedding cake. Thank heavens she got over that stage and never got into piercing."

"She looks beautiful in her white dress. They're a handsome couple." The band stopped playing, and Beth turned in her son's arms. "That's enough, dear. Take me back to the table. These shoes are pretty, but they're killing these old feet of mine. I never thought I would get to the point I would rather watch than dance." She sighed. "But I'm there."

They left the floor, moving across the closely cropped grass to Beth's table, and she dropped thankfully into her chair. "Thanks, love, I think you better go rescue Liz from Dr. Babcock. She looks a little desperate. He will bend her ear until it falls off."

Steve laughed, kissed Beth on the cheek, and went off to rescue his wife.

She was alone at the table. The rest of the wedding party was dancing or mingling with the other guests. Fanning herself with a napkin, she surveyed the remains of the wedding dinner. The stained linen cloths, cluttered with used glassware, coffee cups, dessert plates bearing the remnants of almond cake layered with raspberry filling. The red carnation centerpieces looked dejected; the candles flickering in hurricane lamps were burning low. The tables had looked so pretty when they were first set up.

*We went through dinner like locusts in a wheat field*, she thought smugly. What a wonderful meal: a lovely salad of greens with braised asparagus and toasted almonds, potatoes au gratin with a lovely little steak set atop, all drizzled with a reduction of balsamic vinegar. A feast fit for a king, none too grand for her oldest granddaughter. *It was rather expensive*, Beth thought, *but her finances were in very good shape, and at seventy-eight, money was for spending, not hoarding.*

She picked up her wine glass, and as she did, she noticed her hand and sighed. She used to have such pretty hands—long fingers with well-shaped nails. Now they were covered with knotted veins and sun-caused blotches. Hard working hands, a nurse had remarked once as she started an IV to prepare Beth for a hip replacement. Oh well, they still worked. That was the most important thing.

She finished her merlot as she watched the wedding guests. May was dancing with a rather stout balding man whose name was Willard. She had stayed true to her pledge of not remarrying, but she and Willard had been keeping company for almost a decade. They were very compatible and content in their separate but close relationship. *I'm happy for her*, Beth thought as her eyes followed the couple along the floor.

She shifted her focus to a young couple dressed in Western wear. Jeff and Sue Willamont were the current owners of Nancy and Len's property. Beth still missed her old neighbors. They had retired to the warmer climate of Arizona five years ago because of Len's bad back and feet. Beth thought of Nancy every time she ate a bar of dark chocolate.

The Willamonts raised horses, and Beth had pastured their foals after they were weaned. Far Horizon had watched over the youngsters, guarding them protectively. Until she turned seventy, Beth would halterbreak them and get them used to having their feet worked on. Now she would sit in the pasture in a chair to let them come to sniff at her. She would sing and whisper to them so she could smell them and put her hands on their velvet noses. She missed working with the babies.

She quit riding when Far Horizon died. Putting him down had been one of the hardest things she had done in her life. Quick tears came to her eyes now at the thought of her wonderful Arabian gelding.

Beth heard footsteps coming from behind, and she looked up as a woman pulled out a chair and sat with a groan of relief. "That was the best wedding cake I ever ate. In fact it was the best meal I ever had, and I ate way too much."

"It helps when the groom is a professional chef. I wondered if he was going to make it to the altar. He was so busy making sure things were going right in the catering truck." Picking up the bottle of red wine, Beth raised an eyebrow. "A little more merlot, Gloria?"

Gloria put up her hand. "Thanks, I've had enough."

"Me too, but maybe one more little splash. Red wine is supposed to be good for the blood." Beth sighed as she put the bottle down. "A perfect evening, but I wish your dad had lived to see this." Fresh tears threatened and she blinked hard.

"I miss him so. How do you stand it? I know you loved him. You fought so hard for him. Against me," Gloria whispered brokenly.

"Oh dear, I wasn't going to spoil this evening missing Dale." Beth's voice trembled. "I was lucky enough to have fifteen good years with your father. It hurts, terrible at times, but I wouldn't give those years up just to avoid the pain. I get through it day by day and I'm lucky. I have a loving family and friends. And I have you." Beth turned in her chair and patted Gloria on the knee. "I'm very glad we've been able to become friends."

Tears trickled down the other woman's face. "I don't know how you can . . ."

"We've been all over this. You're my husband's daughter. It would have been very hard on Dale for his wife and daughter to have hated each other all those years, don't you think?"

Gloria nodded and wiped her eyes.

"It wasn't easy for either of us, but it was worth it. Dale's gone, but I still have a connection to him through you." Beth struggled to her feet. "Now would you be a sweetheart and help an old woman to the house? I don't want to fall and break something and spoil the wedding. I'm tired. I want to just sit on the deck and look at the moon."

Dale's death had brought Gloria and Beth closer together. For Dale's sake, they had done their best to be friendly. Gloria had agreed to get some badly needed counseling. But it had been difficult. *It was a complete waste of time to hold on to bitterness*, Beth thought as the two women walked slowly toward the house. *It solved nothing and made so many people unhappy.*

Gloria had decided several years ago to specialize in rehabilitation. One of her cases, a man recovering from a near-fatal auto accident, seemed to be developing into a relationship. Beth was keeping her fingers crossed. Perhaps Gloria would finally have a chance to love.

Gloria settled Beth in a chair, kissed her cheek, and left.

It wasn't long before the party began to break up. People waved at Beth or came over and said good-bye. *I'm in danger of being hugged to death*, she groused to herself, but it felt good. *What had that health report said years ago? A person needs eight hugs a day to have good mental health? I got enough tonight to live another decade and be all right mentally*, she thought. *Too bad it doesn't do anything physically.*

Beth was about to go into the house when she saw Carrie coming toward her, carrying a covered basket with a big bow tied to its handle.

"Grandma, I've been looking for you everywhere."

"I needed some peace and quiet, sweetheart. How's my youngest grandgirl? You look so pretty in that red dress."

"I'm not a girl, Grandma, I'm a woman." Carrie sat in a patio chair and turned it so their knees were touching.

"I can see that, but you're still my little girl. You always will be. How soon before you start at the hospital?"

"Next month, Grandma. I'll have time for a little vacation. I'm so glad to be done with nurse's training." Carrie sighed.

*Just like me*, Beth thought, hearing the sigh. "With two nurses in the family, will we get discounts?"

"Probably not, and don't you get sick. You're my only grandma," Carrie said with a frown.

"I don't plan to, my love. I'll keep going until I'm as wrinkled as a toad and you'll be glad to be rid of me."

They chattered happily until a sound from the basket Carrie was holding grabbed Beth's attention.

"What's in the basket? Did I hear a meow?"

"I have something for you I think you need." Carrie opened the basket and carefully removed a kitten. It blinked sleepily at them and yawned widely, exposing its tiny pink tongue.

"Carrie, honey . . ."

Beth's faint protests stilled when the kitten was placed on her lap. Her hands automatically started stroking the little beast. It looked up at her, its blue eyes wrinkled with uncertainty.

"You miss Tazmeralda, Grandma, and with my Grandpa Rob and Grandpa Dale gone too . . . I don't want you to be all alone."

"Oh honey, I'm too old for a kitten. What if something happens to me while she's still alive? I'm almost eighty after all." Beth's hand never paused in its stroking.

"I promise to take her. Doesn't she look a lot like Taz? I had to look at a lot of cats." Carrie gave her grandmother an impish smile. "I got one too."

"Well, looks like I can't talk you into taking this one back then, can I?" Beth gently stroked the tiny ears of her gift.

"Oh good. That's a yes, I can tell." Carrie jumped out of her chair and put the basket on the deck. "I'll get the rest of her things and be right back."

As Carrie hurried away, Beth picked the kitten up and rubbed her cheek with its furry body. A tiny pink tongue rasped her, and she chuckled. Snuggling the kitten in the crook of her arm, she thought of her old pet, who had lived to be twenty. "Tazmeralda, I think I'll call this little girl Ralda. She'll be a lot of company, and if I'm lucky, she'll be a good mouser like you were."

*I'm already talking out loud to this one like I did Taz.* As she looked down at the little cat, she felt coolness around her shoulders. It wasn't the wind. She had felt it occasionally after Rob first died when she would be close to sleep or thinking of him and their life together, and the same thing had happened after Dale died. It felt like a hug.

*It's the next life breaking through,* Beth thought drowsily. *Soon, my loves, I'll be there soon.*

The kitten started a buzzing purr, and the two sat on the deck in the balmy summer night, content.

CPSIA information can be obtained at www.ICGtesting.com
Printed in the USA
LVOW13s2158260614

391961LV00001B/175/P